The Secret

LEE CHILD and ANDREW CHILD

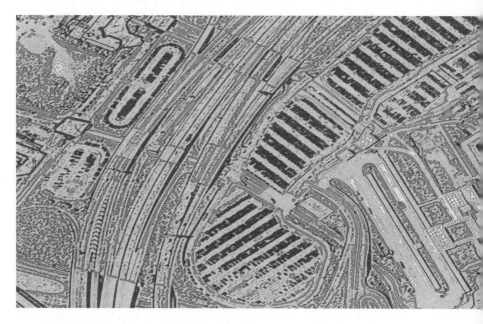

Delacorte Press | New York

The Secret

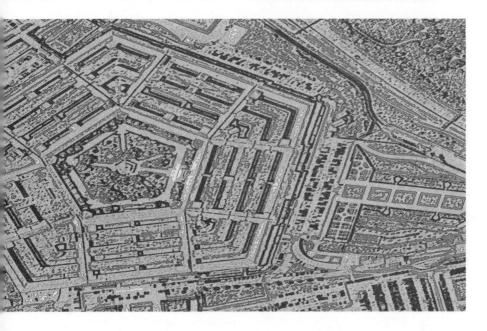

A JACK REACHER NOVEL

Published in the United States by Delacorte Press, an imprint of Random House, a division of Penguin Random House LLC, New York.

DELACORTE PRESS with colophon is a registered trademark of Penguin Random House LLC.

LIBRARY OF CONGRESS CATALOGING-IN-PUBLICATION DATA

Names: Child, Lee, author. | Child, Andrew, author.
Title: The secret / Lee Child and Andrew Child.
Description: First Edition. | New York: Delacorte Press, 2023. | Series: Jack Reacher; 28
Identifiers: LCCN 2023033072 (print) | LCCN 2023033073 (ebook) | ISBN 9781984818584 (Hardback) | ISBN 9781984818591 (Ebook) | ISBN 9780593871454 (International)
Subjects: LCSH: Reacher, Jack (Fictitious character)—Fiction. | LCGFT: Thrillers (Fiction) | Novels.
Classification: LCC PS3553.H4838 S43 2023 (print) | LCC PS3553.H4838 (ebook) | DDC 813/.54—dc23/eng/20230720
LC record available at https://lccn.loc.gov/2023033072
LC ebook record available at https://lccn.loc.gov/2023033073

Printed in the United States of America on acid-free paper

randomhousebooks.com

9 8 7 6 5 4 3 2 1

First Edition

Book design by Virginia Norey
Title page art: gokturk_06/stock.adobe.com

For Larry, with thanks

The Secret

Chapter 1

Keith Bridgeman was alone in his room when he closed his eyes. The morning medical rounds were over. Lunch had been delivered and eaten and cleared away. Other people's visitors had clattered along the corridor in search of relatives and friends. A janitor had swept and mopped and hauled off the day's trash. And finally a little peace had descended on the ward.

Bridgeman had been in the hospital for a month. Long enough to grow used to its rhythms and routines. He knew it was time for the afternoon lull. A break from getting poked and prodded and being made to get up and move around and stretch. No one was going to bother him for another three hours, minimum. So he could read. Watch TV. Listen to music. Gaze out of the window at the sliver of lake that was visible between the next pair of skyscrapers.

Or he could take a nap.

Bridgeman was sixty-two years old. He was in rough shape. That was clear. He could debate the cause—the kind of work he had devoted his life to, the stress he had suffered, the cigarettes and alcohol he had consumed—but he couldn't deny the effect. A heart attack so massive that no one had expected him to survive.

Defying odds that great is tiring work. He chose the nap.

These days he always chose the nap.

Bridgeman woke up after only an hour. He was no longer alone. Two other people were in the room with him. Both were women. Maybe in their late twenties. They were the same height. The same slim build. One was on the left side of his bed, nearer to the door. The other was level with her on the right, nearer to the window. They were standing completely still. In silence. Staring at him. Their hair was pulled back, smooth and dark and tight. Their faces were expressionless like mannequins' and their skin shone in the harsh artificial light as if it were molded from plastic.

The women were wearing white coats over hospital scrubs. The coats were the correct length. They had all the necessary pockets and badges and tags. The scrubs were the right shade of blue. But the women weren't medics. Bridgeman was sure about that. His sixth sense told him so. It told him they shouldn't be there. That they were trouble. He scanned each of them in turn. Their hands were empty. Their clothes were not bulging. There was no sign of guns or knives. No sign of any hospital equipment they could use as weapons. But Bridgeman still wasn't happy. He was in danger. He knew it. He could feel it as keenly as a gazelle that had been ambushed by a pair of lions.

Bridgeman glanced at his left leg. The call button was where the nurse had left it, lying on the sheet between his thigh and the safety rail. His hand darted toward it. It was a fluid movement. Smooth. Fast. But the woman was faster. She snatched the button then dropped it, leaving it dangling on its wire, almost to the floor, well out of Bridgeman's reach.

Bridgeman felt his heart quiver and tremble in his chest. He heard an electronic beep. It came from a piece of equipment on a stand near the head of the bed. It had a screen with a number in the center of the top half and two jagged lines that zigzagged across the full width of the lower half. The first line showed his pulse. It was spiking wildly. Its peaks were surging closer together like they were chasing one another. The number showed his heart rate. It was climbing. Fast. The beeps grew louder. More frequent. Then the sound became continuous. Insistent. Impossible to ignore. The number stopped rising. It began to flash. It changed direction. And it kept going down until it reached 00. The lines flattened out. First at the left of the screen and then all the way across until both were perfectly horizontal. The display was inert. Lifeless. Except for the desperate electronic howl.

It told of total cardiac failure.

But only for a moment.

The second woman had grabbed Bridgeman's right wrist when the alarm began to shriek. She had yanked a square blue clip off the tip of his index finger and attached it to her own. The screen flashed twice. Then the sound cut out. The heart rate started to climb. The two lines began to tick their way from left to right. None of the values were quite the same as Bridgeman's. The woman was younger. Fitter. Healthier. Calmer. But the readings were close enough. Not too high. Not too low. Nothing to trigger another alarm.

Bridgeman clutched his chest with both hands. Sweat was prickling out across his forehead and his scalp. His skin felt clammy. He had to make an effort to breathe.

The woman with the clip on her finger lowered herself into the visitor's chair next to the window. The woman on the left of the bed waited a moment then looked at Bridgeman and said, "We apologize. We didn't mean to startle you. We're not here to hurt you. We just need to talk."

Bridgeman said nothing.

The woman said, "We have two questions. That's all. Answer them honestly and you'll never see us again. I promise."

Bridgeman didn't respond.

The woman saw him glancing past her, toward the door. She shook her head. "If you're hoping the cavalry's going to come, you're out of luck. Those clips slip off people's fingers all the time. And what do they do? Stick them right back on. Anyone at the nurses' station who heard the alarm will figure that's what you did. So. First question, OK?"

Bridgeman's mouth was dry. He did his best to moisten his lips then took a deep breath. But not to answer questions. To call for help the old-fashioned way.

The woman read his play. She put a finger to her lips and took something out of her coat pocket. A photograph. She held it out for Bridgeman to take. It showed a gloved hand holding a copy of the *Tribune* next to a window. Bridgeman could read the date on the newspaper. Tuesday, April 7, 1992. It was that day's edition. Then he saw two figures through the glass. A woman and a child. A little girl. Even though they were facing away from the camera, Bridgeman had no doubt who they were. Or where they were. It was his daughter and granddaughter. In the home he had bought them in Evanston, after his wife died.

The woman took hold of Bridgeman's arm and felt for his pulse. It was fast and weak. She said, "Come on, now. Calm down. Think of your family. We don't want to hurt them. Or you. We just need you to understand how serious this situation is. We only have two questions, but they're important. The sooner you answer, the sooner we're out of here. Ready?"

Bridgeman nodded and slumped back against his pillow.

"First question. You're meeting with a journalist the day after tomorrow. Where is the information you're planning to give her?"

"How do you know about—"

"Don't waste time. Answer the question."

"OK. Look. There is no information. We're just going to chat."

"No credible journalist is going to believe a whistleblower without ironclad proof. Where is it?"

"Whistleblower? That's not what this is. The reporter's from a little weekly rag in Akron, Ohio. Where I was born. The story's about my heart attack. My recovery. It's a miracle, according to the doctors. People back home want to read about it. They say I'm an inspiration."

"Heart attack? That's what you're going with? When you're sitting on a much bigger story?"

"What bigger story?"

The woman leaned in closer. "Keith, we know what you did. What you all did. Twenty-three years ago. December 1969."

"December '69? How do you know . . . ? Who are you?"

"We'll come to who we are. Right now you need to tell me what information you're planning to give this reporter from Akron."

"No information. I'm going to tell her about my recovery. That's all. I will never talk about December '69. Why we were there. What we were doing. What happened. Not to anyone. I swore I wouldn't and I keep my word. My wife never even knew."

"So you don't have any documents or notes hidden in this room?"

"Of course not."

"Then you won't mind if I take a look around."

The woman didn't wait for an answer. She started with the locker next to the bed. She opened the door and rummaged through Bridgeman's spare pajamas and books and magazines. She moved on to a leather duffel on the floor near the door. It held a set of clothes. Nothing else. Next she checked the bathroom. Nothing significant there, either. So she moved to the center of the room and put her hands on her hips. "Only one place left to check. The bed."

Bridgeman didn't move.

"Do it for your daughter. And your granddaughter. Come on. I'll be quick."

Bridgeman felt his pulse start to speed up again. He closed his eyes for a moment. Took a breath. Willed himself to relax. Then pushed back the sheet, swung his legs over the side of the mattress, and slid down onto his feet. He looked at the woman in the chair. "Can I at least sit? I'm older than you. I have one foot in the grave."

The woman held up her finger with the clip attached. "Sorry. The cable's too short for me to move. You want to sit, use the windowsill."

Bridgeman turned and looked at the windowsill. Considered sitting on it. But taking orders from one of the women was bad enough so he settled on leaning against it. He watched as the other woman finished her search of the bed. Again she came up empty.

"Believe me now?" Bridgeman said.

The woman took a piece of paper out of her pocket and handed it to Bridgeman. There was a list of names. Six of them, handwritten in shaky, spidery script. Bridgeman's was one of them. He recognized all the other five. Varinder Singh. Geoffrey Brown. Michael Rymer. Charlie Adam. Neville Pritchard. And beneath the final name there was a symbol. A question mark.

The woman said, "A name is missing. Who is it?"

Bridgeman's heart was no longer racing. Now it felt like it was full of sludge. Like it didn't have the strength to force his blood into his arteries. He couldn't answer. It would mean breaking his oath. He had sworn to never reveal a single detail. They all had, twenty-three years before, when it became clear what they had done. And the missing name belonged to the flakiest of the group. Better for everyone if it remained off the list.

The woman handed Bridgeman another photograph. Another shot of his daughter and granddaughter, on foot this time, halfway across a crosswalk. The picture had been taken through a car windshield.

Bridgeman was channeling all his energy into trying to breathe. It was only a name that the woman wanted. What harm could come from telling her? Plenty, he knew.

The woman said, "Bonus question. What happens tomorrow? Or the next day? Is the driver drunk? Do his brakes fail?"

Bridgeman said, "Buck. The missing name. It's Owen Buck."

The woman shook her head. "Buck's dead. He died of cancer a month ago. Right after he wrote that list. So his isn't the name I need. He said there was an eighth name. He didn't know what it was. But he was certain one of you others do."

Bridgeman didn't answer. He was struggling to make sense of the information. Buck's conscience must have gotten the better of him. He was always mumbling about doing something stupid. But that didn't explain why he told this woman there was an extra name. Maybe his mind had gone. Maybe whatever cancer drugs they gave him had fried his brain.

The woman said, "Maybe the driver will be distracted? Maybe he'll be asleep at the wheel?"

"Maybe there is another name." Bridgeman closed his eyes. "Maybe someone knows what it is. One of the others might. But not me. I don't think one exists."

The woman said, "Maybe there'll be enough of your granddaughter left to bury. Maybe there won't."

Bridgeman was struggling for air. "Don't. Please. I don't know. I swear. I gave you Buck's name. I didn't know he's dead. I've been sick. I've been in here. No one told me. So if I knew of some other name I'd tell you it, too. But I don't. So I can't."

"You can. You don't have to say it. You can do what Owen Buck did. Write it down. He gave me six names. You only need to give me one."

She pulled a pen from her coat pocket and held it out. Bridgeman stared at it for a moment. Then he took it and added *Owen Buck* to the top of the list.

He said, "That's the only name I know. I swear."

The woman said, "Have you ever seen a child's coffin, Keith? Because if you haven't I don't think anything can really prepare you for how tiny it will seem. Especially when it's next to the full-sized one your daughter will be in."

Bridgeman's knees started to shake. He looked like he was ready to collapse.

The woman's voice softened. "Come on. One name. Two lives saved. What are you waiting for?"

Bridgeman's body sagged. "Buck was wrong. There isn't another name. Not that I know of. I was there three years. I never heard of anyone else getting brought on board."

The woman stared at Bridgeman for ten long seconds, then shrugged. She took the pen and the paper and slid them back into her pocket. "I guess we're done here." She stretched out and touched Bridgeman's forehead. "Wait a minute. You feel awful. Let me open the window. Fresh air will perk you up. I don't want to leave you like this."

Bridgeman said, "You can't. The windows don't open in this hospital."

"This one does." The woman leaned past Bridgeman, pushed down on the handle, and the window swung out on a broad arc. Then she scrabbled under the collar of her scrubs and pulled a fine chain up and over her head. The key to the window was hanging from it. "Here." She dropped the chain into the breast pocket of Bridgeman's pajama top. "A present. Something to remember us by, because you're never going to see us again. As promised. There's just one last thing before we go. You asked who we are." The woman stood a little straighter. "My name is Roberta Sanson."

The woman with the finger clip climbed out of her chair. "And I'm her sister. Veronica Sanson. Our father was Morgan Sanson. It's important you know that."

Morgan Sanson. The name was an echo from the past. An unwelcome one. Four syllables he had hoped to never hear again. It took a fraction of a second for the significance to hit him, then Bridgeman pushed off from the wall. He tried to dodge around Roberta Sanson but he never stood a chance. He was too frail. The space was too cramped. And the sisters were too highly motivated. Roberta shifted sideways and blocked his path. Then she grabbed his shoulders with both hands and drove him back until he was pressed against the sill. She checked that he was lined up with the open window. Veronica bent down and took hold of his legs, just above the ankles. She straightened and Roberta pushed. Bridgeman kicked. He twisted and thrashed. Roberta and Veronica pushed one more time. Two more times, to make sure there was no room for error. Then they let gravity do the rest.

Chapter 2

Jack Reacher had never been to the Rock Island Arsenal in Illinois before, but he was the second Military Police investigator to be sent there within a fortnight. The first visit was in response to a report of missing M16s, which proved to be false. Reacher was the last to join his unit, following his demotion from major to captain, so he had been allocated a less interesting allegation. Inventory tampering.

The sergeant who had filed the complaint met Reacher at the main entrance. There were maybe ten years between them. They were about the same height, six foot five, but where Reacher was heavy and broad, the older man was skinny and pinched with pale skin and thin, delicate features. He couldn't have been more than 180 pounds. That would be sixty pounds lighter. His uniform hung off his shoulders a little, causing Reacher to worry about the guy's health.

Once the usual courtesies were taken care of, the sergeant led the way to Firing Range E, near the base's western perimeter. He locked the heavy steel door behind them and continued to a loading bench that jutted out from the rear wall. Six M16s were lying on it, neatly lined up, muzzles facing away, grips to the right. The weapons weren't new. They had spent plenty of time in the field. That was clear. But they were well maintained. Recently cleaned. Not neglected or damaged. There were no obvious red flags. No visible indication that anything was wrong with them.

Reacher picked up the second rifle from the left. He checked that the chamber was empty, inspected it for defects, then slid a magazine into place. He stepped across to the mouth of the range. Selected single-fire mode. Took a breath. Held it. Waited for the next beat of his heart to subside and pulled the trigger. A hundred yards down range, the red star on the target figure's helmet imploded. Reacher lowered the gun and glanced at the sergeant. The guy's face betrayed nothing. No surprise. No disappointment. Reacher fired five more times. Rapidly. Sharp *crack*s rebounded off the walls. Spent cartridges rattled onto the cement floor. A neat T shape was hammered into the figure's chest. It was textbook shooting. There was no sign of any problem with the gun. And still no response from the sergeant.

Reacher pointed to the magazine. "How many?"

The sergeant said, "Sixteen."

"Vietnam?"

"Three tours. No misfires. If it's not broke . . ."

Reacher slid the fire selector to its lowest position. Full auto. The model was old, from before the switch to three-shot bursts. He aimed at the target's center mass and increased the pressure on the trigger. The green plastic torso should have been shredded. The ten remaining bullets should have torn through it in less than a second. But nothing happened. Because the trigger wouldn't move. Reacher changed back to single-shot mode and lined up on the target's face.

The crude contour representing its nose split in half under the impact. Reacher toggled to full auto. Again, nothing happened. Which left no doubt. The trigger would not move in that position.

He said, "They all like this?"

The sergeant nodded. "All of them. The whole case."

Reacher crossed to the bench and set the gun down. He removed the magazine, cleared the chamber, pushed out the takedown pins, separated the lower receiver, and examined its interior contours. Then he held it out toward the sergeant and said, "The trigger pocket's the wrong size. It won't accept the auto-sear. And there are only two trigger pinholes. There should be three."

The sergeant said, "Correct."

"This isn't military spec. Someone's switched out the original with a civilian version. It makes the gun semi-auto only."

"Can't see any other explanation."

"Where did these come from?"

The sergeant shrugged. "Admin error. They were supposed to be sent for destruction but two crates got mixed up and these wound up here by mistake."

Reacher looked down at the guns on the bench. "These would be considered end-of-life?"

The sergeant shrugged again. "I wouldn't say so. Ask me, the condition's acceptable for weapons that would generally be held in reserve. Nothing stood out when the crate was opened. Only when a malfunction was reported. Then I stripped the first one down. Saw the problem right away. Just like you did."

"Who decides which weapons get destroyed?"

"A dedicated team. It's a special procedure. Temporary. Lasted a year, so far. Result of Desert Storm. The war was a great opportunity for units to reequip. Assets that are designated surplus as a result come back from the Gulf and get sent here for evaluation.

Firearms are our responsibility. We test them and give them a category. Green: fully serviceable, to be retained. Amber: marginally serviceable, to be sold or allocated to civilian gun safety programs. Doesn't apply to fully automatic weapons, obviously. And red: unserviceable, to be destroyed."

"You got sent a red crate when you should have gotten a green one?"

"Correct."

Reacher paused for a moment. The account was plausible. There wasn't a kind of equipment the army owned that hadn't been sent to the wrong place, some time or other. Which was usually totally innocent. Like the sergeant said, an admin error. But Reacher was wondering if there could be a broader connection. Something to do with the recent report of stolen M16s. Someone could designate good weapons as unserviceable, fill their crates with the right weight of whatever trash came to hand, send that to the crusher or the furnace, and sell the guns on the black market. Officially the weapons would no longer exist, so no one would be looking for them. It was a feasible method. A loophole someone needed to close. But it wasn't what had happened here. Reacher had read the report. The inspection was unannounced. A full crack-of-dawn, shock-and-awe operation. And it had been thorough. All the weapons crates on the entire base had been opened. All had the correct number of weapons inside. Not so much as a pocket knife was missing.

Not so much as a *complete* pocket knife . . .

Reacher said, "When did these guns get delivered to you in error?"

The sergeant looked away while he did the math, then said, "Fifteen days ago. And I know what you're going to ask me next. You're not going to like the answer."

"What am I going to ask?"

"How you can trace which unit owned these weapons in the Gulf. Before they were sent back."

"Why would I want to know that?"

"So you can figure out who's stealing the lower receivers. Someone is stealing them, right? And selling them. So that gangbangers or whoever can make their AR-15s fully automatic. The Gulf's the perfect place to swap parts out. Officially every last paperclip is tracked. But in reality? Different units have different systems. A few have switched to computers. Most are still paper-based. Paper gets lost. It gets wet. It gets ripped. Digits get transposed. People have handwriting that's impossible to read. Long story short, you'd have a better chance of selling bikinis at a Mormon convention than tracking that crate."

"You don't think I have a future as a swimwear salesman?"

The sergeant blinked. "Sir?"

Reacher said, "No matter. I don't care who had these guns in the Gulf. Because that's not where the parts were stolen."

Roberta and Veronica Sanson heard the impact all the way from the street outside. They heard the first of the screams over the background grumble of traffic. Then the cardiac monitor at the head of the bed started to howl again. Its lines had slumped back down to the horizontal. Its display read 00. No heart activity. Only this time the machine was correct. At least as far as Keith Bridgeman was concerned.

Roberta turned left into the corridor and made her way to the hospital's central elevator bank. Veronica went right and looped around to the emergency staircase. Roberta reached the first floor before her sister. She strolled through the reception area, past the café and the store that sold balloons and flowers, and continued out of the main exit. She walked a block west then ducked into a phone booth. She pulled on a pair of latex gloves and called American Airlines. She asked for information about their routes and schedules. Next she called United. Then TWA. She weighed the options. Then she tossed the gloves in a trash can and made her way to the public parking lot in the center of the next block.

The sergeant led the way to a storeroom that was tacked onto the side of a large, squat building near the center of the site. The wind had picked up while they were at the range which made it hard for him to heave the metal door all the way open, and after Reacher had gone through the guy struggled to close it again without getting blown over. He finally wrestled it into place then locked it. Inside, the space was square, eighteen feet by eighteen. The floor was bare concrete. So was the ceiling. It was held up by metal girders that were coated with some kind of knobby fire retardant material and flanked by strip lights in protective cages. There was a phone mounted by the door and a set of shelves against each wall. They were made of heavy-duty steel, painted gray. Each had a stenciled sign attached—*Intake, Green, Amber, Red*—and a clipboard with a sheaf of papers hanging from its right-hand upright. There were no windows and the air was heavy with the smell of oil and solvents.

The shelves held crates of weapons. Short at the top, long at the bottom. There were fourteen crates on the Red shelves. Reacher pulled one of the long ones out onto the floor and cracked it open. He lifted out an M16. It was in much worse shape than the one he had fired earlier. That was for sure. He field-stripped it, checked its lower receiver, and shook his head.

He said, "It's original."

The sergeant opened another crate and examined one of its rifles. It was also pretty scuffed and scraped. He said, "This one's the same."

Each crate had a number stenciled on the side. Reacher took the Red clipboard off its hook and turned to the last sheet. It showed that the crate he'd picked had been signed off by someone with the initials UE. The crate the sergeant had chosen had been initialed by DS. Reacher could only see one other set: LH. He picked a crate with a corresponding number, removed the lower receiver from one of the guns inside it, and held the part up for the sergeant to see.

The sergeant said, "Jackpot."

Reacher said, "LH signed off on this. Who's LH?"

"Sergeant Hall. In charge of the inspection team."

"Sergeant Hall's a woman."

"Yes. Sergeant Lisa Hall. How—"

"UE and DS are men?"

"Yes. But—"

"There are no other women on the team?"

"No. But I still—"

Reacher held up his hand. "Fifteen days ago you received a Red crate by mistake. Fourteen days ago we received a report that M16s had been stolen from this facility. We checked. They hadn't."

"I heard about the raid. I don't see the connection."

"The report was anonymous, but the voice was female. I read the file."

"I still don't—"

"Sergeant Hall realized a Red crate was missing the day after it got mishandled. She knew it could be traced back to her so she made a bogus accusation. A serious one. Stolen weapons. The investigators came running, just like she knew they would. They opened all the crates, including hers. They were looking for M16s. Complete ones. That's what they found, so they closed the case. No crime detected. Then if the missing receivers came to light, Hall had just been cleared of theft. She was hoping an investigator would make the same jump you did. That the doctored weapons arrived that way, from the Gulf."

"No. I know Lisa Hall. She wouldn't do something like that."

"Let's make sure. Where is she today?"

"Don't know, sir."

"Then find out."

"Sir." The sergeant shuffled across to the phone on the wall. Thin clouds of dust puffed up around his feet. He dialed slowly, made the inquiry, and when he was done he said, "Not on duty, sir."

Reacher said, "OK. So where's her billet?"

Veronica Sanson was waiting for her sister, Roberta, on the fourth floor of the parking garage. She was standing at the side of a blue minivan. They had stolen it from the long-term lot at O'Hare when they arrived in the city, two days before. Roberta nodded a greeting and opened the van's rear door. They took turns, one keeping watch, one hunkering down between the back seats and changing their clothes. Off came the hospital outfits. On went jeans and sneakers and shirts and jackets. All plain, anonymous items. When they were dressed the sisters hugged, retrieved their plain canvas duffels from the van's narrow cargo area, wiped the vehicle clean of prints, then made their way to separate exits. Roberta threaded her way west. She pushed through knots of shoppers and tourists, past the wide storefronts and cafés and offices, until she reached the

Clark/Lake El stop. Veronica walked south and kept going to Roo-
sevelt, where the Orange Line emerged from its underground section.

Reacher liked the armory sergeant at Rock Island. He figured the
guy was reasonably smart. Reasonably street wise. Reasonably capable of anticipating the kind of trouble he'd be in if Hall somehow
got word that she was under suspicion. But Reacher was a cautious
guy. He'd learned a long time ago that it can be dangerous to over-
estimate a person. That unit loyalty can run deeper than deference
to a stranger. Especially when that stranger is an MP. So he made
sure that the sergeant was clear about the consequences of any
phone calls he might be tempted to make. He left no room for
doubt. Then he requisitioned a car from the base's motor pool and
found his way to Hall's address.

Hall lived in the last of a little knot of houses stretched out along
a river about four miles east of the Arsenal's main gate. Her home
was small and neat. Set up for efficiency, Reacher thought. No fancy
décor to maintain. No complicated yard work to stay on top of.
There was no answer at the door when Reacher knocked. No sign
of anyone through the windows, front or back. Just an array of bud-
get furniture laid out as if someone had tried to re-create a picture
from a low-cost catalog. There was nothing personal. No photographs. No ornaments. None of the knickknacks people use to im-
pose their identity on a place. Reacher understood that. Aside from
his four years at West Point he had spent his life bouncing from one
base to another. Six months here. Six months there. Different countries. Different continents. Never anyplace long enough to feel at
home. First as a kid, because his father had been an officer in the
Marines. Then as an adult, as an officer himself. Maybe Hall had the

same experience. Maybe she was anticipating her next change of station and didn't want to waste effort on a place she knew she was soon going to quit. Or maybe she had another reason to be ready to leave in a hurry.

Reacher walked back to his borrowed car and settled in to wait. He wasn't worried about how long it might take. He was a patient man. He had nowhere else to be. And he was naturally suited to two states of existence. Instant, explosive action. And near-catatonic stasis. It was the in-between he struggled with. The sitting through pointless meetings and reviews and briefings that made up so much of army life.

Chapter 3

The phone rang at 9:00 P.M. Eastern. That was 8:00 P.M. Central, where the call originated. Which was right on time.

It was answered immediately.

The guy who had dialed said, "Another one's dead. Keith Bridgeman. Massive blunt force trauma resulting from falling out of his hospital room window. United Medical, Chicago. Twelfth floor. Had been recovering from a heart attack. Not out of the woods but was expected to pull through. Fine when the nurses did their rounds a couple of hours earlier. No reported visitors or calls or outside contact. The police are fifty/fifty, suicide or accident. He must have unlocked the window himself—the key was still in his pocket—but there was no note. All for now. More at 0800."

"Understood." The guy who had answered hung up.

Officially the telephone line they had used didn't exist. It was one of the Pentagon's ghost circuits. There were hundreds of them in the building. Maybe thousands. They generate no records, incoming or outgoing. The call that had just ended could never be traced. It could never be correlated with the next call made on the same line, but the Pentagon guy walked through to the outer office anyway. Old habits die hard. He picked up a different phone and dialed a number from memory. A number that was not written down anywhere. Not listed. Not officially in service.

The Pentagon guy's call was picked up in the study of a house four miles away, in Georgetown, D.C. By Charles Stamoran. The Secretary of Defense of the United States of America.

The Pentagon guy repeated what he'd been told a minute earlier. Word for word. Neutral tone. No summarizing. No editorializing. The way Stamoran insisted it was done.

"Understood," Stamoran said when the Pentagon guy stopped talking. "Wait one."

Stamoran laid the handset down on the worn leather desktop, crossed to the window, and peered out from around the side of the closed drapes. He stared across the lawn, toward the pond and beyond that the wall, picturing the sensors and tripwires and hidden cameras, and he weighed what he'd just heard. He received briefings on all kinds of subjects, all the time. It was part of the job. One regular report he got was a list of significant deaths. Foreign leaders. Key military figures, friend and foe. Terrorist suspects. Essentially anyone who could upset the geopolitical status quo. Dry stuff, on the whole. But a perk of the job was that he got to add a few extra names for himself. Nothing official. Just people he had a personal interest in. One of these was a guy named Owen Buck. He had died of cancer four weeks ago. Nothing suspicious about that. On its own. Then another guy on his list had died. Varinder Singh. Electrocuted in his bath. A tape player had wound up in the water with him. Its cord was still plugged into the wall. Fifty/fifty, suicide or accident, the police had said. And now Keith Bridgeman had died. Also on his list. Also fifty/fifty. Not the kind of coincidence that was ever going to pass Stamoran's smell test. That was for damn sure.

Stamoran returned to his desk and picked up the handset. "I'm going to give you three names. Geoff Brown. Michael Rymer. Charlie Adam. They're already on my list. I want them under surveillance, twenty-four/seven, effective immediately. Send our best people. Someone looks at these guys funny, I want them in a cell before they can blink. In isolation. No one gets access until I send someone to question them."

"Covert surveillance, sir? Or can the watchers make contact? Make it known what they're doing?"

"Covert. Strictly hands-off. These guys are Company lifers. If they cotton onto the fact that we have reason to watch them, they'll disappear faster than a politician who's asked to keep a promise."

"Understood."

"And there's a fourth name. Neville Pritchard. He's also on my list. I want him in protective custody. The most secure place we have. The most remote. Now. Tonight. No delay."

Stamoran dropped the receiver into its cradle and walked back to the window. Three guys were dead. Three would be watched. One would be put on ice. Which left one last name. Not on the list. Stamoran knew it, of course. So did Pritchard. But no one else did. Stamoran needed to keep things that way. The secret he had hidden for twenty-three years depended on it.

Stamoran turned his attention to Pritchard. Tried to picture his face. It wasn't easy after so many years. He could remember more about the guy's temper. He wasn't going to be happy about getting dragged out of bed and bundled off to some distant safehouse. Not happy at all. But that was too bad. When you're forced into a game of Russian Roulette you have no time to worry about people's feelings. There's only one move to make. Ensure the bullet that could kill you is removed from the gun.

Sergeant Hall showed up a whisker after 8:30 P.M. She parked her car—a small, clean, domestic sedan—directly outside her house and walked up the path to her door. She was around five foot six and was wearing civilian clothes. Jeans, white sneakers, and an Orioles sweatshirt. Her blond hair was tied back in a ponytail and she moved with fluid confidence, like an athlete. She wasn't in a rush. She wasn't glancing around to see if she was being watched. Reacher was pleased. It showed the armory sergeant had listened. He gave her a couple of minutes to get settled then made his own way up the path.

Hall answered the door right away. She looked surprised to see a huge guy in woodland BDUs on her doorstep, but not worried. "Help you, Captain?" she said.

Reacher showed his Military ID card then slid his wallet back into his pocket. "I need a minute of your time. To follow up on the missing weapons case."

Hall's expression was blank. "There aren't any missing weapons. The MPs searched the entire base. They confirmed it."

"The weapons aren't missing. But something else is."

Hall looked away. She scratched the side of her face then tucked a loose strand of hair behind her ear. "I don't—"

Reacher said, "Some of our paperwork. A couple of pages got lost. Someone screwed up. I need to fix it before our CO finds out. Just need a few details. I was told you were the person to talk to."

"Paperwork?" Hall blinked, twice. "Oh. OK. Sure. What . . . wait. You don't have a briefcase or a clipboard or anything."

"Don't need one." Reacher tapped his temple. "I'll remember what you say. Then I'll call my base and pass the information along to the right person. He needs to do the actual form-filling. Otherwise the handwriting won't match."

Hall didn't respond.

Reacher said, "It won't take long. And we're in a time crunch here . . ."

"Oh. OK. What do you need to know?"

"Mind if I come inside? It's been a long day. I could use a glass of water while we talk."

Hall paused. She looked Reacher up and down. He was practically a foot taller than she. Probably twice her weight. But he was an MP and MPs don't like to be told no. Nothing good ever comes of it. So after a moment she nodded and gestured for him to follow her down the hallway. There were framed pictures on the walls. Three on either side. Prints of animals and birds and scenes from nature. Hall pointed to the door on the right then continued to the kitchen. Reacher followed her direction and found himself in her living room. He stood just off center to avoid hitting his head on a light that hung from the ceiling and waited for Hall to catch up. She appeared a minute later with two plain glasses of water. She put one on a side table next to the couch and then perched at the front of a matching armchair.

"So," Hall said. "Details?"

Reacher sat in the center of the couch, took a sip of water, then said, "The weapons that come back from the Gulf. The ones designated surplus. You're responsible for testing them. Deciding which are kept and which are disposed of?"

"My team is. Not just me. But none of those weapons is missing. The MPs searched and—"

"Who decides who tests which crates?"

Hall paused for a moment, then said, "It's basically random. No method to it."

Reacher said, "Who decides?"

"I do, I guess. From a record-keeping point of view."

"I think you do have a method. And it has nothing to do with record-keeping. You make sure the guns that come to you to test are in good shape. And are older ones. With full-auto capability."

"Why would I do that?"

"Where do you get the civilian-spec lower receivers?"

"Civilian-spec? You must be confused. We have nothing to do with civilian weapons."

Reacher said, "Full-auto capable lower receivers are valuable things. They can turn an AR-15 that any bozo can buy into a military grade weapon. So you swap them out, sell them, then send the complete-looking guns to be destroyed. No one ever finds out. *Should* ever find out. But you heard that a crate of doctored weapons had gotten lost on the base. An admin screwup. That could be a big problem. You had to cover your ass. So you called in a bogus report. You said M16s were being stolen. They weren't, so you knew everyone at Rock Island would be cleared. Including yourself. Then if the doctored weapons came to light, you figured the suspicion would be deflected up the chain, to the original owners in the Gulf. Who would never be traced because the systems are all out of whack."

Hall jumped to her feet. "Doctored weapons? I don't know what—"

"Sit down." Reacher's voice was loud enough to have knocked her over.

Hall sat. She wriggled back into the chair, looking small and de-flated.

Reacher said, "You're in a hole. So you know what you should do?"

Hall shook her head. Just a tiny, nervous motion.

Reacher said, "Stop digging. You're only making things worse for yourself. Now's the time to be honest. Tell me everything, right now, no more bullshit, and I'll see what I can do to help you. Maybe I can limit the damage a little. But only if you stop being a pain in my ass."

Hall covered her face with her hands and curled up even smaller. When she emerged a moment later, a tear was running down one cheek. "OK." She sniffed. "I'm not admitting to anything. It wasn't me. But I know things. I'll tell you. Make you look good with your CO. Just let me use the bathroom first. I'll be quick. I need to get my head straightened out."

Reacher said, "Fine. But use the one upstairs."

Hall unfolded herself from her chair and scuttled to the door.

Reacher heard light, fast footsteps on the stairs. He heard Hall's bedroom door slam shut and a couple of seconds later he heard her bathroom door close, more quietly, on the far side.

Sergeant Hall knew Reacher would have heard the doors. She wanted him to hear them. Needed him to, for authenticity. But she prayed that he did not hear the next sound she made. The slight, unavoidable squeak as she eased her bathroom window open.

Susan Kasluga was in the kitchen, waiting for the kettle to boil, when Charles Stamoran found her. It was a wide rectangular space with an island in the center. The countertops were plain white, polished to a high shine. The cabinets were also white, with smooth fronts and no ornamentation. The backsplashes were made from sheets of stainless steel, and the few appliances that were on display were organized into logical groups. Kasluga had specified every detail herself and when a journalist had once described the place as feeling like a laboratory, she had been delighted.

Stamoran said, "Got a minute, Susie? We need to talk."

Kasluga crossed her arms. "Better not be about my *tea*." Her tone was fierce, but a smile was playing around the corners of her eyes.

The pair had been together twenty years and married a month shy of seventeen. They weren't a typical couple. She was ten years younger. Six inches taller. She had wild red hair that reached her waist when it wasn't tied up for work—to match a suit or, less often these days, a lab coat. She had high cheekbones and bright green eyes. When she walked into a room, people noticed. They couldn't help it. They couldn't avoid staring, even now that she was on the wrong side of fifty. Physically, Stamoran was the opposite. The wrong side of sixty, short, compact, forgettable face, hair innocuously cropped—what was left of it. He could be by her side throughout a party or a reception or a dinner and people would have to check the press photos the next day to tell if he'd been there at all. They worked in different worlds. They had different interests. Different hobbies. Different tastes in food and books and movies. But when it came to brains and guile, they were a perfect match.

"This has nothing to do with your . . . drink." Stamoran smiled, too, but there was no warmth in it. He was a precise man. Pedantic, even. He couldn't stand that she called a bunch of foul-smelling herbs infused in hot water *tea*, because there wasn't any tea in it. He hated the lack of accuracy and thought that as a research scientist she should know better. It was one of the few things about her that rankled with him, even after two decades. "I have some news. Not good. Three people who worked at Mason Chemical when you were there have died. All in the last month." He paused. "Owen Buck. Varinder Singh. Keith Bridgeman."

The kettle managed a first feeble hint of a whistle, but Kasluga didn't wait for it to get louder. She picked it up and poured hot water into her mug. She knew she didn't need the full 212 degrees for that kind of *tea*. And she had no problem with switching between precision at work and vernacular at home. Her husband's single-track rigidity drove her crazy.

She said, "Those names ring a bell. They were in India, in '69, right? They were part of some special development team. Their work was kept separate. Some kind of a secret project. Those guys must all be pretty long in the tooth by now. What happened? Old age catch up with them?"

"Buck, cancer got him. The others, not so clear-cut. The police say fifty/fifty, suicide or accident."

"Both of them?"

Stamoran nodded.

Kasluga said, "They can't both have had fatal accidents, one after the other. So suicide? Really?"

"No. I think someone killed them."

"Killed, as in murdered?"

Stamoran nodded again.

Kasluga shook her head. "Why would anyone want to murder a couple of retired scientists? That makes no sense."

"Susan, there are some things you should know about what happened in '69. Things I didn't tell you before, for reasons that will become obvious. But I need to fill you in now, because I think you're in danger."

"Danger? Me? How? I had nothing to do with whatever work those guys were doing."

"I know."

"It was the 1960s, for God's sake. It was hard enough as a woman to get any kind of research job. No matter that I was smarter than every man who had applied to Mason Chemical in the previous ten years. Probably the previous twenty. And that I could run rings around every man who was already there when they did finally hire me. The assholes wouldn't let me near anything halfway interesting."

"Which is why you took the position in India. I know. And that was a wise move."

"It wasn't. I thought if I got away from corporate HQ I'd have more freedom, but no. I was still stuck on the sidelines. Only over there I was caught in the million-degree heat with no amenities and nothing to do. Not until the shit hit the fan, anyway. Then they wanted a pretty face to stick in front of the cameras until the fuss blew over. Pretty and naïve. I went from unwanted hanger-on to flavor of the month, overnight. Suddenly they couldn't get enough of me. And boy, did I pay the price for that, the minute they didn't need me anymore."

"You were taken advantage of. Used as a PR mouthpiece. That's clear. But it's not why I'm worried."

"So what's the problem? A couple of guys I had basically no connection with, more than twenty years ago, might have been murdered. If anyone should be looking over their shoulders, it's the other members of that team, surely? Maybe you should be talking to them. Maybe someone has a grudge. Maybe one of the surviving scientists."

"I don't think so. This is the work of an outsider. And I'm taking the appropriate steps. The surviving members will all be . . . taken care of."

LEE CHILD and ANDREW CHILD

"You really think someone's going after the rest of the team, then? All of them? Why? What did they do?"

Stamoran didn't reply.

Kasluga glared at him. "And why is someone so upset about it now, after all this time?"

Stamoran took a moment, then said, "There were seven people on that team. On the face of it, all legitimate scientists. But that's not all they were. Two were employed by the army. Five, by the CIA. Their civilian credentials were a cover."

Kasluga lifted her mug, then set it back down on the countertop. "You're joking. The place where I worked was crawling with soldiers and spies? How long have you known?"

Stamoran said, "That's not important."

"The hell it isn't. Why didn't you tell me before?"

"It was on a need-to-know basis. You didn't need to know. Now you do."

Kasluga shrugged. "Explains the secret squirrel vibe, I guess. What were they working on?"

Stamoran shook his head. "That's not important, either. There are only two things that matter right now. First, I do believe someone is going after the whole team. Two dead in suspicious circumstances, one after another, is too big of a coincidence. Second, technically there weren't seven people involved. There were eight. Someone else was connected to that project, indirectly. But significantly."

Kasluga reached for her mug, then pulled her hand back and pressed it against the outside of her thigh. "An eighth person? You sure?"

Stamoran nodded. "Certain."

Kasluga took a breath. "You know who it is?"

Stamoran nodded again. "I do."

Kasluga rested her palms on the countertop and leaned all her weight on them. Her voice dropped to barely a whisper. "Charles? If you have something to say, say it."

"OK." Stamoran paused. "The eighth person? It's me."

Chapter 4

Reacher did not just hear Hall's bathroom window open. He also saw it.

The moment her bedroom door closed he jumped up from the couch and moved silently down the hallway. He opened the front door. Left it open to avoid making a sound. Hurried along the front of the house until he got to the left-hand corner. Lined up so that the reflection in the driver's window of his borrowed car gave him a clear view down the side of the house. And waited. A moment later Hall's head appeared. She glanced both ways then stretched for the drainpipe that ran down just to the side of the casement. Gripped it with one hand. Then the other. She wriggled out backward until she was sitting on the sill, facing the wall. Pulled her right foot up so she was squatting on it. Did the same with her left. Braced herself, pushed back, and stepped her right foot across to the other side of the pipe. Then she started to lower herself, hand over hand, soles flat against the wall, leaning out almost horizontally, like she was rappelling down a rigid iron rope.

Reacher let her get halfway down before he moved. He stepped around the corner and started in toward her. She spotted him right away. Changed direction. Tried to climb up. To dive back through the window. But before she got close Reacher stretched out and grabbed her belt.

"Want to come here, nice and slow and secure?" he said. "Or risk falling on your head?"

Hall climbed down. Her feet hit the path and she slumped back against the wall.

Reacher stepped in close and said, "It's safe to say the confession phase of this interview is done, yes?"

"Asshole. What happens now?"

"Depends on you."

"What do you want?"

"You took the lower receivers?"

"Obviously."

"How many?"

"Forty-eight."

"Hear that?"

Hall looked left and right. "No. What?"

"That's the sound of the window for you helping yourself slamming shut."

"Wait. Ninety-six."

"You sold them?"

"I didn't take them as souvenirs."

"Who did you sell them to?"

Hall shook her head and sighed. "Be honest with me. How much trouble am I in?"

Reacher said, "My guess? A lot."

"Anything I can do to improve the forecast?" Hall pushed away from the wall and looked Reacher in the eye. "Anything you need? Any way to make the outlook a little sunnier?"

"Maybe," Reacher said.

"Wait a minute." Kasluga stepped back, away from the kitchen counter. She was holding her right hand out in front, palm upright, like a cop stopping traffic. "You were at the Mason plant in India in '69? The same time as me? No way. I would have known. I would have seen you."

Stamoran shook his head. "I didn't say I was there, in India. I was based in the States. At Langley. I was in charge of the program those seven guys were working on at Mason Chemical. And five other projects kind of like it in other countries."

Kasluga's hands switched to her hips. "You were in charge? So it's down to you that I got hung out to dry?"

"No. My number two, the point man on the ground, he was responsible for that. He was authorized to act independently if there was an emergency. And this was all long before you and I met. Before I even knew you existed."

"Who was this guy? Your number two?"

"That's not important."

Kasluga snatched a chef's knife from a block next to the stovetop. "Say something I ask you about is *not important* again and I'll stab you. Now, come on! Pritchard, right? Neville Pritchard? He was your number two. He's the guy we're talking about."

Stamoran didn't reply.

Kasluga set the knife down next to her mug. "Pritchard reported to you. So he knows your name?"

Stamoran nodded.

"Does anyone else?"

"Only him. The structure was compartmentalized. For security."

"So he could give you up. If whoever is killing his team members catches up to him, trying to put names in all the frames."

"Theoretically."

"Then this murderer could come after you, too? Oh no, Charles. I don't like that. I don't like it at all." Kasluga moved around to Stamoran's side of the kitchen island and stretched to touch his arm.

Stamoran said, "I'm in no danger. It's you I'm worried about."

"Why? I wasn't involved with that team. I was just a *PR mouthpiece*. You said so yourself. And what I did is hardly a secret. There's no reason for Pritchard to point a finger at me. Or for any of the other survivors to."

"You're not seeing the bigger picture, Susie. Singh was an old man, living alone. Bridgeman was in a hospital bed, half dead from a heart attack. Getting to those guys was easy. But me? After the president, I've got to be the best protected man in the world."

"So what do you think? This guy will come after me to get to you?"

"That's what I'd do in his shoes."

"That's not very nice." Kasluga let go of Stamoran's arm.

Stamoran shrugged.

Kasluga moved back to the other side of the island. "Can't you do something? Catch this guy before he gets to anyone else? Before he even finds out about you?"

"It's in hand."

" 'In hand'? What does that mean? What are you doing, exactly?"

"That's not . . . Suffice it to say, this guy won't be on the loose for long."

"Is it safe to leave the others out there, while he's roaming around, hunting them down? Can't you lock them up somewhere where they'll be protected?"

Stamoran said nothing.

"So that's a no?"

"I can't get into the specifics. You know that. You also know I'm not someone who leaves anything to chance. So I'm going to ask you to do something for me."

"Of course. What is it?"

"Stay here. At the house."

"When?"

"Tomorrow. The next day, too. Don't go to the office. Don't go anywhere. Not till this guy is behind bars."

"You cannot be serious."

"I'm completely serious."

"That's the dumbest thing you've ever asked me to do. I have meetings scheduled all day tomorrow. All day the next. Aside from me, only three women head up a top 500 company. Versus 496 men. You know that. So if I don't show up, what are all those men going to say? She's flaky. Unreliable. Not up to the job. Weak. The knives would be out for me before the sun was halfway up."

"What would people say about your job skills if you got electrocuted? That's what happened to Singh. Or if you *fell* out of a twelfth-floor window? Like Bridgeman. Susie, think about it. You can't be CEO of anything if you're dead."

"Goddamn it!" Kasluga picked up her mug and flung it into the sink. It shattered, spraying rivulets of pale greenish-brown liquid all over the stainless-steel backsplash. "I'm going to work out. We'll talk about this later."

* * *

Roberta and Veronica Sanson caught up with each other at the
New Orleans Airport Hilton, as planned. They had arrived on separate flights, from different airports. They were traveling under fake
IDs. They took courtesy shuttles twenty minutes apart. The only unexpected detail was that Roberta got to the hotel first. The airline schedules had her a quarter hour behind her sister, but the baggage handlers
at Midway were working slowly that day. They were causing all kinds
of delays. But the wrinkle was a minor one. Roberta figured it didn't
call for any major recalibration, so she slid straight into her next task.
She bought an iced tea at the hotel's ground-floor café, carried it outside to a seating area behind a cutesy white picket fence, and settled
in to watch the valet parking station at the side of the curb.

When Veronica arrived she made the valet station her first port
of call. She sauntered up to the guy behind the stand and said, "Evening. How are you doing today?"

The valet shrugged. "Fine, I guess. Thank you for asking. You
collecting your car?"

Veronica shook her head. "Not me. I don't drive. I'm on my way
to check in. But here's the kicker. I hear this is a great party town,
and I'm only here for one night. I don't want to waste my time in
some lame-ass dive. So, I was wondering, do you live around here?"

"Born and bred."

"That's what I was hoping you'd say. What's your name?"

"Riccardo."

"Nice to meet you, Riccardo. I'm Stephanie. And here's my question. If you had a good friend coming to visit who knows how to
enjoy herself but has no time to waste, where would you take her?"

"Enrico's. A block away from Bourbon Street. All the fun but a
lot more class. Can't go wrong there."

"What if this friend wanted to . . . go wrong?"

Riccardo smiled. "In that case, The Vault. A person can get into all sorts of trouble there."

Veronica smiled back. "Sounds like you're speaking from experience."

"Maybe. But we've just met. Maybe I should take the Fifth."

"Or maybe we should meet there, later, and you could show me what's up. Given that I'm a stranger here and you have all this . . . experience."

Riccardo's smile grew wider. "Sure. We could do that. I get out of here at eleven."

"Excellent. See you there around midnight?"

"Count on it."

Veronica walked away, feeling the valet's gaze on her ass, and headed for the hotel entrance. She twisted her hair into a tight knot at the back of her head, approached the desk, and booked herself a room. Just for one night. She paid cash. The ID she used showed the name Cailin Delaney. She signed all the forms the clerk handed her, took her change and her room key, and walked back outside. She threaded her way through a gap in the fence around the café's seating area and paused next to an empty table. She scanned the space like she was looking for someone. She leaned down and rested the tips of three fingers on the tabletop. She didn't look at Roberta. She knew her sister was watching. After a moment she curled her ring finger up, leaving two fingers showing, then a moment later she flexed her hand so that all four fingers were touching the table. She stayed still for a moment. Then she shrugged like the person she'd hoped to find hadn't showed up, headed inside, and made her way to room 324.

* * *

Outside, Roberta continued to watch the valet station. She let a black convertible come and go. Three domestic sedans. A Jeep. Then she drained the last of her tea and stood up. A minivan had stopped by the curb. Its passenger door opened and a woman climbed out. She looked stiff and tired and irritated. She would be in her mid-thirties, Roberta guessed, and was wearing white shorts, a pink blouse, and sandals. The blouse had a large oval stain on it. Her hair looked like it hadn't seen a brush in days. She stretched her back, grunted, then turned and rolled open the rear door. Four kids instantly spilled out. The oldest was maybe twelve. The youngest, six. They were all boys and right away they were chasing and yelling and shoving. Roberta had seen packs of wild dogs fighting over a prize carcass that were calmer. The mother started herding the boys toward the hotel, arms outstretched, shaking her head. A man appeared at the back of the van. Presumably the father. He swung up the load gate and began hauling out a bunch of bright, multicolored suitcases. The valet helped him load them onto a baggage cart. Then he handed the father a claim ticket and looped around to the driver's door.

The father seemed in no hurry to catch up with his family. He slipped his valet ticket into the back pocket of his baggy shorts and started to push the cart with one hand. It was a halfhearted effort. The cart barely moved. It was rolling so slowly that Roberta had to adjust her own pace. She changed her angle slightly then pulled a notebook out of her bag. Pretended to be checking something written inside it as she walked. Made out like she didn't realize she was on a collision course. And bumped right into the guy. Her knee wound up brushing against his inner thigh. She shrieked and dropped her book. It landed right in front of him. He let go of the cart and stepped aside. Took a moment to gather himself. Then leaned down, retrieved the book, and handed it back to Roberta.

She said, "Thank you so much. You're very kind. And I'm sorry I was so clumsy."

The guy grinned and straightened the front of his crumpled shirt. "Don't worry about it. That was the most exciting thing that's happened to me all week." *You say that now,* Roberta thought. *Wait till you try to get your minivan back . . .*

Chapter 5

Two cars were stopped at the side of a road south of Annapolis, Maryland, between Back Creek and the Atlantic Ocean. They were tucked in together, right after the crest of a tight bend, in darkness. Not the safest place to park, but the drivers had no choice. The road was narrow and it was lined with trees, already in leaf, which restricted the view of the old, peaceful houses that were scattered along either side. Soft lights twinkled faintly through the ancient shrubs and bushes that filled most of the gaps between the trunks, making it harder still to observe the buildings.

The first car was empty. Two men were sitting in the second. They had partial sight of one of the houses. They'd brought binoculars, a camera with a long lens, and a pair of portable radios. One of the men was writing in a log book. He had a flashlight in one hand. His fingers were covering a chunk of the lens which smothered most of the beam and turned the little light that did escape a subdued pink. He had a cheap ballpoint pen in his other hand. He jotted down the time. The place. His initial observations. Stuff he would need later for the report he would have to write. He had just finished recording what he could see when his radio crackled into life. It was one of the guys from the other car. They had made their way around back, behind the house, and were reconnoitering on foot.

The voice on the radio said, "Pritchard's here. Positive ID. I saw him through the kitchen window, clearing dishes. Over."

The guy with the pen said, "Is he alone? Over."

"Affirmative. There's no one with him. And he washed only one plate and one wineglass."

"Is he still there?"

"Negative. He's gone upstairs. The first-floor lights went off. The bathroom light came on. Wait. It just went off. Now his bedroom light is on."

"He's getting ready for bed?"

"Looks that way. Wait. His bedroom light just went off as well. So do we grab him now? Or wait for him to get settled?"

The guy with the pen took a moment to think. This wasn't his first rodeo. He liked his targets dopey and compliant. He'd learned the hard way what could happen if they weren't. Pritchard had drunk at least one glass of wine, which was a good start. Then it takes the average person between forty-five minutes and an hour to reach deep sleep. So experience dictated that they should wait ninety minutes. To be on the safe side. To give themselves a good chance that Pritchard would be away with the fairies. Then pick his locks and approach his bedroom with maximum stealth. Nine times out of ten the cuffs would be on before the target's eyes were even open. But this operation was different. The orders came right from the top. Which meant the result would be under the microscope. His performance would be, too. And the word *immediate* had been used. Even if the arrest went like clockwork a delay could take some of the shine off it. And if something went wrong, it would be blamed on his decision to wait. He was under no illusions about that.

The guy with the pen hit the Transmit button on the side of his handset and said, "Egress points at the rear?"

The voice on the radio crackled back, "Seven, as expected. Three windows, second floor. Two windows, one personnel door, first floor. One personnel door, rear of garage."

"OK. Form up. Watch them in case he tries to bail out. We're hitting the front door in ninety seconds."

Charles Stamoran was in his study, rereading one of the day's reports, when his wife found him. She was wearing a white bathrobe, knotted in the front, and her hair was still wet from the shower. Her feet were bare and her skin was glowing from the recent heat and steam. She smelled of all kinds of shampoos and conditioners and lotions. Stamoran found the combination a little overpowering, although he had never admitted that to her. He said, "Well?"

Kasluga crossed the room, perched on the ottoman in front of her husband's armchair, and stretched out to touch his knee. She said, "Charles, I'm sorry about before."

Stamoran didn't reply.

She said, "Two days."

Stamoran frowned. He hated it when his wife dangled an unfinished comment and clammed up until he coaxed the rest of the information out of her. He tried to resist the follow-up, but as always, he failed. He said, "What about two days?"

"I'll lay low, like you asked. Stay here. Keep away from the office. Give you time to catch the guy."

"Why two days? Why set a timetable? Why not stay safe until he's in custody?"

Kasluga shrugged. "It was you who said two days. And I've found a way to turn a two-day absence into an advantage. Any longer and it won't work."

"Two days was just a sensible starting point. Not a maximum duration. And what won't work?"

Kasluga leaned in closer and lowered her voice like she was afraid of being overheard. "I've been working on something. An acquisition. A major one. A game-changer. I've been keeping it under the radar so that if it doesn't pan out, I won't lose face in the industry. I figured I'd wait till the ink was dry then claim credit for it as a fait accompli. But just now I made some calls. Looks like we're home and dry. The lawyers have cleared the final obstacle and swear the papers will be signed within forty-eight hours. So I've whispered in a couple of ears. Seeded some rumors. Made out like the deal is on life support. A bunch of the asshole men will be getting hard-ons, thinking I'm going to publicly crash and burn. And when the result is a triumph, it's going to look like I dropped out of sight to personally intervene. I'll be the hero. But if I stay away any longer, it'll look like I had nothing to do with it. I can't have that."

Two days, Stamoran thought. Maybe enough time to make an arrest. Maybe not. It was out of his control. The remaining targets were being watched. The traps were set. The guy who was picking off the scientists from '69 might try to strike again within forty-eight hours. Or he might not. Stamoran had no idea what was driving the guy's schedule. But he wasn't too worried about it, because Susan was off the money in one important respect. The arrest wasn't the crux of the matter. The key was removing Pritchard from the game. Stamoran checked his watch. The team he had sent should already be at Pritchard's house.

Stamoran looked at his wife. He nodded and said, "Two days will be enough."

The guy with the pen in the car in Annapolis was named Paul Birch. He put his pen away, took out his gun, and turned to his partner, Simon Stainrod. Birch nodded. Stainrod pulled the lever that popped the trunk and the two men climbed out. Stainrod retrieved a tactical battering ram—a heavy metal cylinder nine inches in diameter and eighteen inches long, with two articulated handles fixed to its center line—and they crossed the road, side by side, Birch a couple of feet ahead, six feet apart. They ignored the gate and stepped over the two-foot-high wall. Walked parallel with the path, one on either side, feet in the flower bed, churning up the damp dirt and crushing the shrubs that were growing there. They reached the house and stepped up onto the porch. Stainrod swung the ram back then heaved it forward, hard, waist high, parallel with the ground, gaining momentum as it passed through the air. It slammed into the door near the keyhole for a heavy-looking lock. The wood splintered. The screws tore away from the hinges. The frame ripped off the wall and the door careened back into the hallway like a punch-drunk boxer reeling from a knockout blow. Then it flopped over, landed horizontally, and slid until its top edge was pressed against the foot of a grandfather clock. Stainrod dropped the ram, pulled his gun, and took up a position tucked in tight against the wall near the ruined doorway. Birch ran past him. He left a trail of muddy footprints over the remains of the door, along the hallway, and up the stairs. He knew where the bedroom was. He knew where all the rooms were. He'd memorized a faxed copy of the house's original design before leaving the Pentagon that evening. He found the right door. Held his flashlight parallel with the barrel of his gun. Kicked the door open. Burst through. And lined up his gun on the head of the bed.

Paying for a night in an airport hotel and only using the room for a couple of hours was not strictly necessary. Not an optimal use of funds. Not the kind of thing Roberta and Veronica Sanson would have considered doing even a month before. But under the circumstances, they figured they could justify it. There were some definite benefits. They could hang out without anyone seeing them together. They could order food from room service and eat without the risk of other restaurant guests remembering either of them. And very soon—maybe in only a few days' time—they were going to be rich, so the cost aspect was essentially a nonissue.

How rich they were going to be was yet to be determined. But when Owen Buck's investigator had tracked them down, and they had verified his bona fides, and Buck had tried to salve his dying conscience by revealing what had happened in India back in '69, he had left them with no doubt. A heap of cash was out there. The way they saw things, it had their names on it. They were entitled to it. They were going to take it. And that would be a fitting way to round off what was needed to right the wrong that Buck swore had been done to them.

It took Birch a moment to register the fact, but the bed was empty. He checked all four corners of the room. The bathroom. Under the bed. Inside the closet. And found no one. He cleared the other upstairs rooms. There were two more bedrooms and another bathroom, but no sign of Pritchard and no indication that anyone else lived there. So Birch went back downstairs. He stopped in the hallway and shot a glance at Stainrod. Stainrod shook his head. Birch moved on and searched the living room. The dining room. The kitchen. A tiny laundry room. And finally the garage.

There was no sign of Pritchard in any of them.

Birch returned to the hallway and used his radio to call the pair who were watching the back of the house. He said, "Anything?"

The reply was loud and clear. "Nada."

"Are you certain?"

"One hundred percent."

"OK. One of you come inside. Help me search. Pritchard must be hiding. He must have a bolt-hole somewhere. In the crawl space. The attic. A hollow wall. Somewhere. And he must still be here. His bed hasn't been laid in. His closet is full of clothes. I saw a bunch of suitcases still in there, too. His car is in the garage. And we know he didn't leave on foot. So we need to find him. Immediately."

The sisters ate, and talked, and watched TV, and took turns showering, and were ready to leave the hotel by 11:30 P.M. That gave them a half-hour cushion in case Riccardo's shift finished late. Veronica left first. She walked down the stairs, strolled through the deserted lobby, crossed to the courtesy bus stop, and waited ten minutes for a ride to the airport's departure terminal. Then she made her way straight to arrivals and found the passenger pickup area.

Roberta stayed in the room another five minutes then headed outside, to the valet stand. She smiled at the new guy on duty and handed over her stolen collection ticket.

The guy returned with the minivan after fifteen minutes. Roberta gave him an average tip—not memorably big, not unforgettably small—and climbed in behind the wheel. She drove away from the hotel and followed the signs to the airport, and then the arrival terminal. She drifted to a stop by the curb at the far end of the pickup zone and immediately Veronica stepped out from behind a pillar. A moment later she was in the passenger seat. A minute after that Roberta was speeding toward the city, following a route to an address she had memorized before they had arrived in Chicago.

Chapter 6

The phone in the Pentagon rang at 9:00 A.M. Eastern, the following morning. That was 8:00 A.M. Central, where the call originated. Right on time.

The guy who answered listened in silence then hung up, switched to an internal line, and dialed the extension for an office that was one floor higher up and one ring closer to the center of the building.

Stamoran picked up immediately. He said, "Is it done?"

"Neville Pritchard is not in custody," the guy recited. "Repeat, not. He was positively identified, alone, at his home, but in the short time between confirming the sighting and the team gaining entry, he disappeared. How he evaded capture is unknown. His current whereabouts are unknown. Records indicate he received no phone calls prior to the raid. No other signals were observed or detected. Therefore he is believed to be acting alone. Attempts to locate him are ongoing with the utmost urgency."

Stamoran laid the receiver down, leaned back in his chair, closed his eyes, and silently cursed. He should have sent snipers, not nursemaids. Especially not nursemaids who somehow tipped their hand in the middle of a simple snatch job. Which they must have done. There was no other explanation. Pritchard had been alone. No one had contacted him. The report made that clear.

Stamoran took a long, slow breath. He tried to view the situation rationally. The news wasn't great. They didn't have Pritchard. But equally, the news wasn't terrible. There was no reason to believe that Pritchard had been captured. He was just in the wind. So whoever was going after the scientists from '69 didn't have him, either. The secret was safe. For now.

Stamoran opened his eyes and picked up the phone. "I want the team from last night to understand they have one chance to redeem themselves. I want two additional units assigned. The best we have. I want Pritchard found. Like, yesterday. And when he is found, if he tries to run again, I want him stopped. By any means necessary."

Sergeant Hall was already at her post at Rock Island Arsenal. She was set for a busy morning. A truck was due in from Little Rock Air Force Base, Arkansas. Paperwork was going to be involved, followed by some manual labor. It was a process Hall was familiar with. She had gone through it more than seventy times in the last year. She knew exactly what to expect so was already at the guard post at the base's main entrance, waiting, when the M35 Deuce and a Half rumbled into sight, looking tired and worn in its faded desert-sand paint job.

Hall waited for the gate to clank back into place behind the truck then climbed into her Humvee and led the way to the storeroom Reacher had visited the previous day. It was a step called for by regulations, not necessity. The sergeant who was driving the truck had pulled that duty more than fifty times. He could have followed the route with his eyes shut but was required to have an escort for as long as he was on-site. He didn't mind. And neither did Hall. It was an arrangement that worked very well for both of them.

Hall drove slowly until she reached the front of the building, then parked well clear of the storeroom's steel door. She walked back, unlocked it, and waited for the truck to grind to a halt. She watched the driver jump out. His name was Chapellier but she privately called him *Ape* because of his short body, long arms, and hunched gait. He rolled up the flap at the rear of the truck's canvas cover and opened the metal cage that had been bolted to the load-bed floor. Then together they started to haul out the crates of weapons that had been sent back from the Gulf and stack them up on the storeroom's Intake shelves. They worked steadily and efficiently and when the truck was empty, they moved straight on to refilling it with the crates from the Red shelves. The ones that held the weapons Hall's team had earmarked for destruction.

When the final crate had been squared away and the records had been updated and signed and the doors to the storeroom and the truck's cage had been locked, Hall got back into her Humvee. Her forehead was prickling and she could feel a drop of sweat inching its way down her lower back. She shifted in her seat and watched in her mirror as Chapellier climbed into the truck. She could have made him turn around in the narrow roadway but instead she set off the way they were already facing, planning to loop around and circle back to the guardhouse from the opposite direction. That was the way she always did it. No one watching—in person, or on a screen fed by the site's network of security cameras—would have been remotely surprised.

Hall's chosen way out was a little longer than the route they had followed on the way in. It involved passing through a kind of tunnel that had been formed when a set of classrooms had been extended out over the road due to a lack of space on the site. The covered section was more than 150 feet long. Cameras were lined up along its entire length. There wasn't an inch that escaped observation.

There wasn't an inch that hadn't escaped observation when the cameras were installed. But two of those cameras had been moved. Very gradually, over the course of ten weeks. The pair nearest the center, either side of an alcove formed by a fire escape that provided a convenient marker. They had been moved by Sergeant Hall, far enough to leave a blind spot twenty-three feet long. That was enough space for an M35 truck to stop with five inches to spare, front and rear.

Hall watched for the alcove, made sure there would be room for the truck to pull up alongside her, then stopped and climbed out. She hustled around to the rear of the Humvee and lifted out a crate. A plastic one. Olive green, but not army issue. She carried it into the gap between the vehicles. Waited for Chapellier to open his door then heaved the crate up higher so he could pull it into his cab. The guy balanced it on his knees and loosened the lid. He looked inside. Pulled out a metal object. An M16 lower receiver. He checked its holes and contours. Smiled. Dropped it back into the crate and reattached the lid. Placed it on the cab floor to the side of the gear lever and passed Hall an identical crate from the passenger side footwell. She wedged it against the top step and examined its contents. A wad of cash, which she counted, as she always did. And another stack of gun parts. Civilian spec.

She looked up and said, "You need more? Already?"

Chapellier frowned. "Is there a problem?" Then he heard a sound, behind him and to the side. A metallic screech. Primitive hinges that were starved of oil after a long stint in the desert. He spun around in his seat and saw the passenger door opening. A head appeared. And a torso. Belonging to a man he didn't recognize. A huge, broad man with a ferocious scowl on his face and a gun in his hand.

"Problem?" Reacher said, leaning farther into the cab. "Guess you could put it that way. If you're big on understatement."

Roberta and Veronica Sanson's night had not gone as planned.

It had started out OK. They completed the drive from New Orleans airport to Geoff Brown's house without incident. But when they slowed to look for a suitable spot to stop and keep watch, they saw another car parked at the side of the road. A Ford Crown Victoria. Plain blue. Poverty spec. An extra antenna on the roof. Another on the trunk lid. And two men inside. Neither one was making a move to get out. This wasn't a worn-out detective's car repurposed as a cab. It wasn't someone getting home late after too many beers and fumbling with his wallet so he could pay his fare. The car was positioned deliberately. The guys inside were waiting, perfectly relaxed and still, like they knew they were there for the long haul. Like that was something they were used to.

Roberta figured they could afford one pass-by. They needed at least some idea of what they were dealing with—and in any case, continuing in the same direction was less suspicious than abruptly turning around and slinking away. Brown's house was set back about fifty feet from the road. The area around it was somewhere between rustic and overgrown, like the owner had once been on top of his yard work but in recent years had started to let it slide. Nature was gaining the upper hand. That was clear. The house itself was long and low. It had a deep porch running along the front and the white paintwork was neat and crisp. Brown was keeping up with his property maintenance, at least.

Veronica gestured toward the house and said, "Windows."

All of Brown's shades were drawn. Maybe against the heat that would start building the moment the sun came up. Maybe for privacy. But either way, it meant no one could see in. Not from any of the neighbors' houses. Not from a car parked on the street. And not by anyone prowling around the grounds.

Roberta nodded. "We can work with this."

Roberta had kept up a slow, steady speed until she reached the next intersection, where she took a left and made her way back toward the southeast side of the city. She remembered seeing some kind of abandoned industrial site there. It looked like the place was being set for demolition. A security fence had been thrown up around the perimeter and a handful of portable offices had been dumped in a cluster outside. No vehicles had been parked nearby. No lights were on. There was nothing to suggest it was a twenty-four-hour operation. But there was plenty of scope to conceal their stolen minivan until the morning.

They took turns sleeping and when Veronica woke for the second time she nudged her sister. "The guys watching Brown's house? Could mean he's the one. He could have the name we need."

Roberta shook her head. "Buck said one guy on his list knew the name. The security doesn't mean anything. Someone's connecting the dots. That's all. Former CIA assets start dropping like flies, someone at Langley's going to notice. They'll be watching all the survivors from '69."

"I guess you're right."

"You know I am." Roberta clambered back into the driver's seat and fired up the engine. "Come on. I'm starving. We need breakfast. And supplies. And then you have a call to make."

*　*　*

Reacher climbed up into the truck's cab and settled into the right-hand seat. He said, "OK. There are two ways we can play this."

Sergeant Chapellier sat for a moment with both hands on the wheel. Then he lunged to his left. He grabbed Hall by the front of her tunic and dragged her up and into the truck and kept on pulling until she was sprawled across his lap. He said, "No. Only one way. Get out."

Hall thrashed and struggled. She twisted around onto her back and stretched up and tried to gouge Chapellier's eyes out. Reacher didn't move.

Chapellier pinned both of Hall's arms with one of his and slid his other hand up to her throat. He turned to Reacher and said, "Get out. Now."

Reacher said, "Get out? Is that it?"

"Get out or I'll break her neck."

Reacher checked the guy's name tape. "You're not one of the world's deep thinkers, are you, Chapellier? She already gave you up. I don't need her anymore. Kill her and I can nail you for murder. Much easier than rolling up whatever kind of a racket you've got going on."

Chapellier tightened his fingers around Hall's throat. She wriggled her arms free and grabbed his wrist with both hands. She strained to pull it clear but she couldn't get the leverage. Her legs were hanging out of the open door and her weight was pulling her harder into Chapellier's grip. She was also kicking and squirming like crazy. It was an instinctive response. There was nothing she could do to stop it, but it only made her problem worse.

Reacher stretched out his left hand and flicked the truck's master switch to Off. Its engine rattled to a stop. He waited for the last raucous echo to fade away then said, "First you're going to let her go. Then you're going to tell me who you're selling those gun parts to. Or we're going to step out of the vehicle, pieces of you are going to get broken, and then you're going to tell me."

Chapellier was still for three seconds then he hauled Hall up so that she was sitting. He shoved her in the back with his right hand, launching her out of the truck, then he sprang across toward Reacher. His arms were stretched out. He was trying to grab Reacher's gun. Reacher leaned to his left and raised his elbow. Chapellier plowed into it, hard, face-first. Reacher didn't wait to assess the damage. Instead he heaved his door open and jumped down. He slid the gun into its holster. Then he leaned in and grabbed Chapellier by his right arm. He dragged him sideways. All the way to the door. He kept going until Chapellier slithered off the edge of the truck's seat and bounced down its metal steps and slammed onto the ground. Reacher rolled him over onto his back. Stepped on his neck. And twisted his arm until his shoulder and elbow and wrist were all a hair's breadth away from breaking.

Reacher said, "This is the end of the road, Chapellier. Give it up."

Chapellier whimpered and a bubble of blood billowed out of his nose. His voice was strained and husky. He croaked, "Screw you."

Reacher kept up the pressure on Chapellier's arm. He said, "Tell me something. Did you pick this spot because, A, a lot of cameras are focused on it? Or B, because no one can see what happens here?"

Chapellier grunted. He managed a faint, "Asshole."

Reacher said, "Something else for you to think about. Those gun parts are US Army property. No civilian should ever get their hands on them. So I want whoever you're selling them to behind bars. I'll need your help with that. If you cooperate, I can't hurt you. I'll need you in one piece. Or reasonably close to one piece. But if you don't help me I can do as much damage as I like. *Injuries sustained while resisting arrest.* My word against yours. And you can forget about Sergeant Hall as a friendly witness."

Veronica Sanson pulled a file from her bag, checked a number, and fished a quarter out of her pocket. She was wearing leather gloves, which made snagging the coin more difficult than usual. She finally got hold of it, dropped it into the slot on the front of the payphone, dialed, and waited. It took ten rings for her call to be answered.

"Yes?" It was a man's voice on the line, quiet and slightly breathless.

Veronica said, "Dr. Brown? Geoffrey Brown?"

"Who's asking?"

"Sir, this is Special Agent Holbeck with the Federal Bureau of Investigation. I have some news for you. Bad news, I'm afraid. And I need to ask for your assistance in a very urgent matter."

Brown took a moment to reply. "Go on."

"Sir, I'm sorry to have to tell you this, but two of your former colleagues are dead."

"Owen Buck I know about. Cancer, right? Who else?"

"Dr. Buck died of natural causes, as you say, but I'm calling about two others. Varinder Singh and Keith Bridgeman."

"Bridgeman and Singh? Dead? When? How?"

"Dr. Singh was electrocuted. Dr. Bridgeman fell out of a window. Reports in the press are suggesting their deaths may have been accidental. Those reports are wrong."

"There was foul play? You're sure?"

"One hundred percent. The Bureau wouldn't be involved, otherwise."

"Who killed them?"

"That's where I need your help. Our sketch artists have put together a likeness. I need you to take a look. Tell me if you recognize the person."

"How would I recognize him?"

"He's killing members of your former research team, Doctor. There must be a connection. And he's not going to stop until we catch him. We believe you will be his next target. That's why I've come here, now. So please, take a look at the sketch. It'll only take a minute and it could save your life. I could come to your house and—"

"No. But I'll meet you. Somewhere public. Forgive me. Old habits."

Veronica smiled. "I understand. I'm working out of the local field office while I'm in town. There's no safer place than that, right? I'll give you the address. And if you could come right away, that would be in everyone's best interests. Particularly yours."

Chapter 7

It took Dr. Brown thirty minutes to reach the FBI field office. And another thirty seconds to discover that Agent Holbeck didn't exist.

Brown knew what he should do next. Run. His go-bag was in the trunk of his car. Old habits. He could take it and disappear. Stay out of sight until he figured out who was coming after him. And how to stop them. That's what he would have done at any time during his career. And when he was newly retired. But now there was a problem. Without the human contact that comes with work, for the first time in his life, he had started to feel lonely. He didn't have any friends in the city. He wasn't a sociable man so he wasn't likely to make any new ones. He didn't get on with his neighbors. And he knew no one would ever want to live with him. So he adopted a cat. Hercules. Another creature that no one had wanted. Who was still at his house. With no way to get out. No way to get food. No way to get water.

It took Brown twenty-five minutes to get back to his street. He slowed down and drove past his house. It looked the same as when he had left it. The drapes were all drawn. The door was closed. There were no cars parked at the curb. No strangers loitering on the sidewalk or poking around his yard. That allayed one of his fears, but he was still worried about something else. A couple of times while he was driving home he'd thought he was being followed. He'd thought it, but he wasn't certain. So he took a left. Then a right. Then he stopped dead. No cars steered desperately around him. None screeched to a halt behind him. There was no one in sight in his mirror. He shook his head. Chalked it up to rusty instincts. And too much adrenaline. He was out of practice. That was all. With that concern put to bed he figured it was safe enough to loop around and pull up onto his driveway. Dart inside. Grab Hercules. And race back out. A couple of minutes, max.

Brown opened his front door and paused. He listened. He couldn't hear anything. Couldn't smell anything. But he could feel something. A subliminal disturbance in the silent vibrations he was accustomed to the house giving out. Someone was there. Waiting. For him. Rusty or not, Brown's instincts told him to get out. Immediately. He started to turn. Then he heard a muffled squawk. From the living room. It was Hercules. He was in distress. Brown crept forward. Stopped at the threshold. Listened. Heard another squawk. More anguished this time. He reached for the door handle. Took a breath. And burst into the room.

A woman was standing next to Brown's favorite armchair. Her dark hair was pulled back. She was holding Hercules tight to her chest. Another woman was on the other side of the chair. Same height. Same build. Same hair. They were completely still. Their faces were expressionless, like statues. Neither of them spoke.

Brown took a step forward. "Let go of my cat."

The first woman's face cracked into a smile. She said, "Dr. Brown, we're glad you're back. Your cat doesn't seem to like us. Please, sit. I'll drop him on your lap."

Brown stayed where he was. "I recognize your voice. You called me. Pretended to be from the FBI. Why?"

"I apologize for the subterfuge. We didn't mean to mislead you. We just need to talk. Privately. And two men were watching your house so we couldn't just knock on your door. We figured they would follow you if you went somewhere. Give us a chance to get in, unobserved."

Brown crossed to the window, peered around the side of the drapes, then turned back. "The blue sedan? What the hell's going on?"

"What I told you on the phone? Aside from me being an agent, it's true. Particularly the part about you being in danger. We're here to help you."

"Help me? How? Who are you?"

"We'll come to that. But we need a piece of information first. Please sit. Let me explain."

Brown shuffled across to the chair and lowered himself into it.

The woman handed over the cat. "Your research team in India, in 1969. There were eight people on it."

"India? Never been there."

"Don't waste time. The threat against you is imminent. Believe me. So, eight people."

Brown shook his head. "Seven."

"Eight." The woman took the handwritten list out of her pocket and passed it to Brown. "We know seven names. You need to tell us the one that's missing. So that we can protect the surviving members who were involved."

Brown glanced at the piece of paper. Owen Buck's name was written in a different hand. He must have given up the rest of them. He always had been the weakest. Always talking about coming clean. But he must have been slipping if he could no longer count. "There were seven people. Their names are all here."

"There were eight. See the question mark? One name is missing. You need to tell us who it is."

"There were seven. I was there. You weren't. So I know what I'm talking about. You don't. And you shouldn't be asking questions about '69. No one should. It's time to close the book. Time for you to leave."

"You live in a nice neighborhood, Dr. Brown. Although there are a lot of busy roads around here. Lots of drivers in a hurry, not concentrating, not looking where they're going. It would be very easy for a person to get run down. Even easier for a small animal. Like a cat."

"I'm not going to listen to this. You need to leave. Now."

Brown held Hercules to his chest with one hand and used his other arm to start hauling himself out of the chair. He made it halfway then the second woman darted around behind him and leaned on his shoulders, forcing him back down. His elbow shot out to the side, almost knocking his pipe and tobacco pouch off his side table.

The first woman said, "If a cat did get hit by a car, would it be killed right away? Maybe, I guess. But maybe not. Imagine finding yours, all crushed and bleeding. Scooping him up. Racing to the veterinarian's office."

"No."

"Waiting outside the operating room door. Praying he can be saved. Worrying that the damage is too severe."

"I swear, there are only seven names. Anyone tells you otherwise, they're wrong. You want to cause pain to prove I'm not lying, hurt me. I don't care. Just leave my cat alone. He hasn't done anything to you."

The woman took the list back and slid it into her pocket. "OK. We're done here. I believe you. And I apologize. This is important so we had to be sure. I'm sorry we upset you." She paused for a moment, then said, "You know, you're looking very pale all of a sudden. Can I get you some coffee before we go? Tea? Something stronger?"

"Are you kidding? You break into my house and threaten to kill my cat and think I'm going to drink anything you give me? Forget it. You can show yourselves out."

The women made it as far as the door then stopped and turned around. The first one said, "Where are our manners? We forgot to introduce ourselves. I'm Veronica Sanson. This is my sister, Roberta."

Brown didn't answer. He hugged Hercules a little tighter.

Veronica said, "Our father was Morgan Sanson. It's important you know that."

Brown didn't need to be told. He knew who Morgan Sanson was. He took a deep breath and listened to the footsteps in his hallway. They approached the front door. It opened. Closed again. And there was silence. He breathed out. Gave Hercules a stroke and reached for his pipe. His nerves were shot. He packed the bowl. Brushed away a stray strand of tobacco. Held his lighter so its flame flickered and the tobacco began to smolder. He took a long, deep drag. Gulped down the smoke. Held it in his lungs. Exhaled, slowly. Sucked down some more. Kept the routine going until his head settled against his chair. His eyes rolled back in their sockets. Then globs of off-white foam started to dribble out of his mouth.

Veronica and Roberta stepped back into the room. They had never left the house. They watched as Brown's back arched. The cat jumped down and ran behind the couch. Brown jerked and grabbed his stomach. Then his chest. He vomited, a long greenish watery stream. It soaked the front of his shirt and his pants and sprayed across a wide arc of carpet. He jerked again. His whole body spasmed. Twice. Three times. Then he flopped back and lay completely still.

Veronica and Roberta waited for five minutes, to be certain. Then they moved into the hallway. Brown's telephone was sitting on a low, square table. Veronica put her gloves on and took an object from her pocket. A small tape recorder. She worked its buttons until she found the place she wanted, then picked up the phone. She dialed 911. Waited for the emergency operator to answer. Then she held the recorder up to the mouthpiece and pressed Play.

"Help me?" Brown's voice said, a little muffled but easy enough to make out.

Reacher gave Sergeant Chapellier a couple of minutes to stem the bleeding and stretch his sore joints. He checked that Sergeant Hall wasn't too much the worse for wear after getting flung out of the truck. Then he climbed back into the cab and made Chapellier drive behind Hall's Humvee as far as the Arsenal's guard post. He had formalities to complete. Medical attention had to be arranged. Escorts organized. Paperwork filled out. But first he had to make a phone call. Time was suddenly of the essence. Special arrangements needed to be made and Reacher knew how the machine worked.

The regular cogs would grind too slowly. Shortcuts were called for; otherwise, a golden opportunity was going to slip through their fingers. Meat Loaf may have thought that two out of three ain't bad, but Reacher didn't agree. That was for damn sure.

Roberta and Veronica had expected there to be vomiting. They had researched the side effects carefully when they were deciding what kind of substance would be best to add to Geoff Brown's tobacco. They just hadn't realized how much there would be. And they hadn't anticipated that Brown would put his keys back in his pocket when he arrived home. They'd imagined that he would set them down on a table in the hallway or hang them on a convenient hook. The reality only dawned on them when Veronica dropped the receiver back onto its cradle after she ended the 911 call. Roberta had picked the lock on the front door when they broke into the house but they couldn't leave that way because the agents who were watching the place were on station again, outside. They couldn't climb out of a rear-facing window because there would be no way to lock it and they figured that a single unlocked, accessible window would be suspicious. So they needed the key to the back door. Only now it was on a ring that was encased in vomit-soaked cotton and attached to a corpse. Retrieving it was not an appealing prospect.

Veronica said, "Maybe there's a spare?"

Roberta glanced at her watch. "Go look. Quickly."

Veronica ran to the kitchen. She checked the walls near the door. There were no hooks or shelves with keys on them. She opened the nearest drawers. The cabinets beneath them. Looked inside the refrigerator. And found nothing that seemed like a viable hiding place. She figured she'd used up two minutes. They had maybe two more before the police would arrive, so she ran back to the living room. Roberta was standing six feet away from Brown's body. She looked like she was ready to puke, herself. She said, "Anything?"

Veronica shook her head, then held up her hands. She said, "My gloves are leather. Yours are disposable. You do it."

As soon as everything was squared away at Rock Island, Reacher set out to drive east, to Chicago. He made good time, so when he left the highway and saw a line of large, soulless buildings crammed around three sides of a square, open-air parking lot, he pulled over. He had no civilian clothes with him and he knew he was going to need some later in the day. He figured he might as well get the task out of the way as quickly as possible, so he headed into a sporting goods store and picked up the first things he saw that would fit. Black sneakers. Beige pants with all kinds of extra pockets sewn onto the legs. A blue T-shirt with a logo he'd never seen before. And a lightweight, blue, waterproof jacket.

Reacher paid for the clothes and changed in the store's fitting room. He folded his BDUs, placed them in the bag the clerk had given him, and stowed them in his trunk, alongside his duffel. Then he continued toward the west side of the city, slightly south of the center, which he figured put him closer to the White Sox than the Cubs. He found the building he was looking for without difficulty. The FBI field office. A mid-rise tower of glass and concrete. It had a bowed front but otherwise looked like a child had designed it with a construction set that only had square-shaped parts.

Roberta and Veronica Sanson heard the siren at the same moment. They listened to it draw closer. Crossed to the window and peered around the side of the drapes. Watched a patrol car barrel down the street and slide to a halt outside the house. And saw the two agents jump out of their Crown Victoria and intercept the cops before they made it halfway up the path.

That was their cue. The watchers were occupied, so Roberta and Veronica hustled to the back door. Roberta had already unlocked it. They hurried out into the yard, relocked the door, and retraced their steps to their stolen minivan. They'd left it three streets from Geoff Brown's house, facing away. Veronica climbed up into the passenger seat. Roberta dropped her gloves and Brown's key down a grate in the gutter and slid behind the wheel.

Veronica waited until they were under way, then said, "Where next?"

It was an important tactical decision. They couldn't work their way down the list in order, or whoever had noticed that the former CIA agents were dying would know where to focus their resources. Roberta and Veronica wanted their opposition spread as thin as possible, which meant picking their next target at random. But nothing is truly random. All kinds of studies have been done. Subliminal influences shape people's choices in diverse, subtle ways. So they resorted to a technique they'd learned years ago.

Roberta said, "Three names left to pick from." In her head she allocated a number to each remaining one. "Give me three colors."

"Red. Silver. White."

The next car they saw was white. The third color Veronica had named. The third name on Roberta's mental list was Michael Rymer, who lived in northern Colorado.

Roberta said, "Get ready for some altitude. We're going to Denver."

*   *   *

Reacher dumped his car in the lot and headed inside to the reception desk. He asked for Agent Ottoway, who did exist. She was small and wiry with long black hair and she arrived to collect him after only a couple of minutes. She used a plastic card to let him through a turnstile and escorted him to a bank of elevators and then on to a meeting room at the end of a corridor on the third floor. It was a small, stale space with no windows. It smelled of cigarette smoke and sweat, like half its air was piped in from a bar and the other half from a locker room, and its contents made it look like a dumping ground for redundant furniture. There were half a dozen chairs. Two tables, one balanced on the other, upside down, with its legs pointing at the ceiling. And a handful of squat bookcases that were all missing half their shelves.

Reacher wasn't surprised by the place. He knew the score when it came to interagency cooperation. Choosing a room like that was a way of expressing a lack of enthusiasm on the part of the hosts. Reacher could understand their position. He was on their turf. His request hadn't come through the proper channels. And it had come with next to no notice. It had probably stretched their resources thin on one of their other operations. But if this one worked out, it was going to be worth the inconvenience. He was confident about that.

Agent Ottoway's supervisor arrived hard on their heels and he kept the briefing mercifully short. Just the three of them, huddled together on dilapidated chairs under a flickering fluorescent light. No need for notes or diagrams. No unnecessary complications, which was the way Reacher liked it. Just confirmation of the objective. The time and place. The principal players. And the code word should it become necessary to abort.

When all the details were set, Agent Ottoway led the way back to the elevator. She hit the button and while they waited for the car to arrive, she said, "Captain, can I ask you one question?"

Reacher said, "Shoot."

"What are you planning on wearing tonight?"

Reacher glanced down at his shirt and pants. "What I'm wearing now."

"That's what I was afraid you'd say."

"Is there a problem?"

"You might as well hang a sign around your neck saying *Undercover Cop*. All right. This is what's happening. If you have plans for the afternoon, cancel them. I'm taking you shopping."

Chapter 8

The phone in the Pentagon rang again at 1:02 P.M. Eastern. Not a scheduled time for a call.

The guy who answered it listened, hung up, then moved to his outer office and dialed another number. It was for a cellular phone mounted in a car that was traveling southeast on Pennsylvania Avenue.

Charles Stamoran picked up after one ring. "Tell me Pritchard's been found."

"Sorry, sir," the Pentagon guy said. "This is about Geoffrey Brown. He's dead. The cause is pending confirmation from the lab, but a New Orleans PD officer who attended the scene was confident he recognized the symptoms. Brown suffered a fatal reaction to the venom of the Sonoran Desert toad. He smoked the dried secretions mixed with tobacco in a pipe that was found at his side. People do this for its psychedelic effect, and to combat psychological conditions such as PTSD. If Brown was new to the practice, he could have used too high a concentration. The source of the substance is being traced but is most likely one of the stores in the city that caters for pseudo-religious ceremonies. Brown had no visitors and received no deliveries. He called 911 himself, so the police think his death is likely an accident, but cold feet following a suicide attempt cannot be ruled out."

Stamoran lowered the receiver to his lap and glanced out of the car window at the swarms of people rushing in and out of one office building after another. He felt himself getting angry. He could think of an explanation that couldn't be ruled out. Toad venom? Seriously? Brown did smoke a pipe. Had smoked one for years. And after some of the things he'd done, it would be a miracle if he never had some kind of psychological reaction. But there was no way he would involve himself in New Age hippy designer-drug bullshit. Not voluntarily. A generous pour of bourbon and branch? Yes. Smoking secretions harvested from poisonous amphibians? No. Not in a million years. Someone was adding insult to injury.

Stamoran lifted the handset. "Waiting to catch this guy when he strikes isn't working. We need to get proactive. Leave the agents watching Rymer and Adam in place but I want a task force set up, as well. By tomorrow. Reps from the army, CIA, FBI, Treasury, and any other agency this guy could be from based on his performance and obvious training. I want him identified. I want a focused suspect pool our people in the field can work with. And I want him stopped."

At eight o'clock that evening Reacher was in a bar in River North, Chicago. He was wearing the second set of new clothes he'd bought that day. A pair of black jeans, a dark green shirt, a leather jacket, and black ankle boots that were secured with straps. Agent Ottaway was sitting opposite him across a low, round table. She was wearing a plain black dress and her hair was curlier than it had been earlier.

The bar was fashioned out of an old factory. The walls were brick. They were pitted and stained and riddled with holes and sockets and brackets where all kinds of equipment must once have been secured. Like industrial petroglyphs, Reacher thought, telling the story of the people who spent their lives working there. He spent a few minutes trying to decipher them, then glanced across to a stage that was set up in the far corner. A three-piece band was midway through its set. The performance was competent from a technical standpoint but it was nothing Reacher would call exciting. Nothing that was going to knock Howlin' Wolf or Magic Slim off his list of favorites.

Ottoway nudged Reacher's foot with her own under the table and nodded almost imperceptibly toward the entrance. Sergeant Chapellier had walked in. He was wearing stained jeans and a Metallica tour shirt. He paused for a moment like he was looking for someone then made his way across to an empty table. It was six feet away from Reacher and Ottoway's, in a section that was separated from the rest of the space by a line of vertical iron pipes. There were a dozen of them, three feet apart, four inches in diameter, rusted almost black. Ten were lit from above. They all should have been. But the lamps over two of them had failed and that left them lost in the gloom.

Reacher pretended to be watching the bartender prepare drinks but he kept one eye on Chapellier. He was fidgeting, drumming his fingers on the tabletop, and glancing repeatedly at the door. No one came through. One of the waitstaff picked up a tray of drinks. He was aiming to deliver it to a table at the back. It was made out of an old beer keg with things that looked like upturned buckets as seats. Two twenty-something guys were perched there along with two women who looked a little younger.

One of the guys gestured for the waiter to hurry up. Maybe he was thirsty. Maybe he was trying to show off. But whatever the reason, he wasn't helping. The waiter was doing his best. The space was crowded. The furniture was jammed in at all kinds of crooked angles. There was no set path for him to get through. There was no point trying to make him go faster. A couple of times he nearly dropped the tray. Once he skidded on a wet patch on the floor. And finally, when he was almost at the right table, he knocked into another customer.

The man was hard to miss. He was six foot six with a huge beard, a baseball cap worn backward, baggy jeans, and a plaid shirt with buttons that were struggling to contain his gut. He glanced around. He was checking to see if anyone was looking. He saw that plenty of people were. So he shoved the waiter in the chest. Hard.

The waiter stumbled back a couple of steps then lost his balance. The tray slipped out of his hands. Four drinks hit the floor. Three beers and some kind of fancy cocktail with an umbrella in it. The waiter tumbled over backward and hit his head on the base of another table.

Chapellier paid no attention to the altercation. His gaze was now fixed on the door. No one came through. There were a couple dozen people already in the railed-off section of the bar. None of them lifted a finger to help the waiter. Not even to haul him back onto his feet. He finally rolled over then crawled forward to retrieve his tray. The fat guy pushed it farther away with his foot. Still no one did anything. Still no one came through the door.

The waiter came back a couple of minutes later with a mop and a broom and a bucket. He started to clean up the mess. The fat guy took every opportunity to nudge and jostle him. No one in the bar did anything to help. Then Reacher stopped watching the sideshow. Because someone had finally come in. A man, late thirties, loose shirt, baggy jeans, and a battered leather messenger bag slung over one shoulder. He was scrawny with lank, unwashed hair and a week's stubble on his face. Reacher recognized the look. A dollar would get a dime that the guy was a former soldier. A drug habit had led to stealing had led to a dishonorable discharge. A pattern Reacher had seen play out a thousand times.

The scrawny guy hustled across to Chapellier's table and sat down. The waiter appeared and Chapellier said something, then held up two fingers. The guys sat in silence until the waiter came back with two beers. They nodded, clinked glasses, and both drained their drinks in a single gulp. The scrawny guy belched, then set his bag down on the empty seat next to him. Chapellier picked it up. Glanced inside. Then took a vehicle key from his pocket and placed it on the table. The scrawny guy nodded again, took the key, got up, and headed for the door.

Ottoway turned away and took a radio from her purse. She held it close to her mouth and said, "He's coming out. He'll be heading for a vehicle. Wait till he's in it, then take him."

A minute passed then Ottoway's radio crackled back into life. A man's voice said, "We have him. The contraband, too. It's a wrap."

Susan Kasluga hung up the phone and closed her eyes. She breathed out slowly and felt the knots in her shoulders ease, just a little. She was sitting at her desk in her home office. It was a small room but it was quiet and its view over the pond and the trees made up for its lack of size.

"Trouble at work?" Charles Stamoran said.

Kasluga opened her eyes and saw her husband standing in the doorway. She said, "Are you spying on me?"

"If I were, you'd never know."

"Maybe this is a double bluff?"

The Secret

"It isn't. So what was up? Wrong number?"

Kasluga picked up a bright pink stress ball and flung it at his head. "None of your business. Now get out. I'm working."

Ottoway left the bar first. Reacher was last, and Chapellier was sandwiched between them. The street outside was a blaze of red and blue. Four Bureau cars were lined up with dome lights flashing on their dashboards. The scrawny guy was in the backseat of the last car. Behind it was an old, dented Toyota Corolla. Its driver's door was open. So was its trunk. An agent was standing next to it, and as Reacher watched, a plain white box van pulled up next to it and a pair of technicians climbed out. Ottoway made her way to the lead car and leaned down to talk to someone in the passenger seat. Then two men emerged from the shadows near the wall. They were trim. Lean. Dressed all in black. Like French avant-garde philosophers who had become obsessed with exercise, Reacher thought. Although he knew what they really were. He could recognize soldiers in and around bars in his sleep. Years of experience had honed his instinct. And MPs were even easier to spot. No one else ever hung out with them. They were too unpopular. The only thing Reacher couldn't figure was what they were doing there. He hadn't requested backup.

The MPs stepped forward. The taller one said, "Captain Reacher?"

Reacher nodded.

"Could you verify that, please, sir."

Reacher took out his wallet and showed his Military ID card.

"Thank you, sir." The MP pulled an envelope from his jacket pocket and handed it over.

Reacher tore the envelope open. Inside was a single sheet of paper with the Military Police crest at the top. It stated that he was to relinquish custody of Sergeant Chapellier and report to an address in Washington, D.C., at 11:00 A.M. the following day.

Reacher looked at the MP. "What do you know about this?"

"Nothing, sir."

"What have you heard?"

"We've been told nothing, sir."

Reacher smiled. It was clear that these guys were NCOs. The backbone of the service. And Reacher knew from experience that the NCO scuttlebutt was the most efficient communication medium in the world. "I didn't ask what you've *been told*. I asked what you've *heard*. And if you tell me you've not heard anything I'll have you locked up for impersonating a member of the US Army. So let's start with this. I'm being sent to D.C. How come?"

The MP glanced at his buddy then said, "Word is, a couple of people died."

"Who?"

"Don't know."

"Ours?"

The MP shook his head. "Retired scientists. One got electrocuted. One fell out of a hospital window."

"Fell out?"

The MP shrugged.

"So they were CIA. What's our angle?"

"Word is, it's part of a bigger thing. CIA, plus other agencies. Orders from the Pentagon."

"Then why are they sending me?"

"They wanted an O-3 or higher. No one from HQ would touch it. I guess you must have pissed off the wrong guy, sir."

* * *

Susan Kasluga tapped gently on Charles Stamoran's study door, pushed it open, and took a small step into the room. Stamoran was sitting in his armchair. He was reading a book. A biography of George Meade. He glanced up, then went back to his Civil War history.

Kasluga saw her stress ball sitting on a low table beneath the window. It was leaning against a decanter of whiskey. A pair of cut-crystal tumblers sat on either side. She made her way across to the table and poured two measures. She went heavier on one, which she carried over and handed to Stamoran.

"I'm sorry," she said. "You took me by surprise. That call—"

"You don't have to tell me," Stamoran said.

"I know. It's just . . . it's nothing you need to worry about. Just business."

"Your takeover deal?"

"A vulnerability. Something that could have derailed everything. But it's fixed now. That call was confirmation. Which is why it was so short."

"I've never known a lawyer to be so brief."

"Who said it was a lawyer?"

"Maybe I'm better off not knowing about this."

"See? Another reason I married you. Impeccable instincts. Now let's leave work till tomorrow. It's getting late." She took a long sip of her drink. "And there are much better ways to spend an evening together."

Ottoway watched the MPs lead Chapellier away then crossed to Reacher's side. She said, "What was that all about?"

Reacher shrugged. "New orders."

"Anything good?"

"More likely the opposite."

"Oh. I'm sorry to hear that. So are you shipping out?"

Reacher nodded.

Ottoway said, "When?"

Reacher said, "Tonight, I guess, if I can get a flight. Otherwise first thing tomorrow."

"I vote for tomorrow. Stay in Chicago tonight. That was a job well done. We deserve to celebrate."

"You have a point." Reacher was quiet for a moment. "And there's something else I wouldn't mind taking care of before I leave."

Reacher led the way back inside the building and strolled across to the bar. The bartender looked up then took a step back. He hadn't noticed Reacher approach. He wasn't expecting to see anyone right in front of him. Certainly not anyone who looked like Reacher. Six foot five. Chest like a refrigerator. Arms like other people's legs. Cropped hair. Head tipped quizzically to one side.

On the far side of the bar there was a metal tub about ten inches high and a yard across. At the start of the evening it had been crammed with ice and bottles of beer. Now it was mainly full of water with a few residual cubes floating around. Reacher pointed to it and said, "That thing? Give it to me."

The bartender blinked and said, "Why?"

Reacher said, "I want to borrow it."

"No," the guy said. "But you can rent it. Twenty bucks for a half hour. Driver's license for security. No questions asked. Do what you want with it."

Reacher shook his head. "I borrow it. For two minutes. You

watch what happens. And when I return it, if you still think I should pay, I'll give you forty."

The bartender thought for a moment then called his buddy to help him heave the tub across to a spot close to Reacher. Reacher picked it up and headed toward the fat guy who'd messed with the waiter, earlier. The guy made a point of turning his back. Reacher closed in, paused to make sure the waiter was close enough to see what was happening, then lifted the tub and dumped the icy water over the fat guy's head.

He screamed. He howled. He flailed his arms and danced up and down on the spot. He huffed and gasped and finally spun around to face Reacher. His cap had been washed off. His beard was drenched. His shirt was clinging to his torso.

"The hell was that?" the guy spluttered.

Reacher said, "Training."

"What?"

"Like with a dog."

"You're saying I'm a dog?"

"I read somewhere, you have a dog and it misbehaves, you do something it doesn't like. Then it'll learn to mend its ways. Now, you're clearly not as smart as an average dog. Probably not as smart as a stupid dog. Probably a dog that started out really dumb and then had half of its brain removed is still smarter than you. So maybe I should stick around. Become your personal trainer. Put this tub to work whenever you act like a jackass."

The guy frowned and shook his head. Droplets of water flew in a wide circle like he was a poodle that had been caught in the rain. He was quiet for a moment. Then his frown turned into a scowl. "Enough," he barked. "I'm going to kill you. I'm going to crush every bone in your body."

"You think?" Reacher was holding the tub low in front, base toward him, angled at about forty-five degrees.

"I know."

Reacher glanced down at the tub then ghosted across about a foot to his left. "You sure you're not going to break your own hand?"

"No. I'm going to break your face."

"Are you?" Reacher took a half step back and said, "Are there any bookies in the house? My money's on the lobotomized dog. That's for sure."

The guy flung himself forward and launched a punch straight at Reacher's face. No technique. No finesse. Just a whole lot of weight and momentum and fury. In some circumstances, that could have served him well. But not that night. Because Reacher stepped aside. Away from the unlit iron pipe he had been standing in front of. The guy's fist slammed right into it. His knuckles shattered. His fingers broke. All kinds of little bones in his hand and wrist and forearm were smashed. Tendons tore. Ligaments ripped. And this time he didn't make a sound. The pain took care of that. It caused him to faint, right there on the spot. His knees buckled. His legs folded. He flopped backward and landed on the ground with his head six inches from the little umbrella that had fallen from the drink he had made the waiter spill a few minutes earlier.

Reacher carried the tub back to the bar and set it down.

The bartender said, "No charge."

Reacher didn't let go of the tub right away. He was thinking about a similar situation that had led to him getting busted back to captain. He said, "Anyone asks, who hurt that guy?"

"No one. He hurt himself."

"Correct answer."

Chapter 9

Michael Rymer ate breakfast on the deck behind his house, alone, as usual. He didn't hurry. He had no need. His hurrying days were behind him. He was retired. Happily so. He had no family. No one to mold his days around. Not since his fourth wife had left him nearly a decade ago. All he had to do was soak up some early-morning sun along with his oatmeal and coffee then make his way down to his boathouse and unmoor *Pegasus*. His pride and joy. A day's fishing in the lake lay ahead of him, followed by a bottle of wine and a movie on his VHS player to fill his evening. It hadn't always been this way. Far from it, in fact. But these days life was treating him well. He was under no illusions about that.

Rymer was halfway to his favorite spot to drop anchor—where he could be sure the largemouth bass would bite and the view of the Rockies never failed to take his breath away—when he saw something he wasn't expecting. Another boat. A forty-footer. The owners of the other half-dozen properties scattered around the lakeshore generally only used their houses—and boats—in the summer, and occasionally for the holidays. The rest of the year he could pretty much guarantee he would be alone on the water. The way he liked it. He considered changing course. Finding a more secluded spot. But something about the other boat bothered him. The way it was moving. It seemed to be drifting aimlessly. Not under way. And not at anchor. For a moment he wondered if it could somehow have broken loose from a neighbor's dock during the night and been blown all the way out there by the wind. Then a person appeared from its wheelhouse. A woman. She started waving. But not in a friendly way. Both arms were windmilling wildly over her head. She was clearly in some kind of trouble. Rymer leaned on the throttle and moved in to investigate.

As he drew closer, Rymer recognized the boat. *The Duchess*. It belonged to a couple from Denver. He had never bothered to learn their names. He thought they might be doctors. But he didn't recognize the woman who was on board. She looked like she could be in her late twenties. She was slim, like she kept herself fit, and her dark hair was pulled back in a practical, no-nonsense style. A relative of the doctors, maybe? Or a family friend? Presumably someone who had permission to be there, anyway. Rymer had gotten caught up in a lot of crazy things in his life but he'd never heard of anyone joyriding in a leisure boat on a mountain lake that was so remote it was virtually impossible to find unless you already knew where it was. He dropped a row of fenders over the gunwale, tied them to the cleats, and eased *Pegasus* up alongside the stricken vessel.

Rymer called out, "Everything OK?"

The woman clutched her head in her hands. She said, "Oh my goodness, I'm so embarrassed. I don't know what to do. The engine just stopped and I can't get it to start again and I don't know how the anchor works and the boat keeps floating around all over the place. Can you help me? Please?"

"You're out here on your own?"

The woman nodded. "Claudia and Andreas are letting me use their house for a couple of weeks. They said I could take *The Duchess* out anytime I wanted. But then they also said it was easy to drive. I feel like a total idiot."

"Don't worry." Rymer took a coil of line from the bow of *Pegasus* and tossed it so that it wound up lying across the raised prow of *The Duchess*. He took another from near the stern, handed it to the woman, jumped over, and landed next to her. He took the rope and secured it to a cleat, then did the same with the line at the bow. "I'm sure it's no big problem. We'll get you up and running in no time."

The Duchess was older than *Pegasus*. It had probably started life as a fishing boat, hauling in loads of lobsters or crabs in shallow coastal waters. Now its wooden hull was painted white with blue stripes here and there and comfy chairs had been added to the open section behind the wheelhouse where the catch would have been carried. A red life buoy stood out against the bright paint near the wheelhouse door and a mess of ropes and lines was strewn around all over the deck. Rymer shook his head at the chaos and took a step toward the trapdoor that covered the engine compartment. Then some of the ropes started to move. They seethed across the shiny surface like they were alive. Wrapped themselves around his feet. Whipped up around his ankles and cinched in tight. His ankle bones ground together. He almost lost his balance. He recovered. But a moment later he crashed down onto his back. Something had heaved on the rope, hard. It felt like he'd somehow gotten hitched to a stampeding horse. Most of the breath was knocked out of his body. He struggled to lift his head and saw it wasn't *something* that was in control of the rope. It was *someone.* Another woman. Almost identical to the one who had asked for his help, but maybe two or three years older. She must have been crouching on the far side of the wheelhouse.

The new woman moved in close, gripped the rope with both hands, and heaved Rymer's legs off the deck. The first woman leaned down and slid her hands under his armpits. She lifted his torso. Moved him around so that his head was pointed away from *Pegasus.* Rymer was struggling for air. He didn't understand what was happening. Then the women bundled him toward the vacant side of the boat. The original woman hauled his head a little higher then dumped him down with his shoulders on the gunwale. She rolled him so that he was facing down, staring at the water. And both women pushed and jockeyed and shoved. He slid across the wooden rail until it reached his waist. Then he pivoted forward, slamming his palms against the outer hull to avoid smashing into it face-first and winding up with the top of his head an inch above the water line.

Roberta Sanson gave the rope a sharp tug to make sure she had Rymer's attention, then said, "Michael, can you hear me? And more important, can you understand me?"

Rymer didn't respond.

Roberta took a large step forward. Rymer's legs tipped up. His torso pivoted down. His head was dunked into the freezing water. Roberta let it stay there for ten seconds then started to pull back. The physics were against her so Veronica had to reach over the side and tug on his belt before he could resurface.

Roberta said, "Michael . . .?"

Rymer spluttered and coughed. "Are you nuts? What are you doing? I'm no kind of threat. I stopped to help you!"

"You want to help? That's good. All you have to do is give us one name. One name, and this will be over. You'll never see or hear from us again."

"What name?"

"Your research team in India. In 1969. We know seven names. Including yours, obviously. You need to tell us the eighth."

"What? No. There is no eighth name. There were only seven of us. I swear. Me. Owen Buck. Varinder Singh. Keith Bridgeman. Geoffrey Brown. Charlie Adam. Neville Pritchard. No one else."

"There were eight. I need the other name. You have to tell me."

"There is no eighth name! Why do you—?"

Roberta plunged Rymer's head back into the water. She left it submerged for fifteen seconds this time. Again she needed Veronica's help to pull him clear.

Roberta said, "This isn't pleasant, is it? The only way it stops is for you to give us the name. Come on. It's not hard. Two words. First name, last name. That's better than drowning, surely. You don't doubt that I will drown you, right?"

Rymer was gasping for air. "Can't. Only seven names. Swear to you."

Roberta looked at Veronica, shrugged, and said, "OK. Your choice. But at this point it's important you know our names. I'm Roberta Sanson. This is my sister, Veronica. Our father was Morgan Sanson."

Rymer groaned.

Roberta said, "Any last minute inspiration?"

Rymer was silent.

Roberta shrugged again and lowered Rymer back down. She

braced her feet against the deck and held on tight to the rope. Rymer thrashed and kicked and struggled. His movements were hard and desperate. Then they softened and waned. The tension ebbed out of his body. His energy almost gave out altogether. He arched his back and clawed at the water one last time then he slumped down deeper into the darkness. A final few bubbles floated to the surface and he was left hanging there on the rope, heavy and slack, slapping against the hull in the slight swell.

Roberta switched her grip to the strand of rope that led away from the knot around Rymer's ankles. She pulled. The knot released itself and Rymer's body slid silently the rest of the way beneath the surface. It bobbed back up a moment later and settled, floating facedown, arms and legs stretched wide, hair spread out around his skull like pale seaweed.

Reacher had also woken that morning with a view over a lake. In his case it was Lake Michigan, through a floor-to-ceiling window, thirty-two stories up in a clover leaf–shaped building near Navy Pier in Chicago. It was Agent Ottoway's bedroom.

"Don't worry," she had said when they got back after a night of blues music on Halsted Street and she saw the expression on Reacher's face. "This is not the product of ill-gotten gains. I got it in my divorce."

Reacher and Ottoway drank coffee in bed, then took a shower together. Soap was involved. So was hot water. And steam. But given how long the process took, not a whole lot of cleaning took place. It left them with no time for breakfast. They got dressed, hurried down to the underground garage, and collected Ottoway's car. She drove to the FBI field office and while Reacher retrieved his duffel from the trunk of the vehicle he'd borrowed from the Rock Island Arsenal, she scribbled on a scrap of paper.

"Take this," she said, and handed the note to Reacher. There was a phone number written at the top. It had a 312 area code. "This is my home number. Anytime you're in town, call me."

Reacher said nothing.

The walk to the El stop and the train ride to O'Hare were uneventful. There was time at the airport for a cup of coffee before the flight to Washington National, then Reacher found his way to the cab line and gave the driver the address from the orders he'd received the day before. The route took them across the Potomac then away from the city, nose to tail in a lingering cloud of exhaust fumes for all but the final ten minutes of the journey. They were heading for some kind of business district. The buildings were long and low, no more than twenty years old, all pale brick and mirrored glass, separated by rectangular open-air parking lots and set back behind glossy green hedges. The cabdriver pulled up outside the last building on the street. There were three cars in its lot. All domestic sedans. Two Fords and a Chevy. One green, one blue, one black. All sprouting more antennas than they'd had when they rolled off the line in Detroit.

Reacher gave the driver a respectable tip then made his way through the building's main entrance. Inside, he found cheap, durable carpet, new inexpensive furniture, and walls covered with fresh, bland paint. Which told him two things. The place was owned by the government. And it was up for sale. Reacher had no idea why, but he'd noticed that the government never spent money on buildings it was planning to keep.

There was no one behind the reception desk so Reacher pushed through a pair of double doors and found himself at the head of a long, bright corridor. The first door on the left was marked *Board Room*. Reacher looked inside. Three people were already there, each on a different side of a rectangular table that seemed too large for the space. Two men and a woman. All looked like they were in their thirties. All seemed a little tense, like they didn't know why they were there but assumed whatever the reason, it was certain to not be good. There were a dozen chairs, arranged in two fours and two pairs, and the only other piece of furniture was a table under the window. Two shiny pump-action flasks were sitting on it, along with a stack of upside-down Styrofoam cups and a bowl that was overflowing with cartons of creamer and sachets of sweetener.

Reacher helped himself to a cup of coffee and then squeezed his way around to the chair at the corner of the table that gave him a view of the window as well as the door. He placed his bag on the floor and sat down. The woman was on the same side of the table, midway along. She had short blond hair and was wearing a navy suit coat over a crisp white blouse and a tan leather briefcase was set, closed, in front of her. One of the men was opposite her. He also had on a navy suit, but his could have been slept in. His hair looked like it had won a fight with a comb that morning, and probably did every morning. His face was plump. His eyes were bloodshot and his nose was a mesh of fine, cracked veins. The final guy was at the corner diagonally across from Reacher. His eyes were cold and blue and he had neat, tidy hair like a banker or an accountant. He was wearing a sport coat and staring intently out of the window like he thought if he concentrated hard enough, he could physically transport himself out of there.

No one spoke. Two minutes crawled past then footsteps echoed in the corridor. The door opened and a man bustled through. He was tall, maybe six foot six, with a long face and neatly combed silver hair. He paused, looked at each person in turn, then took one of the chairs at the head of the table.

He cleared his throat and said, "Let's get started, shall we? First things first. Introductions. My name is Christopher Baglin, Department of Defense. Let's go clockwise."

That meant Reacher was next up. He said, "Jack Reacher. US Army."

The woman followed. "Amber Smith. FBI."

The sport coat guy said, "Gary Walsh. Treasury Department."

The scruffy guy went last. "Kent Neilsen. Central Intelligence Agency."

Baglin nodded, clasped his hands on the table in front of him, and continued. "Lady, gentlemen, thank you for being here. I say that on behalf of the secretary himself. I know you were summoned at short notice, but believe me, we would not have done that if your mission here was not of the utmost importance. We—and by *we* I mean the United States of America—have a problem. A serious one. And we need your expertise to solve it."

Baglin paused, as if he was expecting someone to ask what that problem was.

No one spoke. No one was that naïve, which Reacher found encouraging.

Baglin shifted his hands onto his lap. "By way of background, I need to take you thirty years into the past. Now, as we know, the evils of the Soviet Union have finally been consigned to the garbage can of history, but for decades its empire was a formidable enemy. Back in the 1960s the reds were coming at us from all angles. Nukes, of course. Satellites. Submarines. Sleeper agents. Spies. The list goes on, and at the top was something particularly nasty. Chemical and biological weapons. Newly devised strains and variants designed to kill and blind and incapacitate in the most ghastly ways imaginable. And that's where Project 192 originated from."

Again Baglin left an implied question hanging in the air. Again no one took the bait.

Baglin's hands appeared back on the table. "Before I go on, I must stress two things. First, the secretary insists on complete transparency. He feels that you won't be able to operate with the utmost effectiveness unless you are armed with all the facts. Nothing will be held back, so secondly nothing you learn in this room can leave this room. Are we clear?"

"Crystal." "Yes, sir." "Of course." "One hundred percent." Reacher's and the other three voices overlapped.

Baglin said, "Good. Now, Project 192 was an initiative designed to protect us against these diabolical Soviet weapons. Its purpose was to understand their full effects and develop effective antidotes that could be manufactured rapidly and in huge volumes. This was no mean feat. It required cutting-edge equipment and the latest techniques, and it had to be done in absolute secrecy. The fear was that if the Soviets learned we could counteract their weapons, they would develop new ones, which we may have been unaware of or not immediately able to respond to. So, what happened was that we partnered with the best American industrial research corporations. We built discreet, partitioned facilities within their laboratories. But . . ."

Baglin paused. Again no one bit.

Baglin said, "But this was done outside the realm of direct governmental control. It was done in close proximity to civilian workers. In some cases in close proximity to significant civilian populations. And more often than not, in other countries. Sometimes very poor countries. Countries that would have struggled to say no to that kind of work being done on their soil. Now, I stand behind these decisions. So does the secretary. It was right for America at the time. But as you know, times change. Attitudes change. We've weathered the storm caused by all the reporting on Agent Orange and VX gas since then. Lived through the debacle of the final days of Vietnam. Through Watergate. Through the Contra scandal. Et cetera, et cetera. Our concern is that, particularly with the Soviet Union no longer a threat, people would be less likely to accept the necessity of what we did. If details of the Project became public, it could foster unrest. Our remaining enemies could use the information to embarrass the United States and harm our standing on the world stage."

Another pause was left unfilled.

Baglin lowered his voice. "Which leads us to the nub of the issue. In the late sixties, a team of seven scientists worked on neutralizing a particular Soviet nerve agent. They were based within a civilian laboratory owned by a company called Mason Chemical Industries. It was located in India. Recently, one of the team fell victim to cancer, and three of the others have died in extremely suspicious circumstances."

Smith cleared her throat and said, "How suspicious?"

Baglin said, "One was electrocuted. One fell out of a window. One ingested a fatal dose of toad venom."

Reacher said, "Poison."

"What was that?"

"If it was ingested, it was poison. Venom is introduced through a bite or a sting."

"You think that's the relevant fact, here?"

"It's accurate. And I think accuracy is always relevant. Especially when lives are on the line."

Baglin glared at Reacher for a moment, then turned away and said, "Our working hypothesis is that a hostile agent killed these men in an attempt to uncover information that could be used against the United States. Three men from the team are still alive. Precautions are being taken to ensure their safety, but the secretary is not satisfied with a passive response. He wants the perpetrator identified and stopped. That's where you all fit in. The identification of suspects. The army and the CIA because those organizations were jointly responsible for the research operations in the sixties. The FBI in its counterintelligence capacity, in case the initiative is being driven by a foreign country. And the Treasury Department in case we're off the mark and someone is merely trying to steal industrial secrets. An office has been prepared for each of you, with a phone, fax machine, and stationery supplies. Accommodations are being provided at a local hotel for as long as necessary. Any questions?"

Reacher raised his hand. "Have any ransom demands been received?"

Baglin shook his head. "No."

"Have any scientists who worked on other bioweapon programs been targeted?"

"Not that I'm aware of."

"Will you find out?"

"I'll ask the question. Now—"

"One last thing. You said precautions are being taken to safeguard the remaining scientists from Project 192. What kind of precautions?"

"They're being watched, twenty-four/seven, by experienced agents."

"Were any of the victims being watched?"

"Captain, this is not the time for finger pointing or interagency point scoring."

"That's not my intention. If we're going to cast a net, we need to know how fine to make it. So we need to know what we're fishing for. The different methods of killing tells us something. But not enough. The first guy was electrocuted, right? Killing someone that way is one thing. Doing it under the noses of experienced agents is another. It would indicate a higher degree of competence, and confidence, which in turn would imply a certain kind and level of training, and motivation."

"I see. OK. Yes. Dr. Brown. He was at home when he was *poisoned*, and his house was under observation."

"He was the third victim?"

"Correct." Baglin paused for a moment. "Does anyone else have a question?"

The other three stayed silent.

Baglin nodded. "All right, then. We will reconvene here at 0900 tomorrow, at which time I expect you to furnish the names of the first suspects you think should be investigated."

Chapter 10

Roberta and Veronica Sanson gathered up all the ropes from the deck, coiled them, and put them back in their rightful places. They guessed it would be quite a while before the owners would see the boat again. They didn't know how observant those owners would be. But even so, they didn't want to leave any signs that the boat had been used. Especially given what it had been used for. Operating unseen was a habit. It was ingrained in them. Years of intense, arduous training had made sure of that.

When they were happy with the state of *The Duchess* they turned their attention to *Pegasus*. They took every piece of rope they could find and left them strewn around all over the place. Then, with just the stern line attached, Roberta worked the controls until the boat was pointing roughly in the direction of Rymer's house, which by now was just a dot on the distant shoreline. She set the throttle to just above stalling speed. Waited for Veronica to jump back onto *The Duchess* then leapt across after her. Cut the remaining line.

And steered toward the property they had borrowed the boat from that morning.

The sisters had stolen a pickup truck this time. An F-150. So ubiquitous as to be practically invisible. They hoped. But they took no chances. They didn't risk the most direct route back to Stapleton airport because that would involve passing the agents watching Rymer's house for a second time in a few hours. Instead, they started by heading north, then east, and finally turned south for a straight shot back to Denver.

"There are two men left," Roberta said. She was driving with one hand on the wheel. Her right palm was stinging from a friction burn she'd gotten from the rope the first time she'd lowered Rymer into the water. "So it's fifty/fifty the next one will know the name we need."

Veronica said, "I'd rather it was a dead cert."

Roberta smiled. "Nice."

"Who's the next lucky contestant?"

"Give me two car brands. Not Ford. Not Chevy."

Veronica thought for a moment. She said, "Dodge. And Honda."

A minute later Roberta pointed through the windshield. "There. A Honda Civic." Honda was the second brand Veronica had picked, so Roberta matched it with the second name on her mental list. "Charlie Adam. Initials, CA. Lives in California. Symmetry. I love it."

Reacher spent the afternoon in the building outside D.C., closed away in a room farther down the corridor that had been allocated as his office. Its décor was as bland as the reception area's. The desk was small and the chair was a tight fit for someone as broad as Reacher. A window looked out onto an empty section of parking lot, and beyond that a row of pale shrubs that separated the site from the road. It wasn't the kind of place he would choose to spend time, but he wasn't about to complain. Over the years the army had sent him to a lot of places that were much less pleasant. That was for damn sure.

Reacher was pretty certain that Christopher Baglin, the Defense Department guy, hadn't been entirely on the level. He didn't think the guy had been lying, necessarily. What he'd said was likely to be close to the truth. It just wouldn't be the whole truth. Reacher's general position when it came to briefings from the top brass was that they were incomplete unless proved otherwise. That went double for top brass he didn't know. And double again for politicians. But he also knew that made little difference when it came to the task at hand. Some scientists had been murdered. There was little doubt about that. Based on what he'd been told, there was a chance that a soldier was responsible. And three potential victims were still alive. Reacher wanted to help keep it that way, so he picked up the phone. His first call was to the US Army Chemical Corps at Fort McClellan, Alabama. His second was to the Office of Administration at the Department of Veterans Affairs, which was just down the road, also in D.C., a stone's throw from the White House. He needed to make a third call, to the army's National Personnel Records Center in St. Louis, Missouri, but he couldn't do that until the list he'd requested from Fort McClellan came through.

Reacher inspected the fax machine. It wasn't doing anything. He hoped there wasn't anything he was supposed to set or switch on or program to make it work. He checked it from all sides and saw two cables leading out of its rear. A thicker one that was connected to a power outlet, and a thinner one that was plugged into a phone socket. That seemed reasonable, so Reacher picked a button on the front of the machine at random and pressed it. A little gray screen lit up and a shrill electronic tone pierced the air. Reacher guessed that meant the thing was all set. There was nothing he could do to make the information he wanted appear more quickly, so he turned back to the phone. He called Agent Ottoway in Chicago. He left a message on her machine asking if she could find anything out about Amber Smith. He called a buddy in the CIA and asked him to dig into Kent Neilsen. He called his brother, Joe, who worked at the Treasury Department, and left a message about Gary Walsh. Then he grabbed a blank piece of paper and a pen. He wrote down three names. All belonging to soldiers who were AWOL. Low-level offenders who were likely to skulk at the bottom of his unit's nuisance list for the foreseeable future. Then he picked up the phone again. Called a few other MPs who had helped him over the years, or who he owed favors to. Asked if they had any names stuck on their own lists. If it was true that the Secretary of Defense was personally involved in the operation, they were going to throw the kitchen sink at it. That's the way the world works. There was bound to be plenty of spare manpower. Enough to round up a few additional miscreants, and there was no point in letting all those tax dollars go to waste.

The phone in the Pentagon rang again at 3:13 P.M. Eastern. Not a scheduled time for a call.

The guy who answered it listened, hung up, then dialed the number for Charles Stamoran's private extension.

Stamoran answered after one ring. He said, "Go."

The guy recited the message he had memorized a minute before. "Michael Rymer is dead. He drowned. His body was recovered from

the lake behind his house at 11:38 A.M. The security detail watching
his house was alerted when they saw his boat run aground a couple
of hundred yards from his dock. They investigated, found it empty,
and called a rescue helicopter. An initial examination confirmed
there was water in Rymer's lungs. He had a bruise across his chest
consistent with falling against the side of the boat, and there was
chafing on his ankles consistent with getting tangled in a rope.
There were ropes scattered all across the deck, so his death could
have been accidental if he tripped, fell, and went overboard. Or the
injuries could be coincidental if he had become despondent and
jumped into the water in an attempt to commit suicide."

Stamoran took the receiver away from his ear for a moment.
Michael Rymer was the most fastidious man he'd ever met. There
was no way he would have left ropes lying around on his boat. No
way he would have gotten tangled in them and tripped. There was
a zero percent chance of that happening. Which meant someone
else had been on the boat. Someone who murdered him there.
Stamoran felt an unexpected flash of relief. It only lasted a moment
then a flood of guilt chased it away. It had occurred to him that if
someone was in Colorado killing Rymer, they couldn't be anywhere
else tracking Pritchard down and forcing him to reveal his secret.
Not yet, anyway.

Stamoran lifted the handset again. He said, "The second someone on the task force comes up with a name, I want it followed up.
Vigorously. Resources are not an issue. I don't want any stone, big
or small, left unturned."

At ten after five there was a knock on Reacher's door. It opened
before he said anything and Amber Smith, the FBI representative in
the group, stepped into the room.

Smith tucked a loose strand of hair behind her ear and said, "I'm calling it a day. Going to head to the hotel. See what kind of a place they've stuck us in. Want a ride? Looks like you don't have a vehicle with you."

Reacher looked at the fax machine. No new pages had come out since he'd called the army's National Personnel Records Center a couple of hours earlier and he couldn't make any more progress without the list he'd asked for. He said, "Sure. Thank you."

One of the cars had already gone by the time Reacher and Smith got to the parking lot. The black Impala. That left the two Crown Victorias. Kent Neilsen, the CIA guy, was leaning against one of them. The blue one. His suit was so crumpled it looked like he'd just been run down by it.

Neilsen said, "Either of you hungry? I am. I know a place near the hotel. How about we get squared away with our rooms then go and grab a bite?"

Smith shrugged. She said, "Don't see why not."

Reacher worked on the principle that you should eat when you can so that you won't have to when you can't. He said, "I'm in."

Neilsen pushed himself away from the trunk of his car and made for the driver's door. "Meet in the hotel lobby at six?"

The hotel was a hair over a mile away from the office building. Reacher had spent more nights than he cared to remember in hotels. Mainly in the course of hunting down fugitives or digging up evidence or following leads. And mainly in places with rates that wouldn't cause heart attacks when the army saw the bills. Which tended to define the kind of facilities the establishments had on offer. It was fair to say he was used to his accommodations being on the plain and simple end of the scale. But the place the task force had picked was the equal of the blandest building he'd ever seen when it came to functional design. It had absolutely nothing that wasn't one hundred percent necessary. It was four floors high, built of pale brick, with small windows and a flat roof. There was no cover above the entrance. No valet parking stand. Even the signs lacked illumination. They had to make do with reflective paint.

Smith turned into the lot, spun her Ford around, and backed into a parking spot near the building, next to Neilsen's car. On the far side of the lot Reacher could see a line of much larger bays. The right kind of size for tour buses. He doubted they would be for rock bands or sports teams. So maybe for school parties, he thought. He had heard that it was common practice for kids to visit D.C. when they were in eighth grade. That seemed like a good idea. He'd learned about the nation's capital when he was younger than that, but all the information came from the dog-eared pages of a book in a humid classroom on the other side of the world. That was fine for absorbing facts. Not so good for capturing scale and atmosphere.

They sailed through check-in without a hitch, so Reacher took his key and carried his bag to his room on the second floor. He used the stairs and as he was working the lock on his door he saw Smith emerge from the elevator. She had the room next to his.

Inside his room Reacher found that the bare-minimum approach had been maintained. The essential bases were covered. There was a bed. A dresser. A chair. A kind of flap attached to the wall that could be used as a desk, if you were desperate. A closet with hangers that were fixed to the rail to stop people from stealing them. And a bathroom with soap and shampoo in dispensers in brackets on the wall. Reacher guessed it would be cheaper to top them up a little than to provide fresh miniature bottles for every guest.

* * *

Neilsen was already waiting in reception when Reacher got there at a minute to six. Smith caught up two minutes later and Neilsen started for the exit without saying a word.

Reacher said, "What about Walsh? The Treasury guy."

Neilsen kept moving. "No idea. He was gone when we decided to leave the office and there's no sign of his car outside. Guess he's staying somewhere else."

The bar Neilsen had in mind was a couple of hundred yards from the hotel, heading farther away from the city. They decided to walk. It wasn't the most pleasant evening. The air was heavy with exhaust fumes from all the traffic in the neighborhood and it had started to drizzle, but Reacher didn't mind. He'd been cooped up all morning in trains and planes and cabs, and all afternoon in meeting rooms and offices, so he was glad to be able to stretch his legs.

The building they were aiming for had two floors. The higher level was shared between a nail salon and a wig maker. Two places Reacher had zero interest in visiting. The whole of the first floor was taken up with the bar. Its gimmick was that it looked like it was still under construction. A thick plastic sheet with a zipper down the center hung in the entrance in place of a door. The bar itself was made of scaffolding, with roughly formed shelves and nooks and niches for the bottles and glasses. The kitchen was on the other side of a wall with a jagged hole in it that was supposed to seem like it had been smashed with a sledgehammer. The tables were fashioned out of giant cable drums and instead of regular chairs there were a bunch of wooden crates.

Smith paused near the entrance. There were no other customers in the place. She said, "You sure about this?"

Neilsen looked serious. "Wait till you taste the food. And they make a mean Old Fashioned. Trust me."

They took a table in the corner farthest from the bar and a server approached them after less than a minute. She was wearing denim coveralls and giant, unlaced work boots, and she had a red paisley bandanna in her hair. Reacher figured she was going for the Rosie the Riveter look, and wondered if that was her choice or if it was required by the management. Neilsen ordered a glass of champagne. Reacher and Smith asked for beer.

"You celebrating?" Smith said after the server had retreated to the bar.

Neilsen said, "I guess. I mean, I still have a pulse. I'm still upright. Those things have to count for something, right?"

The server brought their drinks. Neilsen took a sip and said, "So, what do you think? Are we going to save the country from a blackmailing fanatic?"

Smith shrugged. "We're going to try, I guess."

Reacher said nothing.

Neilsen set down his glass. His expression suddenly became overbearingly earnest. "Listen. Here's how I see our situation. We need to trust each other. We need to pull together. If we do, we might just get through this. If not, we're screwed."

Smith said, "How do you figure?"

Neilsen said, "We all have skeletons, right? That's why we're here. Why whoever got the call from the Department of Defense put our names forward. They didn't just pick us out of a hat. We're expendable. This whole thing is a train wreck waiting to happen. When it goes off the rails, we need to make sure we don't crash and burn along with it. We need to decide, right now. Are we going to trust each other? Or not?"

Smith and Reacher stayed silent.

Neilsen said, "You know I'm right. Tell me the first thing you did in your little hutches this afternoon wasn't to pick up the phone and ask questions about the other three. See what dirt you could find."

Smith said, "It wasn't the first thing . . ."

Neilsen said, "But you did do it."

Smith nodded. Reacher gave nothing away.

"Good." Neilsen smiled again. "We may be late for happy hour at the last chance saloon but at least you're not total idiots." He turned to Reacher. "Think the blackmailer is one of yours?"

Reacher said, "I don't think there is a blackmailer."

Neilsen nodded. "That's why you asked Baglin about ransom notes and attacks on people from other projects. But if our guy isn't digging for blackmail material, what is he doing? What does he want?"

"Revenge. The murders? They feel personal."

"I came to the same conclusion."

"If someone who was involved with the project is behind the murders, then it's definitely not about blackmail. They would know what happened, because they were part of it. They wouldn't have to force the information out of other people."

Neilsen nodded again. "Right. And it would be impossible to get away with it. If the killings stop with only one guy left alive, he might as well print a confession in *The New York Times*."

Reacher said, "Agreed. Which is why I think it's a relative of someone who was harmed by the project. Some kind of long-term damage or disability."

"And this could be a soldier?"

Reacher breathed out slowly. "Could be. Think about the training the guy must have had. Kill someone in a hospital and none of the staff notices you were even there? Then get in and out, and murder a guy, while his house is being staked out by professionals? Those aren't things that just anyone could do."

Neilsen said, "Could be army, I guess. Could just as easily be CIA. How are you going to find him?"

"Start with everyone who served in those research units. See who has a son or a grandson or a nephew in green. Or who was in green. Then prioritize by those old-timers who've died recently or who just got a terminal diagnosis. Anyone who had or has a reason to set the record straight at long last."

"That's a sound method. Our records are kept differently but I'm doing basically the same. I wonder if either of us will hit the jackpot."

"You won't." Smith swallowed the last mouthful of her beer and set the bottle down. "You're both wrong. The Soviets are behind this."

"They can't be," Neilsen said. "There aren't any Soviets anymore. They lost."

Smith snorted. "Of course there are. The Soviet Union closed for business, sure. But the KGB didn't. The name it uses will make no difference. You'll see. And their agents are still here. These guys are fanatical. True believers. They'll continue the fight till the end of their days, no matter what else is happening in the world."

"Maybe."

"Definitely. Look at the deaths. No one can prove they weren't accidents or suicides, but come on. Anyone with a brain can see those scientists were murdered. The whole thing screams KGB. It's what they do. They even have a term for it. *Assassination by purported suicide.* They're sending a message. They're making clear they can kill anyone, anywhere, anytime, and no one can do anything about it. They'll pick off the rest of the scientists, one by one, in bizarre, eye-catching ways, then whatever dirt they picked up about the project along the way, they'll release it. Could be years from now when they do that. Whenever they think it'll cause the most harm. You have no idea how long a game these guys play."

While Reacher and the rest of the task force were talking, Roberta and Veronica Sanson were driving. They were in California, south of L.A., right on the coast, in a stolen Jeep Grand Cherokee, and they were going with their new MO. Taking one pass of their target's house before withdrawing out of range of the watchers and finding somewhere to spend the night. Only this time they spotted two government cars parked in strategic places.

Roberta glanced across at Veronica as she steered down the twisty road that led away from Charlie Adam's house. "Lights were on. They were home. Which is good."

Veronica said, "But you saw the cars?"

Roberta nodded.

"Adam was home. And so was his wife."

"That's unfortunate."

"What do we do? Wait?"

"No. Waiting multiplies risk."

"What, then?"

"Make it a murder/suicide this time, I guess."

Reacher ordered steak and had one more beer before switching to coffee. Smith had a salmon salad and three more beers. Neilsen had a burrito stuffed with every available option, three more glasses of champagne, and then switched to whiskey. A lot of whiskey. The conversation came in fits and starts as they ate and drank and waited

LEE CHILD and ANDREW CHILD

on refills. Mostly superficial details about places they'd been posted and hints of highs and lows in their personal lives. Smith and Neilsen revealed more than Reacher. And they both seemed to have had more lows than highs. Reacher began to think that Neilsen had been right about why they'd been selected for the assignment. If things went south and targets were needed to pin the blame on, they all had bull's-eyes already drawn on their backs. In fluorescent paint.

Susan Kasluga was standing in her dressing room. She had a clothes hanger in each hand. One held a navy blue suit. One held a black suit. She was trying to choose between them. She always liked to pick the next day's outfit before she went to bed. She believed it helped to counter decision fatigue. She knew most people scoffed at the concept but she didn't care. She would do pretty much anything to give herself an edge.

Charles Stamoran appeared in the doorway before she'd reached a verdict. He said, "What are you doing?"

She said, "What does it look like? I can't go to the office in my pajamas."

"You shouldn't go to the office at all. Not for a couple more days."

"We agreed I'd stay home for two days. I've done that. No more."

"Susie, it's not safe."

"You haven't caught the guy?"

"Not yet."

"That's your problem. Not mine."

"It'll be a problem for both of us if you get yourself caught by this maniac."

"He killed more scientists?"

Stamoran nodded. "Geoffrey Brown. Michael Rymer."

"That's a shame, I guess. I didn't know them very well. But he didn't get Neville Pritchard. So you're safe. So I'm safe. End of discussion."

"He could get Pritchard tomorrow. Tonight."

"He won't."

"You can't know that."

"Call it intuition. Call it anything you like, but I'm going back to work."

Stamoran could hear the steel in her voice. He'd known her long enough to realize there was no point in arguing so he said, "All right. Back to work. But you're going to need a guard detail."

Kasluga dumped the black suit back on its rail. She said, "Already taken care of."

The sky had cleared by the time Reacher, Smith, and Neilsen left the bar. Neilsen went first, weaving slightly and almost tripping on cracks in the sidewalk a couple of times. Smith hung back. She stayed by Reacher's side. She was tucked in a little closer to him than she had been before. Reacher put it down to the beer. When they arrived at the hotel, they saw that Walsh's car was in the lot, two spaces away from Smith's.

Neilsen's room was also on the second floor, on the other side of Smith's. He mumbled something that could have been *good night*, took out his key, and dropped it on the floor. Reacher picked it up. He worked the lock, nudged Neilsen through the doorway, and tossed the key in after him. Reacher turned back and saw Smith standing in her own open doorway. She smiled, then said, "Sleep well."

Chapter 11

Reacher woke himself at 6:00 A.M. the following morning. Two minutes later he heard footsteps in the hotel corridor.
Someone treading slowly and carefully, trying not to make much
sound. Then a note slid into view between the base of the door and
the carpet. The footsteps padded away, faster than before. Reacher
slid out of bed and looked through the spyhole in the door. He saw
a woman's back, distorted in the little lens. But clear enough to
recognize. It was Amber Smith, and she was carrying her shoes.

Reacher picked up the piece of paper and unfolded it. Smith's
handwriting was jagged and bold. She said she couldn't drive him
to the office because she needed to make an early start. She was
expecting an update on some hares she'd set running the day before. She thought something important was about to break. So she
suggested Reacher hit up Neilsen for a ride instead of her and signed
off with her initials.

Reacher tossed the note in the trash, took a shower, dressed, and headed downstairs in search of breakfast. He ate two bagels with cream cheese, drank two cups of coffee, and left the hotel without setting eyes on Neilsen. It took him fourteen minutes to walk to the commandeered building, and when he arrived he found a security guard had been installed since the day before. He showed his ID then made his way down the corridor and unlocked the door to the room he'd been allocated.

Inside, Reacher saw that two things had changed overnight. A new page had emerged from the fax machine, and the light on the answering machine was no longer solid red. It was flashing. Three blinks and a pause, three blinks and a pause, like it was repeating S in Morse code. Reacher squeezed into the chair and turned one of the dials on the machine to Play Message(s). The first voice he heard belonged to Agent Ottoway, from Chicago. She had found someone who'd worked with Amber Smith a year or so ago. Smith had been a good agent, apparently, but had gone off the rails due to some kind of family tragedy. Reacher's CIA friend was up next. He had learned that Kent Neilsen was once a rising star. He'd done enough stellar work to earn a lot of slack with his bosses, but the word was that he was rapidly approaching the end of that particular rope. People were rooting for him, but not many expected him to find his way back. Last was Reacher's brother, Joe. His was the shortest message, which didn't surprise Reacher. Joe simply said he couldn't find any trace of a Gary Walsh at the Treasury Department, then advised caution before hanging up.

Reacher wasn't too surprised by the first two reports. Not after what he'd seen and heard at the bar, and again after they left. Joe's information was more troubling. He was a thorough guy. If Walsh's record was there to be found, there was no way Joe would have missed it. Reacher would need to dig deeper. But not just then. He had work to do before the morning's meeting. He picked up the new fax. It was from the army's National Personnel Records Center. He set it on his desk next to the two reports that had come through the day before and began scanning the names, looking for connections that might unmask a murderer.

It was the dog that saved Lucy Adam's life. Sophie. A golden retriever.

Lucy and Charlie ate breakfast together on their patio, tucked between the glass railings at the top of the cliff and the back of their house. Yogurt, fruit, coffee, and orange juice. Charlie would have preferred an omelet or something involving bacon and sausage, but given the struggles he'd been having recently getting his pants to fasten, he figured he needed to make some changes. He wasn't happy about it. He was never at his sunniest in the mornings and his new diet did nothing to improve his mood. He scowled his way through the meal, hunched and grumpy and silent, and when Sophie dropped her toy at his feet he just kicked it away.

"Come on, girl." Lucy stood up and glared at her husband. "Ignore Mr. Personality. Let's go for a nice walk."

Charlie waited for his wife to find her shoes and fetch the leash and disappear to the north along the cliff path, then he pushed his bowl away. He struggled out of his chair and went into the kitchen. He came back out a minute later with a bag of croissants in his hand but he didn't sit down. He paused by the table, straining his ears. He thought he'd heard a voice. Then it came again. A little louder. From somewhere on the clifftop. It was female and it said just one word. "Help!"

Charlie dropped the pastries on the table and rushed toward the railing. He leaned over, looked down, and saw someone. A few feet below. A woman. Maybe in her late twenties. Slim and fit with dark hair. She was lying on one of the narrow, natural ledges that the wind and water had cut into the rock face over the last several millennia. She must have climbed up from the beach, far below. It wasn't easy, but it could be done. Charlie had plotted a couple of different routes, years ago, when they had first bought the house. When he was much younger. And much lighter. There were some sketchy places, for sure, but they were all much lower down. The woman was safe where she was. There was no danger of falling from there. Not unless she rolled off deliberately. Charlie looked her over, scanning for injuries. As far as he could tell, there was nothing wrong. No blood on her head or seeping through her clothes. No limbs bent into unnatural positions. He said, "You need help?"

The woman said, "No. But you do."

Something slammed into Charlie's back. The force threw him against the railing. His hips crunched against the top edge and his torso jackknifed over it, leaving him bent double and scrabbling for grip. He tried to straighten up but he couldn't move. A weight was pushing him. Two weights, he realized. A pair of hands planted squarely between his shoulder blades.

Roberta Sanson sat up. She said, "Only one person can help you now, Charlie. Yourself." She took a piece of paper from her pocket and held it in front of Charlie's face. "Read these names. Tell me whose is missing."

Charlie said, "I can't. I don't have my glasses."

Roberta shook her head and put the list away. "OK. Recite for me. The names of everyone connected to your research team. India, 1969."

Charlie didn't respond.

Roberta grabbed his wrists. Veronica took the pressure off his back, took hold of his ankles, and started to lift.

"No!" Charlie kicked and wriggled. He was trying to free himself but all he did was grind his pelvis against the narrow glass rim. "Let me go!"

Roberta said, "We will. As soon as you tell us the missing name. We'll let you go and you'll never see us again. I promise."

Charlie was silent for a moment longer. The pain in his hip bones was becoming unbearable. He whimpered, then reeled off six names.

"And?"

"And what? That's everyone."

"No. You're missing one."

"I'm not."

"You are. Come on. Complete the set."

"There's no one else. I should know. I was there from the start."

"Owen Buck told us there was."

"Buck was crazy. He was paranoid. He was always going on about secrets and running to the authorities. But he never did. You know why? Because there was nothing to tell."

"There was plenty to tell. He told us. We believed him. So now we want the name."

"I don't know any other name."

"Last chance."

"There's no one else!"

"OK. If that's how you want to play it."

Veronica pushed Charlie's legs higher until he slithered down and his hands touched the ground. Roberta stood and wrapped her arms around his knees. Veronica vaulted over the railing and took his right leg. Roberta kept hold of his left. She looked at her sister and mouthed, *One, two, three*. Then they heaved his legs forward, toward the ocean. The momentum carried him over the little ledge Roberta had been lying on and out, away from the cliff. He plunged down, cartwheeling and picking up speed and bouncing off the rocks until he hit the beach. He landed headfirst, drilling a couple of inches into the sand and snapping his neck clean in half.

Christopher Baglin opened the meeting with the news of Michael Rymer's drowning.

No one spoke after he had finished. The air in the room felt heavy. Gary Walsh stared out of the window. Amber Smith looked like she was angry. Kent Neilsen looked like he'd slept in a hedge and wasn't sure how he came to be inside.

Baglin said, "The fact that another man was killed despite being kept under close observation shows the kind of threat we're up against. So, I need names. Reacher, you first. What have you got?"

Reacher slid a piece of paper across the giant table. It had five names on it. Four of them came from the lists he had correlated in his office along the corridor. He had expected more, but that was all the data would support. There had been 3,798 officers and men in the Chemical Corps in 1969. Of those, 157 had kids who followed them into the army. And only one of those kids had been AWOL at the time of the murders, plus another three who had left the service.

Baglin said, "Confidence level?"

"Low to very low."

Baglin nodded. "Smith?"

Smith handed over a page, folded in half. Baglin straightened it out and Reacher saw six names laid out in an orderly column. They were scrawled in the same jagged script he'd read at the hotel.

Smith said, "Due respect to the other people here, sir, but I believe their approach is wrong. My investigation suggests that we're not dealing with one individual who has committed multiple murders. We're dealing with a number of killers who work for the same organization. Same head, different hands. This explains the inconsistent MOs that are reflected in the crimes."

Baglin sat a little straighter. "Interesting theory. And the organization?"

"These men are KGB lifers. Same game, different name."

"Confidence level?"

"High to extremely high."

"Good. They will be checked first. Now, Walsh?"

Walsh dragged his eyes away from the window and said, "Nothing from me."

"Nothing? Not one name?"

"Nothing. The kind of work those guys were doing, the kind of material they were involved with, it doesn't really have a civilian application. Safe to say my well is dry."

Baglin glared at Walsh, then moved on. "Neilsen?"

Neilsen took a sheet of paper from his jacket pocket and held it out. It was surprisingly smooth and crisp, and four names were neatly written in cobalt blue ink. "Confidence? Also low to very low. I wish I could say otherwise but the facts just aren't there."

Baglin stacked the three pages, straightened their edges, and got to his feet. He said, "Keep working. Wrack your brains. Think laterally. Read tea leaves or cast chicken bones if you have to. Just get me more names in case none of these pan out. I'm going to have pagers delivered to you this afternoon. Wear one at all times. If anything breaks out of hours, you're to be back here within fifteen minutes. Any questions?"

Reacher said, "Any word of attacks on scientists from other projects?"

Baglin shook his head. "No. This is the only one."

The phone in the Pentagon rang again at 11:21 A.M. Eastern. Not a scheduled time for a call.

The guy who answered it listened, hung up, then moved into his outer office and dialed the number for Charles Stamoran's car phone. Stamoran had just settled into the car's backseat after a meeting at the White House, which had not gone as well as he'd hoped. He picked up the handset and said, "This better be good news."

The Pentagon guy took a breath, then said, "Charlie Adam is dead. He fell off a cliff from the patio behind his house. His wife returned from walking their dog and found he was missing. She thought he'd gone to the store but his car was still in the garage. Then she noticed more gulls than usual circling and swooping toward the beach. She looked down and saw his body. It was in bad shape. The ME confirmed he died from injuries sustained in the fall. A safety rail that meets the local construction code is in place, so the fall could not have been an accident. Not unless Mr. Adam climbed over voluntarily, then slipped or lost his balance. The agents confirmed that no one entered or exited the property, so foul play is unlikely. Mrs. Adam admitted that her husband had recently exhibited signs of depression but rejected the idea that he committed suicide."

Stamoran leaned his head back against the soft leather. Charlie Adam was the guy from the project he knew least well. He'd always found him prickly and a little vain. He couldn't offer an informed opinion about what Adam would or wouldn't do in any given situation. Except this one. He was sure Adam hadn't jumped. And he was sure he hadn't fallen. However *unlikely*, this was foul play. He had no doubt. Because this wasn't about Adam. It was about whoever was picking the scientists off, one by one. Now there was only one left. Pritchard. And Pritchard was still missing. Which was a circumstance that might play in their favor. But equally, it might not. Much as Stamoran hated to admit it, maybe it was time to think about contingencies.

Stamoran straightened up and said, "There's an upside here. We know where the guy will strike next. We know Pritchard won't be there. We can make sure a surprise is in store. But I want something to fall back on, if it becomes necessary. Baglin is running the task force?"

"Yes, sir."

"Tell him to keep mining for names. If we can identify this asshole before he gets to Pritchard's house, so much the better. But also tell him to shift his focus. There's something else I want him to find."

A pager was delivered to Reacher's office at 1:00 P.M. He had seen doctors and businesspeople wearing pagers clipped to their belts but he didn't want to do that, himself. He thought it would look pretentious, so he shoved it into his jacket pocket. At 1:05 it started to beep. Quietly at first, but by the time he'd fished it out and found a button to press, it was loud and angry. Reacher put it back in his pocket. He figured the sound must have been some kind of a test procedure, or confirmation that the device was activated.

Then he heard doors slamming and footsteps hurrying down the corridor and realized the alert must be for real.

Christopher Baglin was already in his seat at the head of the table when Reacher got to the boardroom. The other three were getting settled. Reacher made his way around to his place, sat, and folded his arms. He could see from Baglin's expression and the stoop of his shoulders that more bad news was on its way.

"We've lost another one." Baglin looked at each person in turn. "Another scientist from Project 192. Charlie Adam. Officially, he jumped, or fell, off a cliff behind his home in California. But let's be realistic. No one's buying that kind of coincidence. He was murdered by the same person who killed his colleagues."

"Or by another person from the same organization," Smith said.

Baglin glared at her, then said, "I guess we can't rule out a team effort, at this stage. But here's the thing. Only one scientist is still alive. Obviously efforts to protect him will be ramped up to the max. But we've already seen that our perp is pretty adept at getting around security. It's like he's a ghost. It would be far safer to intercept him before he gets close. To do that, we need to identify him. So I need you to cast your nets wider. To think more creatively. In short, I need more names. And I need them yesterday. Understood?"

Four heads nodded around the table.

Baglin said, "Good. If you come up with anything hot, page me. Failing that, we'll reconvene at 0900. Now, one more thing. Reacher and Neilsen, you've been looking for relatives of scientists from the sixties in your services. Anyone who died very recently, or who is seriously sick. I like that. It's sound logic. But I want you to expand on it. It doesn't follow that the scientist and the killer have to be related. They could be friends. Comrades in some kind of counter-culture movement. Hell, the current guy could be getting paid by the older one. So I want you to stop worrying about the precise connection for a moment. We can piece that together afterward. Just look at anyone connected, however loosely, to the program in the sixties. Understood?"

Roberta and Veronica Sanson did the closest thing possible to making their stolen Jeep disappear. They parked it in the long-term lot at LAX, wiped it for prints, just in case, and walked away.

There was no debate about where to go next. No need to pick at random from a list of targets. They knew exactly what their destination was. And they had a plan to get there without attracting attention. Roberta took a Delta flight to Washington National. Veronica flew United to Dulles. Both used cash and fake IDs. And then, to mix up their routine, they figured on staying one night at an airport hotel, each stealing a car the next morning, and making their way toward the coast.

The meeting wrapped up and Reacher's afternoon played out much like it had the previous day. Phone calls and faxes and lists of names. Nothing to get his pulse racing, but nothing to complain about. Not directly.

Smith knocked on his door at ten after five and offered a lift to the hotel, which Reacher accepted. Neilsen was waiting in the parking lot. He suggested dinner at the same place as the night before, which Smith and Reacher didn't object to. They met in the hotel reception at 6:00 P.M. and again they walked. Again the drizzle started to fall. The bar wasn't crowded, so they took the same table as before. The same waitress came to take their order.

Neilsen skipped the champagne and went straight to the whiskey. Reacher and Smith stuck to beer. Reacher waited until the food had arrived and the others were on their second drinks, then he said, "One of the names I gave Baglin was for an AWOL soldier. Nothing to do with the task force. I did it to save myself the trouble of tracking him down later."

Neilsen drained his glass and set it down. "Why are you telling us about it? You were Mr. Cagey last night."

"Because of something you said. About the importance of trusting each other. It's even more important now."

"Why?"

"I met a navy guy, years ago. He had this expression. He said if you don't know which port you're heading for, every wind is an ill wind."

"Do you get that?" Smith said to Neilsen. "I don't follow."

Reacher said, "It's like if you don't know what you're aiming for, you're always going to miss. Like with this detail we're assigned to. How can we draw valid conclusions when we don't know what's going on?"

Smith said, "Have you not been listening? Bioweapon research, dead scientists, revelations that could embarrass the country. That pretty much covers it, right?"

"Wrong. The dots don't connect the way Baglin says they do. Think it through. Someone claims the United States did some secret research to find antidotes to bioweapons? So what? Why deny it? Of course we did it. We had to. It would be embarrassing if we hadn't. It would be worse. It would be criminal."

"You're being too logical. We're talking about the general public.

Civilians. They're weirded out by bioweapons. They think of people bleeding out of their eyeballs and babies with two heads."

"That's why we need antidotes."

"Again, forget your logic. This is about emotion."

"It's about something we're not seeing yet. Think about the last thing Baglin said today. He wants names of scientists from the sixties. Why? They can't be behind a plan to find out what was done. They know, because they were the ones who did it."

"I guess."

"And there were a bunch of these bioweapon antidote projects. None of the others has been targeted. Why this one? What's special about it?"

"I don't know. Does it matter?"

"The tide is about to turn. I can feel it. If that last scientist buys the farm, or if some other kind of secret gets revealed, the whole focus is going to switch to blame. The thing itself won't be the problem. Us not containing it will be the problem. And like Neilsen said, we all have some dings on our records right now. Do you have people lining up to go to bat for you? Because I don't."

"So what do we do?"

"We start by getting the truth about Project 192."

"How? Turn inward? Do some digging? Twist some arms?"

"No. That's not going to get the job done. If we're going to save that scientist, and our own asses, we need to go off-base a little bit. Together. Hence, trust."

There was silence for a moment, then Neilsen said, "Two of the names I gave were for my own reasons. Bad guys, sure enough. The world will be better with them behind bars. Or in unmarked graves. But they have nothing to do with the task force."

Smith said, "Same goes for all six of mine. All murdering assholes, but nothing to do with the dead scientists." She paused. "So.

Project 192 was a joint army/CIA thing. Are you suggesting you and Neilsen lean on some people? Cut some corners? Break some rules? Is that what you mean?"

"No. There's no point. We would only come across two kinds of people. Ones who don't know anything. And ones who do know but won't tell us. If we want accurate information about what our side was doing in the sixties, there's only one place to get it. That's where you come in."

"The FBI?"

"No. The KGB."

Chapter 12

The odds were that they would walk into a trap before the morning was out, and Roberta and Veronica Sanson knew it. There was only one name left on their list. Neville Pritchard. The last guy who had worked in the lab in India in '69. Whoever was responsible for keeping him alive would know they were coming. Would focus their resouces. It would be crazy to expect anything less. The smart move would be to walk away. To be content with what they had already achieved. But there was a problem with that. Pritchard was the only one who knew the identity they needed to discover. The key to the secret they needed to unlock. So dumb move or not, they were going to take a trip to Pritchard's house. Their decision was set in stone. But that didn't mean they had to go in with their eyes closed.

Roberta and Veronica rendezvoused at first light at an abandoned gas station five miles outside Annapolis, as planned. Roberta was driving a white Toyota Corolla she had stolen at Washington National airport. Veronica was in a Dodge Caravan she had taken from an off-airport hotel at Dulles. Previously they had done their drive-bys together, but with the likely extra surveillance in mind they decided to keep both vehicles. Make two passes, one from each direction, then compare what they had seen.

Roberta went first, heading south toward Back Creek, sticking close to the speed limit and obeying every stop sign and red light she came to. Veronica followed, sometimes five cars behind, sometimes six, and when she was two streets away from Pritchard's she coasted to the side of the road and stopped next to a stretch of tall, ancient hedge. Three minutes later she saw Roberta's Toyota coming back toward her. She gave no sign that she recognized it. She sat for another minute then pulled out and made her way to Pritchard's house. Drove past it, slowly enough to get a good look, quickly enough to not attract attention, then made for a stretch of scrubby grass that overlooked the ocean and pulled up alongside her sister. She wiped the interior of the van for prints, jumped down, and slid into the Toyota's passenger seat.

Roberta said, "I saw four cars watching."

Veronica said, "Same. Four cars, but one way in. We're going to need costumes. Props. And a different kind of vehicle."

Reacher was awake, dressed, and sitting on his bed when Amber Smith knocked on his hotel room door. It was 8:00 A.M. Right on time.

Reacher let Smith in. Her eyes were wide and she was bouncing on the balls of her feet. She said, "We're getting somewhere. I had people working on it all night. They've hit on three possibilities. Three KGB defectors. I'm still waiting on the details."

Reacher and Smith rode down in the elevator together. They took a detour via the breakfast room to pick up coffee and bagels, then

Smith drove them the mile to the building the task force was using. She spent the remaining three-quarters of an hour in her office, staring at the phone, willing it to ring. Reacher was happy for his not to. He picked up a couple of pages that had spilled out of the fax machine, ran through the names listed on them so that he would have some ammunition for Christopher Baglin at the morning meeting, then settled back in his chair, closed his eyes, and let Magic Slim loose in his head.

Baglin was late. Not catastrophically, but enough to leave him red-faced and out of breath when he finally bustled into the board-room. The other four were in their customary places, in silence. Reacher was on his second refill of coffee. They each handed over their next tranche of names, except for Walsh. He had drawn another blank. Reacher was beginning to wonder if the guy was trying to get returned to the Treasury. If that was really where he was from. He made a mental note to follow up with his brother, Joe.

No new information was forthcoming, and no new orders were issued, so Reacher was back in his office inside ten minutes. Five minutes after that Smith knocked on his door and rushed in without waiting for an answer. She said, "I've heard from my people. One option is a dead end. Literally. The guy got killed while he was training for a dogsled race up in Alaska. He should have known better, at his age. The other two leads are promising, though. One guy is based in Oregon. The other's here, in D.C."

Reacher said, "What do you know about the local guy?"

"He runs a Russian-themed café. And honestly, he sounds like a complete headcase. He was a KGB colonel. Defected in '74. Declined the whole new name, relocation package in return for more money and the chance to stay in town and build his own fake identity. And earn a fortune feeding politicians weird shit they'd never eat at home. He goes by—and I checked this to make sure I was getting it right—His Royal Highness the Prince Sarb of Windsor."

"As in Windsor, England?"

"It's a nod to a legend he supposedly created before he bailed on the Soviets. He claimed he was stationed in London in the late fifties and MI5 picked up his scent. They were closing in fast, his escape routes were blown, so he went to the Brits and pretended to be the illegitimate son of an aristocrat who had been living in Hungary. He said he was on the fringes of the intelligence community there and he had a line on the Russian spy they were chasing. Said the Brits took the fact that he knew who they were looking for as a sign he was legit, and they bought it. So effectively he got them to hire him to catch himself. Which he clearly did not do. If his story is true. Which I doubt."

"What was his specialty?"

"His last two postings were in Southeast Asia. He had a lot to say about chemical and biological stuff when he was debriefed, post-defection."

"Sounds like he's worth a shot."

"I guess. Although . . . Reacher, are we crazy? Is this guy really going to talk to us if we just show up on his doorstep? Normally this sort of thing takes months of negotiating to set up."

"Oh, he'll talk. Strangers always open up to me. I'm a people person. Haven't you noticed?"

Eight pairs of eyes watched the UPS truck as it dawdled along Neville Pritchard's street. It was moving erratically, speeding up and slowing down like the driver was searching for an address. The agent in the lead car picked up the handset of the phone that was mounted between his front seats. He called a number at the Pentagon. Asked his control to find out which UPS depot covered the area, then check whether the truck was one of theirs. The truck drew level with Pritchard's driveway. It turned and crept toward the house. The agent's phone rang. It was his control. He confirmed that the local UPS manager had vouched for the truck. The agent was happy with the news but not completely satisfied. Pritchard hadn't received any other deliveries the whole time they'd been watching his house, and he wasn't home now so it didn't make sense for him to be expecting anything. The agent swapped the phone for his radio. He pressed the Transmit button and said, "Possible contact. Stand by. Over."

The truck made it all the way to Pritchard's garage, then stopped. It sat for a moment, shaking slightly and rattling and pumping exhaust fumes into the morning air. The driver didn't get out. Then the truck began to turn around. It sawed back and forth, back and forth, lurching and swaying each time it changed direction. It paused when it had gotten halfway, perpendicular to the driveway, like the driver was taking a breath. Then it started moving again, even more abruptly, like the driver's patience with the whole situation was wearing thin.

The truck finally got back to the road and turned so it was heading the same way as before. It drove another ten yards then stopped again. It was right in the line of sight of the third agents' car. The only one with a view of Pritchard's garage door. The agent in the driver's seat wound down his window. He saw the UPS driver was a woman. He nudged his partner as if to say, *that explains it*, then waved and yelled at her to move. She may have said something back but it was hard to tell because the side of her face was covered with a large square of gauze bandage, like she'd recently been in an accident. She did return his wave, though. Only she used fewer fingers than he had done.

Roberta Sanson crouched inside Neville Pritchard's garage and leaned against the door. She was wearing a balaclava that covered her ears as well as her face, but she could still hear the truck's engine. She listened to it wheeze and groan and then run and stop and she pictured each step of its progress. Each step they had carefully mapped out. The truck was stationary out on the road for longer than she'd expected. She held her breath. Pictured agents from the watching cars swarming around it. Sliding back the door. Pulling Veronica out. Ripping off her disguise. She held her breath. Then the truck puttered away. It kept going this time. There was no sound of squealing tires. Nothing to suggest pursuit. She relaxed. Just a little. She could see the door that led into the house, but she had no idea what was waiting on the other side.

Roberta inched her way along the side of Pritchard's car until she reached the connecting door. She took hold of the handle, gathered herself, then twisted, pushed, and dived through the gap. She rolled. Pushed back onto her feet. Spun around 360 degrees, fists raised, ready to block or strike. And saw no one. No sign of Pritchard. No sign of any agents.

Roberta moved forward, slowly, planting her feet carefully, making next to no sound. She didn't know Pritchard. She wasn't familiar with his habits but she figured it was probably too late for him to be asleep. There was no sound of water running so he wasn't taking a shower. No sound of kitchen equipment being used so he probably wasn't cooking. Based on the window configuration she'd seen from outside, she guessed the last door in the corridor would lead to the living room. She decided to start there. She kept moving. Passed the first door. Which opened. A man came out. Late twenties, cropped hair, stocky. Dressed in black. Holding a gun.

Not Pritchard.

The guy sneered at Roberta then took a radio from his belt and held it to his ear. He said, "Contact. You owe me fifty bucks. He did show up. Only get this—he's a she. Hold your positions. We'll bring her out in a minute."

Roberta thought, *Of course I showed up. Why would he think I wouldn't? Because they've got Pritchard in custody?* Then she punched the guy in the throat, knuckles extended. He fell back. His gun and his radio rattled against the shiny wooden floor and he grasped his neck, gurgling and gasping as he fought to suck air through his crushed windpipe.

Two more doors opened. Two more men appeared. Both young and fit. Both with guns.

Roberta thought, *Why would they think I'd expect Pritchard to be in custody? None of the others were.*

Another guy appeared at the top of the stairs.

Roberta thought, *Wait. Maybe Pritchard's not in custody?* She darted forward. The guy closest to her stayed still. He let her get close. Which was a mistake. She shaped up like she was going to throw another punch but instead she smashed the side of her foot into the guy's knee. Weight wasn't on her side but she did have strength and momentum, and they were enough. The guy shrieked and fell sideways. He bounced off the wall and whimpered and tried to wrap his arms around his injured leg. Roberta kicked him in the side of his head. Hard. After that he was still and quiet.

Maybe Pritchard ran? Got a tip-off? Heard about the others?

The third guy took a step toward Roberta. He raised his gun. Aimed it at her chest. She grabbed his wrist with her left hand.

Twisted, to stress his elbow. Crashed her right forearm into it, shattering the joint. Punched him in the solar plexus, knocking the wind out of him. Punched him under the jaw to rattle his brain. Then she let go of his wrist, took a half step back, swung her leg up and around, gaining speed and power all the way, and kicked him in the temple. She wasn't exceptionally tall but she was flexible and she was fast. The guy was out cold before he hit the floor.

Maybe they assumed I know his location. Maybe they don't know it themselves? I'll have to be careful how I play this. There are still four cars outside . . .

The fourth guy was already at the bottom of the stairs. He turned to face Roberta. He raised his gun but stayed well out of her reach. He said, "I've got to thank you, miss. These fellas are never going to live this down. Getting their asses handed to them by a girl? The fun I'm going to have? Priceless. But today's fun is over. You're a skinny little thing but no one could miss you from this range. Especially not me, because I'm a hell of a good shot. So give it up. Turn around. Hold your hands out behind your back."

Roberta was still for a few seconds like she was weighing up words of such profundity she could barely grasp their full meaning. Then her head slumped forward, her shoulders sagged, and she turned so that she was facing away from the guy. He wasted no time. He didn't want her changing her mind or pulling any tricks so he stepped in close, wrapped a PlastiCuff around her wrists and pulled it tight. He leaned in so close that Roberta could feel his breath on her neck and said, "That really was quite a performance. I never saw that coming, I'll be honest. Was it you who put an end to the other five guys, too?"

Roberta said, "They never saw it coming, either. But then men have a long history of underestimating women, don't you? If you didn't, maybe more of you would be alive."

"Maybe so. Maybe not. Either way, it's time to go." He pushed Roberta toward the door. "There's someone who wants to talk with you."

"I'm not saying a word. Not unless you tell me something first. I have to know. Did you find it? Was it here? Or was Pritchard lying?"

"The hell you talking about?"

"Pritchard's black book. With the dates and the times and the places, all written down. It's what I came here for."

"Bullshit. You came to kill Pritchard, like you did the others. You admitted it. Only you're behind the curve. You didn't know Pritchard's gone. You don't know where he is."

"I know exactly where he is. He's where I left him."

The guy spun Roberta around. "You have him?"

Roberta winked at the guy.

He said, "He's alive?"

"For the time being. Until his book is safely in my hands. You know how much money I could make off of that thing? A king's ransom. We could split it . . ."

"Where is he?"

"Safe. For now. But if I don't get back to him sometime soon, that could change."

"Tell me where."

"How can I make this clearer? No."

The guy glared at Roberta. "You don't get how this works, do you?" He touched the muzzle of the gun against her chin, held it there for a moment, then slid it down over her neck. He kept it going, across her chest, between her breasts, over her stomach, all the way to the tops of her thighs. "This operation is being run from the top. The very top. I could tear you into a dozen pieces and they'd give me a separate medal for every one of them. And if I felt like doing anything else to you before then, nobody would ever be the wiser. Same goes for my buddies, when they wake up. I don't think you're top of their Christmas card lists. Do you?"

Roberta's eyes opened wide. Her voice shot up an octave. She said, "Go back to town. Head east on 450, then north on 2. Just past mile marker 17 you'll see a boathouse on the right. It's blue. He's in there. In a sail locker. Tied up and gagged."

The guy patted Roberta on the cheek. He said, "See, that wasn't hard." He took his radio and repeated her directions, then said, "Go. All cars. Everything's under control in here. I'll take her for questioning, myself. Out."

Roberta waited until the sound of the cars' engines had faded into the distance. She said, "Under control?" Then she sprang forward and drove her knee into the guy's groin. She put every ounce of strength and fury into it. She would have left the ground without his bulk to stop her. He screamed. His knees buckled. He toppled forward, clutching himself. He puked, spat, rolled onto his side, and settled into a drawn-out, shrill howl. Roberta looked at him and said, "There you go. Underestimating a woman, again. Will you never learn?"

Chapter 13

Amber Smith dropped the car in a loading zone a block from the Soviet defector's café. She climbed out, Reacher and Neilsen joined her on the sidewalk, and together they walked the rest of the way. The place they were looking for was called the Tsar's Tearoom. It took up the first floor of a small, low-rise office building on the edge of a fashionable part of town. A red awning jutted out over its entrance and its facade was covered with garish paintings of onion domes and fairy-tale cathedrals and double-headed eagles. It was a look. There was no doubt about that. Reacher was no design expert but he was pretty sure it wasn't a good one.

Smith went in first. There was a waiting area near the door with green velvet armchairs lined up along the wall. A coat check closet. A lectern for a maître d'. And plenty of tables. Four-tops in the center of the space, neatly set out like squares on a chessboard, and rectangular six- and eight-tops around the edge, all laid with white tablecloths and shiny silver cutlery and delicate cups and saucers. Reacher shook his head. The owner wasn't re-creating a slice of his past. He hadn't experienced anything like this in the Soviet Union. That was for damn sure. What he was selling was pure fantasy.

There were three customers in the place, spread across two of the smaller tables, and one waiter was on duty. He strolled across to the lectern and said, "Table for three? Breakfast or brunch?"

Reacher said, "We want to see the owner."

The waiter looked startled. He said, "He's not here."

"We'll wait."

"OK. I guess. As long as you place an order and don't block a table if other guests—"

"We'll wait in his office."

The waiter shook his head. He said, "That will not be possible."

Reacher said, "Are you sure?" He started toward the back of the room. The waiter set off after him, fussing and flapping in his wake like an anxious child. Smith and Neilsen followed a few steps behind. Reacher weaved through the tables until he got to an embroidered red and gold curtain that was hanging across a doorway in the back wall. It was between two giant paintings of old guys in antique military uniforms sitting astride docile white horses. Reacher pulled the curtain aside. He saw a tiny vestibule and a staircase, leading up. A guy was by the bottom step, perched on a wooden stool. He stood up. He was the same height as Reacher but his chest was so wide that his arms couldn't hang straight down at his sides. He glared, but didn't say a word.

The waiter hustled up and said, "I'm sorry, Sergei. This guest is . . . lost. He didn't mean to trespass, I'm sure." The waiter went up on tiptoes and leaned over, closer to Reacher. He lowered his voice and said, "Come on. Let me take you to a table. If you place a large enough order—champagne, caviar, a suckling pig perhaps— then this little mistake can be overlooked. Sergei will stay here. You can leave. He won't hurt you."

Reacher said nothing. He had hoped someone like Sergei would be waiting there. It confirmed that the stairs led somewhere important. With luck, to the owner's office. In which case there would be more bodyguards. Probably the same size, or bigger. Probably armed. Ready to rush down and snuff out any threat at the first sound of trouble. Which was bad luck for Sergei. It meant there was no time for Reacher to offer him the opportunity to surrender. He had to get straight down to business, so he tipped back his head. Just a little. Just enough to provide some leverage. He engaged the muscles in his neck and chest and abdomen. Then he flung himself forward, jackknifing at the waist and driving his forehead straight into Sergei's face. It was a brutal, primitive, devastating move. The kind Reacher liked best. Sergei had no warning. No time to react. No chance to defend himself. His nose and cheekbones shattered. Cartilage was crushed and torn. Teeth showered down onto the carpet. Blood gushed onto his shirt and he fell back and landed crumpled, inert, half on the floor, half on the staircase.

Reacher turned to the waiter, wiped a trace of blood from his forehead, and said, "We're going upstairs. If anyone's waiting for us, I'll come back down—and what I did to Sergei, I'll do to you. Are we clear?"

Reacher picked his way around Sergei's immobile limbs and led the way upstairs. It took Smith and Neilsen a moment to catch up. Reacher's outburst of violence had wrong-footed them. Reacher stepped out into a corridor that ran perpendicular, the whole width of the building. There was a window at each end, six doors on one side, and four on the other. The walls were painted a dull almond color with scuffs and dents scattered all the way along at various heights. Light came from naked bulbs in plastic holders at intervals on the ceiling. One was flickering and hanging down on its wires. Outside of the public area the place fell somewhere between dump and fire hazard, Reacher thought. Maybe the café wasn't doing so well, after all. Maybe the Soviet guys weren't too familiar with high standards of decoration. Or safety. Or maybe they just didn't care.

Smith and Neilsen arrived in the corridor behind Reacher and straightaway the nearest door flew open. A guy strode through. He could have been Sergei's twin. He was the same height. The same weight. He had the same bulked-up stance. Only this guy didn't stay still. He put his head down and started to charge.

Reacher pointed to the other half of the corridor and said, "Move!" He glanced to his right to make sure Smith and Neilsen were at a safe distance, then he stepped the other way. Toward the onrushing guy. He squared up. Waited until impact seemed inevitable, then danced aside and flattened himself against the wall. The guy was level. Almost past Reacher. On course to demolish the other two. Reacher stretched out. He grabbed the guy's collar and belt, planted his feet, and pivoted, hard. He felt like his arms were getting wrenched out of their sockets but he held firm. He waited until the other guy had swung through 90 degrees. So he was no longer in line with the corridor. He was facing down the stairs. Then Reacher let go. The guy's velocity had dropped a little but he still had plenty of momentum. Enough to carry him half the length of the staircase in midair. When he finally made contact, his arms were stretched out above his head. It was an instinctive response. An attempt to break his fall. Which it did in the extremely short term. It also broke his wrists and his collarbones. It slowed the front half of his body. But not his legs. It caused them to flip up, over his head, and sent him cartwheeling down onto the floor beyond the bottom step. He landed in a solid heap, half on top of his doppelganger.

More bad news for Sergei, Reacher thought.

LEE CHILD and ANDREW CHILD

Reacher checked both ways along the corridor. Nothing was moving. He had ten doors to pick from. The guy they needed to find would be behind one of them. Assuming he was in the building. And the presence of the heavies suggested he would be. Reacher figured the kind of guy who used fake titles and grandiose made-up names must have quite an ego, and a guy with an ego would want his bodyguards close, to show how important he was. So Reacher closed in on the door that Sergei's lookalike had rushed out of. It was still open, but just a crack. Reacher listened. He heard papers rustling. A creaking sound like someone shifting their weight in a stiff leather chair. And breathing. Calm. Relaxed. No sense of tension. And from more than one person.

Reacher nudged the door with his shoulder and strolled casually through like he was returning home from a boring day at the office. Like he wasn't expecting to face any kind of a challenge. The room was rectangular with a window at the far end and dark wood paneling on the walls. There was a desk three-quarters of the way in. A man was sitting behind it. He had broad shoulders. His head was large and square. He was bald, and he had narrow eyes that were set close together beneath a giant slab of a forehead. There were four other men in the room. Two were sitting on plain wooden chairs in front of the desk. Two were on identical chairs near the left-hand wall. All were wearing expensive suits and ties but they looked child-sized compared to the last two guys Reacher had faced. Even though they were sitting down, he could tell they were not very tall. He guessed maybe five feet eight. Five feet ten at the most. They had shaved heads. Their eyes were bright and constantly moving. They looked lean and rangy. The kind of guys who could run all day and all night with huge packs on their backs. Special Forces types. Probably former Spetsnaz operators. The big lunks who were now at the bottom of the stairs were just window dressing. Their job was to scare people who didn't know better. These guys were the ones who would get the job done if a threat got serious.

Or so someone hoped.

Reacher stopped in the center of the room and looked at the man behind the desk with an expression that said he'd been more impressed with the contents of his Kleenex the last time he'd blown his nose. Smith and Neilsen had followed Reacher in but hung back near the doorway. The two guys near the wall got to their feet. So did the pair by the desk. They shifted around so the four were in a square. None had their backs to Smith or Neilsen. Reacher was boxed in. It was a promising position for them. Their numerical advantage and the close quarters negated Reacher's natural strengths—his weight, and the length of his arms and legs. Had it been one against one, or two against one, with more room to maneuver, they wouldn't have been able to get anywhere near him. If they tried to get in range for a punch or a kick he could pick them off at leisure. But here they could swarm in from all sides. One or two of them would take some damage, most likely severe, but if the others sustained the attack, there was every chance they would succeed. And the way they were formed up was smart. Two of them were behind Reacher, outside his field of vision. The odds were against him. That was for sure. But the odds had been against him before. Countless times. All the way back to his childhood when he and his brother, Joe, had been forced to slug it out with the local tough kids the first day of every new school they attended, all around the world. Reacher knew what was going to happen. He didn't need to see the guys in his blind spot. One of them would be the first to attack. It didn't matter which. Not as long as Reacher moved before he got hit. So he spun to his left. He raised his arm as he turned. Brought it up to horizontal. The side of his fist was like the face of a sledgehammer and it was accelerating as it swung around. It caught the first guy under his chin and lifted him off his feet. The force threw him back. His head hit the wall and he slid down to the floor, out cold.

Reacher pushed off his back foot, reversed direction, twisted at the waist, and launched the same fist at the guy in the opposite corner of the square. He was aiming for his face. Going for power rather than placement. But the guy was fast. He anticipated Reacher's move. Given the weight difference he opted to block with both forearms. It was effective. He knocked Reacher's fist off target. Deflected it so it was set to sail harmlessly past his ear. Only the moment they made contact, Reacher bent his arm. His elbow shifted sideways and the tip crunched into the guy's nose. He fell like a suit slipping off a hanger and before he hit the floor Reacher had reversed course again. He was back in the first corner. The guy who'd started to the right of that was moving, too. Going forward into what was now empty space. Their roles had flipped. Now he couldn't see Reacher. For a moment he was defenseless. And Reacher had a rule. You get the chance to put your enemy down, you take it. Every time. No hesitation. No pearl clutching about whether that's a gentlemanly thing to do. No Marquess of Queensberry rules. So Reacher stepped in close. He punched the guy in the right kidney, hard and fast, middle knuckle extended to multiply the force. He did the same to his left kidney. And when the guy collapsed forward onto his knees, Reacher kicked him in the head like he was trying for a sixty-yard field goal.

One guy was left standing. He had shifted across, directly in front of the desk, and was pulling something out of his pants pocket. A knife handle. He hit a round brass button and a blade snapped into place, bright and sharp and mean.

Reacher said, "Bring that thing near me and I'll make you eat it."

The guy held the knife out in front and moved it from side to side in a slow, fluid, mocking motion.

Reacher said, "Don't say I didn't warn you." He stretched to the side and picked up the chair the guy had been sitting on. He flipped it around so that its legs were pointing straight out, then charged. He drove the guy back. The guy's arms were flailing and his knife was nowhere near finding a target. Reacher kept going. The guy bumped into the edge of the desk and fell, sprawling onto its scratched wooden top. Reacher dropped the chair, pinned the guy's wrist with one hand, and used his other forearm to crush the guy's throat. He lifted the guy's wrist then hammered it down, dislodging the knife from his grip. Swung his leg up and planted his knee on the guy's chest. Picked up the knife. Folded away the blade. And pinched the guy's nose.

The guy held his breath for thirty seconds. Forty-five. His face turned red. His eyes started to bulge. He finally opened his mouth. He spluttered and gasped. Reacher shoved the knife so far in it jammed against the guy's tonsils. Then he lifted the guy up and flung him headfirst into the wall.

The man behind the desk had rolled his chair back to avoid getting slashed. He waited a moment then stood up and came around and set the fallen chair back on its feet in its place by the wall. He stared at each unconscious body in turn, then turned his attention to Reacher. This guy was a good five inches shorter but must have been fifty pounds heavier. His legs were relatively short and his waist was narrow, which made his chest and shoulders look cartoonishly big. He was still for a moment, then he launched himself forward, arms spread wide, straight toward Reacher. He was trying to grab him and wrestle him to the floor. Reacher moved at the same moment. Straight toward the guy. One arm rising. Elbow out front like the tip of a steel bar. It connected with the bridge of the guy's nose. His head stopped dead. His legs kept moving. His feet left the floor and he crashed down, flat on his back, still as a rock.

Smith moved up alongside Reacher. She jabbed him in the arm and said, "The hell have you done? How can we talk to him now?"

Reacher said, "Don't worry. This isn't the guy we want. He can't be. It was too easy."

Roberta Sanson wanted the agent to suffer for as long as possible so she left him writhing on the floor, grasping his groin, until she heard the UPS truck pull up outside Neville Pritchard's house. Then she kicked him in the side of the head, made sure he was out, lay on the rug, and pulled her arms as far apart as the PlastiCuffs would allow. She slid her wrists down the back of her legs and out from beneath her feet. Stood, and went to let Veronica in through the front door.

Veronica took out her knife and freed Roberta's hands. She gave her a hug, then looked at the agents' bodies slumped in the hallway and said, "You OK?"

Roberta said, "Fine," and peeled off her balaclava. "You?"

Veronica pulled the bandage from her cheek. "Did Pritchard give up the name?"

"He's not here. It was an ambush."

"Where is he?"

"He's missing. They don't know where he is. We need to figure out where he went. And we don't have much time. I sent the surveillance guys on a wild-goose chase but they'll be back soon. Ninety minutes, max."

"He ran?"

"Must have heard about his old buddies' accidents."

Veronica was quiet for a second then she turned and looked at the doorframe. She opened the door and ran her fingers over a patch near the lock. She said, "I'm not sure about that. This door's been busted in, then fixed. Recently. I think they came to snatch him up, botched it, and he slipped away somehow."

"Maybe. But *why*'s not important right now. It's *where* that matters."

"He was a career agent. A cautious guy. He would have had a go-bag ready. Is his car here?"

"In the garage."

"So he left on foot, or he had another vehicle nearby. Something untraceable."

"Must have had a vehicle. He's no spring chicken and he'd need to carry supplies. And if he was seen walking or running, that could be suspicious. Especially if they came for him at night."

"So what kind of vehicle? Where would he have kept it? How would he have gotten to it?"

"If they hit the house from the front, they'd also have been watching the back. The east side is pretty exposed. Not a great place to bail out from. What about the west? We need to check the garage."

Roberta led the way, retracing her steps from when she had snuck into the house. The garage was small by modern standards. There was room for one car plus just about enough space for a workbench at the far end and some shelves running along the side walls. The workbench was kept clean and a whole assortment of tools was laid out on a pegboard on the wall above it. The shelves were sagging under all the stuff that was piled on them. Years' and years' accumulation of car parts and tools for yard work, and redundant kitchen gadgets and cans of dry food. And the car was a beauty. A blood-red 1969 Camaro with a black stripe down the hood. It looked well cared for. Pritchard was clearly conscientious when it came to its upkeep. Cosmetically, it was flawless. Its paint was gleaming and there was not a scratch or a ding to be seen. A maintenance pit stretched the whole length of the floor so the sisters figured maybe he handled the mechanical stuff himself, too.

They inspected every inch of the walls. Roberta made her way around clockwise. Veronica, the opposite way. They pushed and pulled and prodded every plank and board and panel. Nothing gave an inch. They even poked the ceiling with a broom but it was rock solid, too.

Roberta started toward the door. She said, "Come on. We're wasting time."

Veronica stayed where she was. She said, "Wait. I have an idea. Have you seen a flashlight in here?"

"I don't think so."

Veronica nodded and made her way around to the Camaro's hood. She crept down the steps to the maintenance pit. A moment later, an inspection lamp flickered to life beneath the car. Veronica was out of sight for more than two minutes. When she climbed back up, she had a smile on her face. She said, "This is it. The pit branches off to the side and comes up under a fake coal hatch on the other side of the garage wall. It's how he got out. It has to be. So follow me. Quick. We need to figure out where he went next."

Chapter 14

Reacher crouched down and started to work his way through the guy's pockets. He pulled out a wallet and opened it. He held it up for Smith to see. There was a driver's license in the center section behind a clear plastic window. It gave the name Valery Kerzhakov.

Reacher raised his voice and said, "I wonder what the Russian community in D.C. would do if they found out that Maksim Sarbotskiy is such a pretentious freak he doesn't just make up names, he also hides behind a body double? Laugh, I bet. Certainly stop coming to his little café."

There was a scraping sound from the side of the room. A section of the wood paneling on the wall behind the pair of chairs slid to one side. A man appeared in the gap that had been created. He was wearing a suit with a telltale bulge under the left armpit. His head was shaved. He was tall, but not giant. Broad, but not imposing. Somewhere in size between Sergei and the whippy guys who were now lying unconscious on the floor.

Reacher said, "Got any buddies in there? Because no offense, friend, but you're not going to get very far on your own."

The guy said, "I'm not here to fight you. If I were . . ." He patted the bulge in his suit coat. Then he stepped back and gestured for Reacher to follow him. "Please."

Reacher stepped through the hidden doorway. Smith and Neilsen followed. It led them to another room, the same size and shape. This one also had a window and a desk with a pair of chairs in front of it. It had a leather couch off to the side. Paintings of nineteenth-century battle scenes on the walls. And a console in the corner with a bank of small, square TV screens. There were six. All black and white. They showed live feeds from the room Reacher had just left, the corridor, the stairs, two from the café, and one from the side-walk outside. Reacher turned to the guy who was sitting behind the desk. He said, "Enjoy the show?"

The guy looked remarkably like Kerzhakov, except that he was still capable of sitting upright. He had the same barrel chest and wide shoulders. The same kind of square head and beady eyes and neolithic forehead. He stared back at Reacher and shrugged as if to suggest he'd seen better.

Reacher said, "You're Sarbotskiy?"

The guy prickled. "I am His Royal Highness the Prince—"

"Cut the crap," Reacher said. "This is America. Son of a king or son of a whore, it's all the same here."

Sarbotskiy scowled. He said, "And you are?"

"Jack Reacher. US Army."

"Army? All of you?"

"Close enough."

"What do you want?"

"I'm here to do you a favor."

"What kind of favor?"

"Not burning this place to the ground."

"Not the most generous of favors."

"Best offer you're going to get."

"Undoubtedly. And I assume you want something in return."

"Not much. A little information."

"Why would I trust you?"

"Why would you not?" Reacher gestured toward the TV monitors. "You've seen this isn't a social call."

"You can't force me to cooperate. I have protection."

"You do?" Reacher looked around the room. "Where is it?"

"From the US government. We have an agreement. A contract. It's watertight."

"Watertight. Huh. But is it fireproof? Does it make this property and everything else you own impossible to burn down?"

Sarbotskiy didn't answer.

"Is it soundproof? Does it guarantee that word of your whereabouts won't spread to the guys back home? The ones you no doubt sold out to get this agreement?"

Sarbotskiy crossed his arms. He didn't reply.

"I hear your homeland is falling apart. Collapsing like a house of cards. I bet a lot of those guys are planning to relocate. Looking for a cozy little business to buy into. Only not by using money."

Sarbotskiy leaned back and steepled his fingers. "Maybe I could help you with this *information* you want. But I can't just give it to you. I have principles. I'll need something in return."

"What?"

"A wrestling match would have been nice. You and a couple of my guys. It's one thing watching a bout on a screen, but nothing beats violence up close and personal, does it? I love wrestling." Sarbotskiy sighed. "Tell you the truth, I miss it."

"I never had time for it. Never saw the point. Too many rules."

"All right. Then we drink." Sarbotskiy opened a drawer, pulled out a cut-crystal decanter full of clear liquid and a pair of glasses. Also cut crystal. Tumbler-sized, not shot glasses. He plonked everything down on the desk, filled the glasses, and pushed one toward Reacher. "Come. Sit. The first is for good faith. Then you can ask your question."

Reacher moved toward one of the chairs. Reluctantly. He would have preferred the same kind of approach he'd used with the army driver at Rock Island Arsenal. He wasn't much of a drinker. But not because of some moral scruple. It was a practical thing. Alcohol degrades performance. He'd seen the effect a thousand times. So going shot to shot with a giant Russian wasn't an ideal solution. Especially when the shots were super-sized. That was for damn sure. On the other hand he had a lot of experience with interrogations. Some subjects crumble, given the correct incentive. Others would die before they talked. His gut was telling him that despite his bluster, Sarbotskiy was from the second category.

Reacher kept going, slowly. Neilsen was faster. He darted forward, dropped into the nearer chair, picked up the glass, and downed it in five long, thirsty gulps. He smiled and said, "I believe this is my area of expertise."

Sarbotskiy shook his head. "No." He pointed at Reacher. "The deal's with him."

Neilsen said, "Forget him. You want to loosen someone's tongue with this stuff? Maybe pick up a few secrets, quid pro quo? Then he's not your man." He tapped his forehead. "There's far more interesting stuff in here. Believe me."

Sarbotskiy thought for a moment, then he refilled Neilsen's glass. He said, "The rate's double for you."

Neilsen drained the glass again. "Very generous. We could be friends. Now, we want to know about Project 192. It was a thing in the sixties."

Sarbotskiy drained his own glass then refilled both. He said, "That was your project. Not ours." Then he blinked and started to laugh. His whole belly shook. "You know you can't trust your own government, so you come to the KGB when you need the truth. I like you people. OK. Project 192. I assume you know the basics. It was a program to make antidotes against our chemical and biological weapons."

Neilsen nodded and drained his glass.

Sarbotskiy said, "Your government probably even admits that, in private at least. Yes? But you suspect there's more. You can sense it." He drank, then poured refills for both of them. "Well, your instincts are correct. There was more."

Sarbotskiy gestured for Neilsen to drink.

Neilsen downed the drink in one gulp, again, and slammed the glass down on the desk.

Sarbotskiy emptied his own glass and said, "There was a parallel project. A secret within a secret. We never even learned its official designation. Moscow called it *Typhon*. The deadliest of the mythical monsters. And who says communists don't have a classical education?" He laughed again, as deeply as before.

Neilsen said, "And the purpose of this second project was?" His voice was growing a little slurred.

Sarbotskiy refilled both glasses and said, "One ninety-two was defensive. Countering our weapons. The ones you knew about, anyway. Typhon was the opposite. It was one hundred percent offensive. Literally and figuratively. America was brewing up newer and nastier weapons to attack us with, and all the time pretending to be a passive victim of Soviet hostility." He took another drink. "Western hypocrisy in overdrive."

"Is there any proof? Or is this the potato juice talking?"

"Proof exists. I've seen it. I don't personally have it."

LEE CHILD and ANDREW CHILD

"Who does?"

"A guy named Spencer Flemming." Sarbotskiy took a pen and a pad of paper from a drawer and wrote down an address. "He's a journalist. He has everything. Even pictures."

"Bullshit. If a journalist had pictures like that, it would have made his career. He'd have sold them for a fortune. They'd have been all over the front pages."

Sarbotskiy leaned forward and tapped his forehead in an exaggerated imitation of Neilsen's earlier move. He said, "There can't be much interesting stuff in there if you're so naïve. He has copies. Your government took the originals. They thought they'd taken everything. And they made it clear there was a jail cell with his name on it at that so-called secret facility you guys have in Cuba, in case any of those pictures ever saw the light of day."

Reacher stepped forward and said, "And you know this, how?"

"We communicate."

"You put this Flemming guy onto the story?"

"I may have nudged him in the right direction. The truth can be elusive, sometimes."

Reacher picked up the piece of paper Sarbotskiy had written on. "We're going to visit this guy. Soon. When we do, will he be expecting us?"

Sarbotskiy said, "Do I look like I have a crystal ball?"

"Remember what I said about this place burning down? If Flemming doesn't faint with surprise when I knock on his door, that's what's going to happen. You're going to be inside when it does. You're going to be wide awake. And you're not going to have a drop of vodka to dull the pain."

* * *

Veronica Sanson held the lid of the coal hatch open until Roberta had climbed out, then the sisters stood together and surveyed the area to the west of Neville Pritchard's house. The garage wall was behind them. The street was to their left but they couldn't see it because of a line of shrubs. They had been planted close together and laid out carefully to look like they happened to have sprung up there, naturally, on their own. Over the years they'd grown thick and tight and impenetrable. They formed a perfect screen. Impossible to see through. They were standing right there in the open and yet a thousand people could walk by and not realize their purpose. It was the same story to their right. There was another set of bushes, sprouting apparently at random but totally blocking the view from the rest of Pritchard's yard. Someone could be watching the back of the house with binoculars and they'd still have no idea what was happening in that space. The ground was covered with some kind of short, wiry grass. It was silent to walk on and didn't reach high enough to leave suspicious damp patches on the cuffs of anyone's pants. Ahead was a fence separating Pritchard's property from his neighbor's. It was a standard affair, six feet tall, with vertical planks attached to horizontal rails strung between sturdy posts. Veronica and Roberta moved across to take a closer look. At first the planks looked uniform, but Roberta noticed a set of five that had an extra row of nails. She pushed near the top of the central one and the lower edge of the group swung up and away from the fence frame. It left plenty of room to crawl through.

The neighbor's yard was tidy, but plain. It suggested older residents, happy to pay a college student or grandchild to go through the place occasionally and do just enough to stop the trees and shrubs from getting out of hand. Nothing was neglected, but there was no sign of any new planting or recent attempts at cultivation. A house sat on the far side of the lot, away in the distance. Another structure was much closer. A standalone garage. Which was strange given that all the properties on that street had been built with garages attached. Roberta and Veronica crept closer. There was a window in the side wall. They peered through. There was no vehicle inside. The space looked like it was empty.

There was a personnel door next to the window. Roberta took hold of the handle but Veronica grabbed her arm before she could turn it.

"Stop." Veronica pointed to the top corner of the window. A pair of wires was just visible through a wad of cobwebs. Part of a security system.

Roberta pulled her arm free. She said, "I bet that it's connected to Pritchard's house. Not the police. Not the neighbors. I bet Pritchard built this place. Probably pays rent, or does them some other kind of favor."

"You can't be certain of that."

"Only one way to find out." Roberta pushed on the handle. The door didn't give. It was locked. She turned around, raised her knee, then drove her leg back. Her foot hit the wood, the frame split, and the door swung open. No bells rang. No siren sounded. Not anywhere in their earshot, anyway. Roberta darted inside. She said, "Come on. We're burning daylight. The watchers will be on their way back."

The garage was just as empty on the inside as it had seemed from the outside. There was no workbench. No tools. Nothing hanging on the walls. Nothing stacked in the corners. Nothing shoved in the rafters. But there were two things dangling from the roof trusses. An electric cable and a hose. The cable was thick. It was heavy gauge and it had an elaborate cylindrical plug at the end. The hose had a brass connector attached and faint white writing stamped along its length. Roberta turned her head sideways and read it. She said, "Approved for potable water. This is a hookup for an RV."

Veronica pointed at the floor. Four tires had left dark traces where the vehicle had been parked. They looked wide and splayed out. She said, "Right. And it was heavy. Carrying a full load. Pritchard was ready to disappear for quite a while."

The sisters went back outside and around to the front of the garage. The vehicle door opened onto a driveway. The other houses they'd seen nearby all had driveways made of gravel. This one was made of compacted dirt. It would be silent to drive on. It sloped down toward the street. And its curve led away from Pritchard's house. A heavy RV could roll down and coast a considerable distance without needing to start its engine. A near perfect setup for a covert getaway.

Roberta said, "I'm starting to like Neville Pritchard. I like his style."

Veronica said, "Me too. Shame we'll have to pump him full of LSD and let him loose in rush-hour traffic."

"If we can find him. He could be anywhere."

"I have an idea about that. We're going to need a phone. And the Yellow Pages."

Reacher let Neilsen go down the stairs first. He felt that was a sensible precaution, given the quantity of vodka Neilsen had sucked down. He was still moving on his own, but unsteadily. He took each step slowly and kept his palms pressed against the walls on either side. He made it to the bottom without falling. Sergei and the other guy were no longer lying there. That was fortunate. Their tangled limbs and outsized torsos could well have been one obstacle too many.

Neilsen fought his way through the curtain, took a moment to catch his balance, and started for the exit. Reacher and Smith followed close behind. The waiter stopped in his tracks when he saw them. He stood and stared with an expression of half shock, half admiration on his face. Neilsen plowed on, weaving between the tables, and the three of them got to the sidewalk unscathed. They walked around the corner to where they'd left the cars. Both had tickets on their windshields. Smith tore them off and dropped them into her purse.

"I'll take care of those," she said.

Neilsen stumbled past her, heading for his driver's door. He pulled out his keys. Reacher stretched across and took them.

"Hey!" Neilsen scowled. "I'm fine to drive."

Reacher said, "What you think you can do and what you're going to do are two different things. Go around. Get in the other side."

Neilsen didn't move.

Reacher said, "Or walk. Your choice."

Reacher followed Smith's car through the downtown traffic and back to the hotel. She drove fast. He had to work hard to get close to keeping up. She was already parked in her regular spot when he pulled into the lot. He stopped by the hotel entrance and kept the engine running. Smith opened the passenger door, leaned in, and unfastened Neilsen's seatbelt.

Neilsen said, "Why are we here? We should be at the office. There's no reason I can't work."

Reacher said, "There's no way Baglin won't notice something's up if he calls a meeting. Is that something you want?"

Neilsen struggled forward in his seat. "Maybe I'll just spend some time here, in my room. Meet at six for dinner?"

"Sure. Take it easy. And thanks for doing the heavy lifting back there."

"Please. You know me. And you know the two best words in the English language. *Free alcohol.* Not to be confused with the worst two words. *Alcohol free.*"

Reacher and Smith took both cars to the task force building in case Neilsen got any bright ideas about trying to drive someplace. They showed their IDs to the guard and parted ways in the corridor. Reacher let himself into his office. Three new faxes had arrived. He gathered the pages, selected one, and dropped the others onto the desk. He scanned the list of names. Then he squeezed into the chair, picked up the phone, and dialed the number for the Chemical Corps at Fort McClellan. His call was answered quickly but he spent the next twenty minutes bouncing from one desk to another, listening to one feeble attempt at stonewalling after another. When he finally hung up he figured he had accomplished two things. He had beaten plenty of bushes. He hoped enough to rattle anyone who knew about Typhon. The offensive counterpart to Project 192. Maybe cause a little panic. Maybe bring them out into the open. And he had identified a couple of people who had been on the fringes of the work in the sixties and who were big enough assholes that he wouldn't lose sleep if Baglin tried to stick them with some blame if everything went sideways.

Reacher tried his brother's number again and this time his call was answered.

"Reacher," Joe said.

"Joe."

"You OK?"

"Fine. You?"

"Fine. Listen, I've got an update for you. This guy Gary Walsh. Turns out he's using a cover name. He just got through with a spell undercover. A long one. It was rough. He came back with his head bent out of shape a little, plus there's a suspicion the group he infiltrated had picked up his trail. I guess he got sent to your task force partly as therapy, partly as a safe haven. Aside from that, I'm hearing he's a solid guy."

They shot the breeze for another couple of minutes, mainly about music, then Reacher hung up. He leaned back in his chair, closed his eyes, and filled his head with Howlin' Wolf. A pleasant hour passed and then the music was interrupted by a beeping sound from his pocket. It was his pager. He was being summoned again.

Christopher Baglin was already in his place when Reacher walked into the boardroom. Smith got there right after him, before the door had swung all the way shut. Walsh was sitting at the far end of the table, staring out the window, looking like he hadn't moved since the morning.

Reacher lowered himself into his seat and said, "No need to wait for Neilsen. He's out sick. He had to go back to the hotel."

Baglin frowned. He said, "Names from the sixties?"

Reacher handed him a page with two names. Smith had nothing. Neither did Walsh.

Baglin folded Reacher's piece of paper, slid it into his pocket, and said, "OK. Listen up. We've had a major development. The perp showed up this morning at the house of the final scientist, Neville Pritchard. Got past the watchers, all the way inside."

Reacher said, "So Pritchard's dead?"

"No. Pritchard wasn't there. Four agents were waiting inside, in his place."

"So was the guy captured? Killed?"

"Neither. The agents inside the house attempted to make an arrest but were unsuccessful."

"The guy got away?"

"Correct."

"Did the agents get a good look? Do we have a description?"

"A partial. But the big news is that our guy is actually a girl. A woman. Not a man. So your new top priority is to recalibrate your search parameters."

No one moved.

Baglin said, "What are you waiting for? Go!"

Smith stood up. Walsh struggled to his feet a moment later. Reacher stayed where he was. The news made no difference to him. It had never occurred to him to exclude women from the equation. Instead of moving he said, "Question. Pritchard. Is he in protective custody?"

Baglin hesitated. "Not at present."

"So an attempt was made to bring him in?"

"It was."

"Where is Pritchard now?"

"That's not known. He's proving hard to find. Which is our only silver lining right now. The killer didn't know Pritchard was missing or she wouldn't have come to his house. Therefore she doesn't know where he is, either. Which gives us a reprieve. Maybe only a short one. We need to find her before she finds him. And kills him."

Chapter 15

Reacher, Smith, and Neilsen met in the hotel lobby at 6:00 P.M., as agreed. They walked to the same restaurant as before and sat at the same table. Reacher and Smith ordered beer. Neilsen started straight in on the whiskey.

"What?" he said when he saw the others' expressions. "You think I should stick to vodka?"

Smith cupped her hand to her ear. "What's that I hear? Oh. It's your liver. It thinks you should stick to water."

Reacher and Smith brought Neilsen up to speed on the outcome of the afternoon's meeting while they waited for their food. When it was delivered, Neilsen ordered another drink and said, "Covering up the existence of a secret nerve gas factory is a much stronger motive than keeping antidote testing under wraps. I like that much better. I made some calls this afternoon. Shook some trees. We'll see if anything falls out."

Reacher said, "I did the same."

"This new information about Neville Pritchard means he must be key to potentially exposing the whole illicit program. That's why he's the only one they tried to take into protective custody. My guess is that he was more spy than scientist. Langley's point man on the ground. Or the Chemical Corps'. Whoever's pulling the strings now must have been in overall charge then. Because he has the most to lose if the lid gets blown off. With public opinion the way it is these days this could be career-ending stuff. Legacy destroying."

Reacher said, "Whoever's pulling the strings is a cynical bastard. He could have had all the vulnerable guys taken into custody. But he didn't. He was happy to leave the other scientists out there in harm's way, like bait. He tried to use them to catch the killer before she caught up with Pritchard."

Neilsen breathed out, slowly. "That's cold, man. You can see how this guy got to the top."

Smith said, "Right, but what I don't get is this. Look at it from the killer's point of view. If Pritchard is key to revealing the secret, why leave him till last? I'd go after him first. Get the info I needed. Move on to stage two—embarrassing the USA, blackmailing the government, whatever. Then I wouldn't need to kill the others. I'd save time. Avoid risk."

Neilsen took a large swig and said, "Maybe she deliberately left Pritchard till last to ramp up the tension he was under. She would need him stressed to make him cooperate."

"I guess."

Neilsen said, "Or maybe she didn't know all the names up front. She might have had to start at the bottom and work her way up the food chain, getting a new name out of each victim in turn."

Smith shrugged. "Possible."

Reacher said, "Maybe she did know all the names, but not which the important one was. It could have been chance that Pritchard was last."

Smith shook her head. "Surely he couldn't just randomly be last."

Reacher said, "Sure he could. It's a version of the gambler's fallacy. It's just as likely for Pritchard to be picked last as in any other position. Hitting on his name doesn't get more likely after each failure."

"You certain it works that way?"

"Absolutely. But that might not be relevant. The murders still feel personal to me. Killing everyone on the list could be the whole point. If she just wants to kill all seven, the order won't matter. And if she knows Pritchard's significance, leaving him till last would make sense because his security is the highest. Right now she's batting a thousand. If she went for Pritchard first, she could have struck out right away."

Neilsen said, "Right. But that's academic. Maybe she wants to expose Typhon. Maybe she's just on a homicidal spree. But whether she wants information or to complete her set of corpses, she'll still go after Pritchard. She has to. So we have to find him, to stop her, and avoid the blame landing on us."

"No." Smith put her empty glass down. "You're missing something. If she wants information, she doesn't need Pritchard. Someone else knows about Typhon. Someone who allegedly has proof. Photographs. A secondhand source, but maybe good enough. Maybe better."

Neilsen said, "Flemming. The journalist."

"She could change tack. Go after him instead."

"If she knows about him."

"We know about him, and we've only been involved in this for two days. How long has she been researching? She seemed to know plenty about all her other victims."

"We'll visit Flemming tomorrow. As soon as Baglin's morning briefing is over."

Reacher said, "No. Tonight. Now. Tomorrow could be too late."

The address Sarbotskiy had given them for Flemming turned out to be an abandoned building perched on a narrow strip of land between I-295 and the Potomac. It was three stories high, built of strangely orange bricks, and it was a wildly irregular shape. Sections bulged out here and dropped back there in a way that suggested some kind of complex hidden purpose behind the design. The tops of the walls had a series of bites taken out of them like an ancient European castle. All the windows were blocked up with sheets of rusting metal and the whole place was surrounded by a fence like contractors use to secure construction sites.

Smith pulled her car over at the end of the building's driveway. She didn't switch off the headlights or kill the engine. Neilsen was next to her in the front. Reacher was sprawled out in the back.

Neilsen said, "Whatever is this place? It looks evil. Like an asylum in a horror movie. Maybe Jack Nicholson's in there."

Smith said, "I think it is a kind of asylum. Or was. An annex of St. Elizabeth's. It closed in the sixties. The main site is still open. It's notorious. It was one of the first psychiatric hospitals in the country. Every bad thing happened there. Electroshock treatment. Forced lobotomies. Trials of truth serums during the Cold War. All kinds of stuff they can't do anymore. The operation's much smaller now. Rumor is, they're going to close it soon, too."

Neilsen said, "It gives me the creeps. Let's go. We're clearly on a wild-goose chase. We should buy a can of gas and some matches and pay that prick Sarbotskiy another visit."

Smith shifted into Drive but before she lifted her foot off the brake, Reacher said, "Wait." He could feel a prickling sensation at the base of his neck. An instinctive response. A signal from his lizard brain. The part that was hardwired to sense when he was being watched. The kind of signal Reacher had learned not to ignore. "We're here. It can't hurt to check."

Smith and Neilsen stayed silent. Neither of them moved.

Reacher said, "Stay in the car if you like. I'll go."

"No." Smith turned the ignition key, pulled it out, stretched up and switched off the dome light, then opened her door. "I'll come. Let's just stick together, OK?"

Neilsen fumbled for his door handle. "Guess I better come, too. Keep an eye on you guys."

Reacher led the way around the perimeter of the site on the outside of the fence. He moved slowly. His gaze was constantly switching from the ground in front of him to the sides and top of the building. He was looking for wires, or the glint of metal or glass. He saw nothing. It was too dark to make out much detail. But he could almost feel the presence of the hulking structure like it was some kind of giant prehistoric creature, alive, but asleep.

They completed their circuit without incident and wound up in front of what must have been the asylum's main entrance. A giant portico jutted out from the wall. It was supported by ornate columns, originally to protect new arrivals from the rain or the sun. Reacher checked the join between the nearest sections of the fence. All the others he'd seen were secured with two clamps shaped like butterfly wings with a nut and bolt through the center of the body. This one only had a single clamp, and the nut was missing. The bolt was just pushed through its hole. There was nothing to hold it in place. Reacher pointed down at the concrete base that supported the fence's metal posts. One was scuffed. Something had carved a portion of an arc into its rough surface. Reacher popped out the bolt and opened the clamp. He lifted the post. He pushed and it moved. The clamps holding it to the next section of fence were acting like hinges. And they were silent. They had seen some oil in the recent past.

Reacher squeezed through the gap he'd made in the fence and crossed to the portico. Smith and Neilsen followed. He continued to a pair of double doors. They were huge, made of dark wood, shot through with black metal studs and divided into panels covered with intricate carving. The workmanship had been high quality. That was clear, even though now the surface was dull and rough. The result of years of neglect and damp air, Reacher guessed.

Neilsen was staring at a padlock that secured one door to the other with a hasp and eye. It was a substantial item. Designed to exude strength, and discourage wannabe trespassers from wasting their time trying to pick it. But it was old. It was caked in rust. It couldn't have been opened in years. Neilsen shook his head and turned to go. Reacher grabbed his arm and stopped him.

"What are you doing?" Neilsen whispered. "This is a waste of time. That lock's seized solid. We'll never get it open."

"We don't need to," Reacher replied. "That's not the way anyone gets in or out. Think about it. You can't work a padlock from the inside."

Reacher crouched down and inspected the doors' lower panels. The bottom edges were in the worst shape. He figured that was due to rain splatter so he switched his attention to the next row up. He pressed one of them. It was solid. So was the next one he tried. But the third gave a tiny bit. He tried its opposite edge and it swung back, under tension from some kind of spring. It left a gap about six inches by eight. Reacher stretched his arm through. The surface was contoured and uneven. More carving, Reacher thought. Then his fingers brushed against something smooth and straight and narrow. A small plank. Reacher pushed and pulled and twisted until it came loose. He dropped it, pulled his arm out, and pressed on the next panel. This time a whole section swung inward. Nine panels by nine. Like a tiny door within a door.

It took a lot of squirming and wriggling and struggling but Reacher managed to squeeze his body through the hole. He stood up and stepped to the side, sliding his feet and stretching his arms into the empty darkness. Smith joined him. Then Neilsen. They all stood still and waited for their night vision to kick in. After a couple of minutes a few details started to emerge. The floor was covered with black and white tiles. They were submerged under a thick layer of dust. The cornice around the ceiling, high above them, was crusted with dirt and cobwebs. Hunks of plaster were hanging off the walls at random intervals. There was the indistinct outline of a piece of furniture ahead of them. Maybe a reception desk.

Smith said, "Close your eyes for a second."

Reacher heard rustling, then a click. He opened one eye and saw Smith was holding a slim flashlight. She had pinched the beam down to a narrow shaft and was playing it around the space. A chandelier was hanging from the center of the ceiling. There was a pair of double doors on each side. Ahead was a wall of glass, now obscured by layers of grime. It felt like a grand hotel gone to seed. Reacher could imagine it with uniformed bellhops ferrying fancy luggage and gussied-up guests flitting between dining rooms and ballrooms and the formal gardens that lay outside. Though he knew in reality living there could hardly have been more different. Being forced to live there. There could have been few worse places in the country if Smith's recollection was correct.

Smith lowered her flashlight beam to the floor. The extra illumination revealed multiple sets of footprints going back and forth along a path through the dust. She started to follow them.

Reacher said, "Stop."

He was too late. He had seen a small break in the line of footprints. A narrow patch that hadn't been stepped on. That meant one thing. There was a tripwire above it. Then the flashlight confirmed it. The line was colorless. As fine as a hair. It ran the whole width of the room. And Smith caught it with her right shin. Immediately the room filled with light from somewhere above them. It wasn't harsh and bright, like it would be in the movies. It wasn't enough to blind them. Or to blind the guy who stepped out from the doorway on the right. He was maybe six feet tall, but he was stooped. His hair was long and gray and thin and it hung down on either side of his face in no particular style. His skin was pale. His feet were bare. He was wearing jeans with huge bellbottoms. A bright paisley shirt with a massive collar. And he was holding a shotgun. An old one. A Winchester Model 97. A Trench Broom, as the infantry in the First World War used to call it. He was aiming it at Smith but Reacher and Neilsen were so close behind that they would get torn to shreds along with her if the guy pulled the trigger.

Chapter 16

The guy with the shotgun said, "Stop. Who are you? Why did you break into my home?"

Reacher drifted to his right. He wanted to put some distance between himself and the others. He kept his eyes on the guy's trigger finger and raised his hands to shoulder height. He said, "We're looking for Spencer Flemming. Is that you?"

"Stop moving. What do you want?"

"Are you Flemming?"

"Who's asking?"

"My name's Jack Reacher."

"Are you police? FBI? CIA? What?"

"US Army."

"For real?"

"For real. My ID's in my pocket." Reacher started to lower his right hand.

"No. Stay still. What's the army doing here? You can't operate on US soil."

"We're here to help you. If you're Spencer Flemming."

The guy didn't reply.

Reacher said, "Come on. What's the harm in telling us your name? You're the one with the gun. Are you Flemming?"

The guy nodded. Just the tiniest of gestures. "Might be."

"Then you're in danger. Someone's out to kill you. We're looking to stop that from happening."

"Kill me? Impossible. They'd have to find me first. No one knows I live here."

"We know."

"Yeah." Flemming hitched the shotgun up a little higher. "You do. How come?"

"A friend of yours told us. Maksim Sarbotskiy."

Flemming was quiet for a moment. Then he said, "Who?"

"Maksim Sarbotskiy. He said you were a journalist."

"Oh. That guy. Short, skinny. Albanian. Remind me—which arm is his tattoo on?"

"He's Russian. We didn't see his arms. And he's not short and skinny. He's huge, like a wrestler."

"He goes by a French name now. What is it?"

"It's English. Or it's supposed to be. Prince Sarb. But I doubt anyone takes it seriously."

"OK." Flemming paused. "Go on. Why does someone want to kill me? And why do you care?"

"Because of Project Typhon."

"What do you know about that?"

"Not enough. Which is why we care. It's why we're here. We want you to tell us about it. That will help us stop the person who's coming after you. But if you don't want our help, fine. We'll leave. We won't bother you. We'll just watch for your name in the obituary columns."

Flemming didn't respond.

Reacher lowered his hands and turned away. "Fine. See you. But you should know the person we're talking about has already killed five people."

Flemming said, "Random people?"

"Specific people. All scientists who worked on the project."

"Then why should I worry? I'm not a scientist. I wasn't on the project."

"The killer wants information about Typhon. The only remaining scientist who has it is MIA. The only other person who knows about it is you. Go ahead. Do the math."

Flemming took a step back. "I'm not leaving this place. I won't run. I won't hide."

"Help us and you won't have to."

"How do I know this isn't a trap?"

"How could it be a trap?"

"I've been here twenty-two years. You know why?"

"You have an eccentric taste in décor?"

"Because of the piece I wrote about Project 192. In '69, going on '70. I was a reporter back then. A damn good one. The article was dynamite. The best thing I ever did. It was locked and loaded, two days from going to press. We were all set for a big splash on a Sunday. Going for maximum impact. I was walking home from a date, happy, dreaming of promotions and Pulitzers and book deals. I saw a van waiting outside my building. A blue Ford. I thought nothing of it then. I'll never forget it now. And I'll never forget the smell of the hood they pulled over my head. My world went black. And it stayed black for what felt like weeks. It was actually three days. First I was in the back of the van. Then in a tiny room. I don't know where it was. Somewhere cold. The floor and walls were hard concrete. There was no bed. No chair. No toilet. They gave me hardly any water. No food. Then finally a light came on. It hurt my eyes. A guy came in. He stood. I lay on the floor. I couldn't move. He gave me a choice. Hand over all my notes and early drafts and photos and never tell a soul what I knew, or spend the rest of my life in a room like that. In the dark. Cold. Hungry. Alone."

"And Sarbotskiy helped you with the article?"

"He was a source, sure. He thought he was using me, I expect. I thought I was using him. The truth? A bit of both, probably. But I never printed anything that wasn't true. I triple-checked every detail. I wasn't a Soviet asset. I'm no traitor."

"So you gave this guy in the room what he wanted, then you came here?"

"Damn straight I gave him what he wanted. And I didn't come here right away. I tried to go back to work. But it was no good. The guy said they'd be watching me. If I ever made a nuisance of myself, if I poked my nose where it didn't belong, if I attracted attention in any way, all bets were off. He said they would keep the room ready for me, just in case. He said they had already hung a sign on the door with my name on it. I'll be honest. That messed with my head. I couldn't write a story without thinking about how it could be interpreted. Couldn't walk down the street without having a heart attack every time I saw a van parked at the curb. I figured it would be best to disappear."

"You think we're here to test you. See if you're ready to make waves again."

"In my life, when people show up out of the blue it's to hurt me, not help me. Why should this time be any different?"

"What if someone vouched for us?"

"Who?"

"Sarbotskiy. You know him. And he's already done his deal with the government. He's got what he wants. There's no mileage for him in selling you out."

Flemming took a moment to think, then said, "OK. I guess that could work."

Reacher said, "We'll take you to him. You guys talk. We'll bring you right back."

"I'm not leaving. I told you that. We'll call him."

"How?"

Flemming gestured to a door in the glass wall at the far end of the space. "You three go first. Don't try anything."

The door led into a square courtyard. It was totally enclosed by the four sides of the building except for a vehicle-sized gate that was now barricaded with old tires. Reacher figured the gate had originally been for deliveries, and the space for allowing light into the inner side of the wards. It could also have been a place for patients to exercise. Maybe there had been gardens and paths and benches. Maybe conscientiously maintained. But now there was nothing growing on the ground apart from a few weeds that peeped out from between hunks of rubble. The center of the area was empty. There was nothing against three of the walls apart from graffiti. But against the west wall there were three travel trailers tucked in close to the brickwork. Their skin was aluminum. It was dull, but Reacher guessed it would have been shiny when they were new.

Flemming pointed toward the one on the left. He said, "That one's my office. The center one's my living room. The other's where I sleep."

He folded back the office trailer's door and latched it open. He leaned in, flicked a switch, and a light came on. He gestured for the others to climb in ahead of him. There was a desk under the window. It was plain and utilitarian, with a metal frame and plain wood surfaces. A chair on wheels, which had seen better days. Its fabric was torn in multiple places and stuffing was spilling out in dirty orange clumps. And a leather armchair which wasn't in much better shape. The rest of the area was stuffed with shelves. They looked homemade. They were crammed with books and files and sheafs of papers and piles of magazines. One wall was covered with things in frames. Diplomas. Awards. Reprints of articles. And a single picture. It was of Flemming when he was a much younger man. He was thinner and his hair was dark brown. He was on a boat crossing a river in a jungle. It looked like Vietnam.

Reacher nodded toward the heap of papers on the desk and said, "You still working?"

Flemming shrugged. He said, "I keep busy. I don't write anymore. Not under my own name. That's too risky. But I help a few folks out with things. Research. Copyediting. Like that." He moved some papers around on the desk, uncovered a phone, and lifted the receiver.

Smith said, "That thing works?"

Flemming said, "You think I'm going to have a pretend conversation? Of course it works. Everything works. You spend as much time as I did working in some countries I could tell you about, you get pretty good at borrowing things. A little power here. Some water there. A bit of dial tone in between. I've got cable hooked up in the other two vans."

Flemming kept hold of the shotgun, wedged the phone between his shoulder and his chin, and dialed a number from memory. Reacher could hear the slow, lazy ringtone. Then a deep rumbling voice. He couldn't make out the words.

Flemming said, "Sorry, man. Yes, I do know what time it is. But this is an emergency. I've got three guys here who say you sent them." He described Reacher, Smith, and Neilsen, then listened for a few moments. Then he said, "Thanks. I'll let you know how it goes."

Flemming dropped the receiver back into its cradle and lifted the gun. He braced it against his shoulder, pointed it at Reacher, and said, "Sarbotskiy doesn't know you."

Reacher said, "Call him back. Remind him about the fire. I was very specific about where he's going to be when I start it."

Flemming lowered the gun. A tiny hint of a smile flashed across his face and he said, "Sarbotskiy told me if you came back with that, you're OK. So. What do you want to know?"

Reacher moved closer. He said, "Is it true that there was a program running parallel with Project 192? One that created offensive bioweapons? Project Typhon?"

"Yes. Absolutely. Although that name came from the KGB. It was never official."

"How do you know about it?"

"Research. I was good, once, remember. I put in the hard yards. Here, and in India. I know partly because of the facts I pieced together. The kind of chemicals that were shipped to the site. The equipment that was used. The protective clothing that was brought in. The precautions that were taken. Snippets I picked up from lab techs and cleaners. But mainly because of the bodies."

"People died?"

Flemming nodded. "'Fraid so."

"They were experimented on?"

"No. There was an accident. A leak. One night in December '69."

Reacher said, "An accident? Are you sure? Because I hear about an accident and I know the CIA was involved, and my bullshit meter goes off the scale. No offense, Neilsen."

Neilsen said, "None taken. I was thinking the same thing."

Flemming paused. "Let me back up a minute. I'm not explaining this right. The incident that caused the deaths was sabotage. One hundred percent. There's no doubt about it. But it was aimed at Mason Chemical Industries. The civilian corporation that was used to shelter the covert operation. The guy who did it was just a disgruntled employee. Morgan Sanson, he was called. He had no idea Project 192 even existed. Let alone a parallel project to produce offensive weapons. He impacted those by accident."

"So what was his story?"

"It was sad, really. He had all kind of beefs. You name it. Pay. Conditions. Not enough vacation days. Lack of opportunities for promotion. No one in management would listen to him. There was no union so he couldn't get any traction as an individual. So he had the genius idea to mess up some equipment. Cost the company some money. Get attention that way. One night he switched off the water supply that fed a cooling system. He thought it was something minor. It was actually totally critical to 192 and Typhon, but obviously there were no signs saying so. Nothing in the site manual about it. The increase in temperature caused an over-pressurization in a storage tank, which burst, and a bunch of gas leaked out. A lot of people died. Civilians. Locals. It wasn't pretty. I was there. I took pictures."

"How many casualties are we talking about?"

Flemming held up his finger. "This is where it gets interesting." He crossed to one of his shelves and stared at all the stuff piled up there for a second. Then he pulled out a binder, blew some dust off it, leafed through until he found the right page, and handed it to Reacher. Smith and Neilsen closed up on either side and together all three read the article. It was from *The New York Times.* Its date was January 13, 1970. The paper was yellow and it looked thin and fragile inside its protective plastic sleeve. There was a photograph of a woman in a lab coat at the top of the page. Her hair was tied back. She was wearing glasses. She looked young and earnest and pretty. The text that surrounded her picture reflected some of what Flemming had said. It told of a radical employee. Vandalism. A gas leak. An experimental disinfectant that would bring major benefits to underprivileged communities as soon as it gained regulatory approval. It mentioned seven fatalities, and stressed that the toll would have been much worse if not for the rapid response from the company's emergency team. A second photograph showed the bodies. They were lying in a field of long grass and flowers. They were dressed in clean, pale-colored clothes. Their faces looked calm. Almost serene. It was like they were returning home from a stroll in the countryside and had decided to take a nap in the afternoon sun.

Reacher looked at Smith and Neilsen in turn. That was not what he'd expected to read or see. He could tell from their expressions that they were surprised, too. And not in a positive way. He felt like the ground had shifted a little beneath his feet. The article told of a tragedy. That was for sure. But it was pretty light on shock value. It didn't establish much of a motive for multiple murders. He could feel their theory begin to wobble.

Flemming took the binder and said, "That's what appeared in the *Times*. It's not what I wrote." He took a different binder from the shelf and passed it to Reacher. "My piece is in here. Remember, I'm not supposed to have this. I swore I'd handed everything over. You can't tell anyone you've seen it."

This binder didn't contain newsprint. Just regular letter paper covered with double-spaced, typewritten text. It told a story that was similar in some respects. It included a saboteur. A gas leak. Dead civilians. But in other ways it was very different. It involved secret government research. The CIA. Nerve agents. A corporation panicking over a potential PR disaster. A cover-up operation. But the most dramatic discrepancy came in terms of the death toll. This version didn't tell of seven fatalities. It claimed that 1,007 people had lost their lives.

"Turn the page," Flemming said when he saw from their faces they had finished reading. "But only if you have strong stomachs."

The next plastic sleeve held a photograph. It was ten inches by eight. This one was in color and it was sharper than the newspaper image. It showed a different kind of field. There were no flowers. No plants. Nothing living at all. Just dust and rocks and corpses. It was a wide shot to establish the scope of the scene. It captured a huge expanse and the whole space was filled with bodies. They were twisted into alien, distorted shapes like the victims had been convulsed in unspeakable agony at the moment of release.

"Turn again," Flemming said.

The next sleeve held another photograph. A close-up of a victim's face. Her eyes were screwed shut. The flesh was pulled tight over her cheekbones. Her mouth was stretched open in an eternal scream. Her skin was stained with weird purple blotches.

"Again."

There were thirty-four more pictures in the binder. All of corpses. Some on their own. Some entangled. All having clearly perished in hideous pain.

"Awful," Smith said. "Just awful. I can see why the government was desperate to stop the story getting out. That doesn't justify what they did to you, though."

"Thank you." Flemming took the binder back and replaced it on the shelf.

Reacher said, "I want to know more about the saboteur. This guy Sanson."

"There's not much else to say. He was a scientist. Frustrated at work but content at home, by all accounts. He was married. His wife's name was Alisha, I think. They had four kids. Robbie, Ronnie, Ritchie, and what was the other boy's name? Ryan, maybe?"

"What happened to him after the incident?"

"He got crucified in the press. His role didn't come out for a couple of days but when it did, things got ugly, fast. Even when people believed he only had seven deaths on his hands. Whether it was the vilification or whether he knew the truth about the numbers and that was too much to bear, I don't know. But two weeks later, back in the States, right before Christmas, he killed himself."

Reacher said, "I hear suicide, the CIA's involved . . ."

"I know, I know. But there was no Company connection. I checked long and hard when I was researching the article. Plus it would make no sense for the CIA to kill him. They wouldn't have derailed their own project. Maybe he knew the truth about the death toll, but so did I. So did my editor. They didn't kill me. Or her."

"Could he have been KGB?"

Smith said, "No way. The KGB is loyal to its agents. If one of them had spiked a major US weapons program, they'd have been taken back to Moscow, a hero. Given a medal. Maybe a slightly larger-than-average apartment with a marginally less depressing view. Sanson still might have killed himself, but not in the States, and not for that reason."

Reacher said, "What about the victims? Do we know their IDs?"

Flemming shook his head. "And you'll never find out now. It was too long ago. Too far away. It wasn't in the corporation's interest to keep records of them. It certainly wasn't in the CIA's. Or the army's. And the families were all paid off to keep silent, so there's no way in there."

"What about witnesses. A thousand is a lot of corpses to hide."

"Hide? You're thinking like a westerner. We're talking about a place where famines regularly kill millions of people. Plus a large proportion of the population believe in pre-ordained destiny. And for anyone who was looking to make waves, there was always good old-fashioned hush money."

"One other thing's bothering me," Reacher said. "The woman in the photo in the *Times*. I didn't see a name. Why does she look familiar?"

Flemming said, "That was a very young Susan Kasluga. It was her first job out of college."

"Susan Kasluga, as in Charles Stamoran's wife?" Reacher said. "The Secretary of Defense?"

"Right." Flemming nodded. "She came back from India after the incident, quit her job at Mason Chemical, and founded AmeriChem Incorporated. She grew it into one of the largest companies in the world. She still works there. She's the CEO."

"Anyone else find that weird?"

"What's weird about it?"

Reacher said, "Stamoran set up the task force to stop Project 192 from getting exposed, and now we find his wife was part of it? That's got to be self-interest, at the very least."

Flemming said, "But Kasluga wasn't part of Project 192. Or Typhon. She worked for Mason Chemical, which was purely civilian. The government was using the inevitable overlap between weapons development and civilian research to conceal the covert programs they were running. No Mason employees knew anything about the secret work. Look at Sanson, the saboteur."

"Kasluga's picture was in the paper. She was part of the cover-up."

"Don't believe everything you read in the papers. I checked her out for the article. Everyone said the same thing. It was the sixties. She was a woman, fresh out of college. The closest she'd have gotten to the lab where they did the secret stuff was if they let her in to clean it. If they hadn't needed a pretty face to stick in front of the cameras, she wouldn't have gotten a mention. The original version had her take an active role on the emergency team. By the time it went to press, she was just a talking head. She was no more part of Project 192 or Typhon than those bodies in the *Times'* picture were the actual victims. Wait a second. Let me show you something else."

Flemming went back to his shelves and searched through a pile of manila envelopes. He pulled one from near the bottom, tipped the contents onto his desk, and selected a sheet with a kind of flow chart traced out on it. "This is an organizational diagram I made when I was researching another article about a chemical plant in Sri Lanka. It was the same deal as in India. A public-facing civilian plant hiding a secret government laboratory. The secret lab had two missions. To develop antidotes to Soviet weapons. And to create weapons of our own. The local point man coordinated both of these, and he reported to a control in the States. There were no leaks or fields full of bodies, so the story got bumped to the back burner by 192 and Typhon."

Reacher took the diagram from Flemming and studied it. The names of the scientists were all different, which didn't come as a surprise. But the box representing the head of the program was empty. No name. No rank. No job title.

It wasn't going to stay that way for long, Reacher thought.

Chapter 17

Reacher's third full day in D.C. started in pretty much the same way as the previous two. He took a shower, dressed, ate a quick breakfast, grabbed an extra cup of coffee to go, and covered the short distance to the task force's office. That day he chose to walk. He hadn't slept well and he hoped that a little exercise combined with caffeine and what passed for fresh air in the capital would get him going. All night he had been plagued by a recurring image from something he'd heard about in Flemming's RV. He pictured a guy, creeping furtively in the shadow of a complex piece of machinery. Shutting off a valve or a faucet. Looking to make some kind of a point. Not trying to hurt anyone. And waking up to the news that he'd killed a thousand innocent people. Now, decades later, on the opposite side of the world, five more people were dead. It had to be part of the same picture, but something was missing. Reacher was sure of it. He felt like all the elements were there in front of him but he couldn't quite see some of them. Like he was looking at a distant panorama through a blanket of patchy fog. He knew it would clear, and that when it did, the connections would come into focus. There was nothing he could do to speed up the process. He knew that from experience. But that didn't mean he was happy about it.

Christopher Baglin started the morning meeting with another announcement.

He said, "Listen up. The agents who were involved in yesterday's debacle at Neville Pritchard's house have finally completed their after-action reports, now that they're all out of the hospital. One further piece of useful information has emerged. The killer is not working alone. She had a partner, or an accomplice. Another woman. She drove a stolen UPS truck that deposited the killer outside the house. She then blocked the view of the corresponding watcher while the killer gained entry. We presume she was also involved in the killer's escape. It's not clear at this stage whether she was involved in the other murders, but personally I'd be surprised if she wasn't. The two clearly have a rapport. The exact relationship or dynamic between them is not known. It is still important information, clearly, so you'll need to update your search parameters again. This should help to narrow the field considerably."

Reacher said, "Not in the army's case, unfortunately. There were no female soldiers AWOL within the relevant time frame, so it makes no difference whether we're looking for one or two. And I found no record of any female veterans with relevant experience or training who are related to anyone involved with Project 192 in the sixties, either by blood or marriage."

Neilsen said, "Same. We're looking at a dead end, from the Agency's perspective."

No one else spoke up.

Baglin said, "Agent Smith?"

"I'm getting no hits for anyone currently on our radar," Smith said. "It's conceivable that there's a sleeper—a pair of sleepers—that we didn't previously know about who've now been activated. Or a pair of clean skins recently infiltrated. But both those scenarios are highly unlikely, in my opinion."

Baglin nodded and said, "Walsh, is there any point asking you?"

Walsh looked away from the window. He said, "None." Then he turned back and carried on staring into the distance.

Baglin said, "OK. You all know what we're trying to find. Go look. Hard."

The time Veronica Sanson spent on the phone proved fruitful. She had started with the premise that Neville Pritchard would have wanted to spend as little time on the road as possible. A basic principle of escape and evasion. Minimize your exposure. She also assumed that given Pritchard's state of readiness, he would have prepared a safe haven in advance. So she called all the RV parks and campsites within a fifty-mile radius of his home. That was made easier by the fact that he lived so close to the coast. Almost half the potential area was discounted by the ocean. She explained to each person she spoke to that she'd recently moved to Annapolis with her husband and was keen to find a place where they could enjoy regular weekend getaways. They had no kids or dogs so would prefer somewhere without too many young families. In fact, the more private and secluded, the better. They were experienced RVers so didn't need a ton of facilities. And they weren't big on change, so if they liked the place they'd want to make a long-term booking to make sure the same plot was always available to them. Two places ticked all the boxes. They decided to try the nearer one first.

*　*　*

Reacher had been back in his office for less than ten minutes after the morning meeting finished when there was a knock at his door. It opened before he said anything and Smith walked in. Close up she looked pale and there were dark circles under her eyes.

She said, "Reacher, can we talk?"

He said, "About what?"

"I think we need to tell Baglin what we know. What we learned from Flemming last night."

"You do? Why?"

"The way I see it, our goal hasn't changed. We need to stop the killer. Save Pritchard. Keep Project 192 a secret. There's no reason to assume the killer's motive has changed. It's still revenge, exposure, maybe both. But what has changed is the subject pool. It's been transformed out of all recognition. We're not talking about a handful of KGB holdouts any longer. Not a few soldiers or spies with relatives who were harmed by the project. No. We're talking about the relatives of a thousand bereaved families. That could be, what? Five thousand people? Ten thousand?"

"Could be."

"That's way too many. And think of the logistics. We'd need to liaise with the civilian company, Mason Chemical, if it's still in business, and if it keeps records so far back. We'd need cooperation from the Indian government. The Indian army, too, if we're right about the military training. Which we probably are."

"Which is another problem. The Indian army only just started admitting women. No time for our suspects to have gotten trained."

"So we'd have to look for families or individuals who had emigrated to countries with armies that have accepted women for at least, what, five years? More complication. And then we'd need help from INS, to confirm who was in the States at the relevant time. Three people can't do all that. It's just not possible. Especially from thousands of miles away. And when we can't work the way we normally would. The families were paid off, right? Well, we can't follow the money because it was paid by the CIA, in a foreign country, so no doubt it was funneled through a bunch of shell companies and cutouts. We'd have more chance of finding Bigfoot."

"We could look for the effect the money had. Families that suddenly bought big new houses. That set up businesses, flush with cash. Or left the village and moved to the city. Or abroad."

"All good suggestions. But again, all things we can't find out on our own. Which is why we should hand it off to Baglin. We should brief him, then he can make all the approaches and line up the resources."

"Makes sense. But there's yet another problem. There's no way to do that without revealing that we know about Typhon. The thousand dead. Which didn't work out too well for Flemming."

"True. And it's not like I want to live in a dark cell, or in a bunch of ruins like a rat. But there's a moral obligation here. A man's life is on the line. The reputation of the country as well, potentially."

There was another knock at the door. Neilsen came in. His eyes narrowed when he saw that Smith was already there. He said, "What are you guys talking about?"

Reacher said, "Last night. What we learned. What we should do about it."

Neilsen said, "What we should do? That's obvious. Pass the buck to Baglin. Let him earn his corn. Look, if we keep doing what we're doing, we'll continue getting what we're getting. In other words, nowhere. Neville Pritchard's going to turn up dead sooner or later, or word of 192 will leak, or both, and we'll be left sitting here with *Blame Us* tattooed on our foreheads. I don't know about you, but I don't want that."

Reacher said, "OK. But there's no way to involve Baglin without burning Flemming. Is that what you want to do? Seems like the guy's had enough bad luck for one lifetime."

Neilsen shrugged. "I don't want to burn him, no. But hey. Omelets. Eggs. And look, they might lock him up, I guess. But it's not like he's living like a king now. And as long as the story doesn't go public, I can't believe they'd throw him in the hole."

"There might be implications for us, for knowing what we know."

"I don't think so. We're professionals. Not reporters looking to shout scandal from the rooftops. We know how to handle secrets. We do it all the time."

Smith said, "So, Reacher, what do you think? Do we tell Baglin? Or not?"

Reacher said, "I think there's another dimension we need to consider before we decide. A thousand people were killed. Innocent people. Their deaths have been swept under the rug. Feels like there could be a moral obligation here, too. We know what happened. We've seen the pictures. Would it be right to turn a blind eye?"

"It would be right to let sleeping dogs lie. No crime has been committed. No one has profited. Justice has not been cheated. We can't bring the dead back to life. What happened was that sabotage led to an accident. The saboteur is dead. The victims' families have been compensated. So we should focus on the problem in front of us. Not on digging up the past. Especially when the past is buried in a minefield."

Smith said, "I'm not so sure. I agree with Reacher. We need to think about it more. I mean, what if it wasn't sabotage?"

Neilsen said, "What else could it be? The Agency didn't rain on its own parade. You can be sure of that. And it wasn't the KGB. You said so yourself."

Reacher said, "It could have been negligence. Or corner cutting. Or something that was just inherently dangerous. Look at the location they chose. American lives weren't at risk. If it was safe, why didn't they do it in New York or California?"

Smith nodded. "We need more data before we make a decision. We should start with Morgan Sanson's family. He had a wife. Four kids. What kind of a guy was he? Happy? Depressed? Did he keep a diary? Is it true he was in dispute with the chemical company?"

Reacher said, "Good. Can you make a start on tracking them down? In the meantime we should talk to Neville Pritchard. If the structure was the same as the site in Sri Lanka that Flemming looked at, Pritchard could have been on point for Typhon as well as 192. He could tell us who his control was in the States."

Neilsen said, "Are you forgetting? Pritchard's missing."

"Then we'll find him."

"How?"

"I need to see his house. Figure out where he went."

"You can't. His whole neighborhood will be swarming with agents in case he comes back."

"I don't need to physically go there. A satellite photo will be good enough. The CIA has those, right?"

"Maybe."

"I need you to get a copy of the latest one for the area."

Neilsen shrugged. "I can try."

"I'll need a map, too. Maryland and the surrounding states."

Smith said, "I have one in my car."

Neilsen said, "We're wasting our time. Even if we find him, he won't talk."

Reacher said, "Sure he will. If we ask nicely."

Roberta and Veronica Sanson figured that a Ford Explorer would fit the bill. The kind of vehicle that outdoorsy people use for towing trailers and carrying bikes and transporting kids and dogs. Versatile, but not flashy. So they stole one, twenty years old or so, from the parking lot at a Walmart, five miles outside of town. Then they turned north and west and drove for another thirty miles until they found the entrance to the Whispering Pines campsite and backwoods resort.

The site covered a hundred acres. It was mainly forest, but there were a couple of ponds for fishing, some rocks for scrambling, and plenty of tracks for walking and trails for riding. In the center there was a cluster of buildings known as The Oasis. There was an office. A store that sold food and basic maintenance items for RVs. A restroom block. And a shower block. Spread out to the east were the full service RV plots with hookups for power, fresh water, and drainage. Roberta and Veronica ignored those. They were too close together. Too near the buildings that would attract other people. Maybe nosy people. Maybe people with good memories. Instead they drove around the site looking for remote plots. The more isolated and inaccessible the better. Any time there was a choice, they took the smaller, less obvious road.

After twenty minutes of circling around and crisscrossing back and forth, Veronica spotted a glint of white paint through a distant stand of trees. Roberta continued for a quarter of a mile then pulled off the road. They jumped down from the Ford and made their way back on foot. They slowed right down as they approached the gap Veronica had glimpsed the vehicle through. They crept close. Took a good look. It was definitely a promising candidate. An RV. White with green and brown stripes. A dated, angular shape. Windows dotted along the side and a sleeping pod bulging clumsily out over the cab. It was sitting low on its springs. So it was heavy. With tanks full of water, like they were sure Pritchard's would be.

They worked their way around through the undergrowth so that they could approach the RV from the front. They figured that Pritchard—or someone else if this wasn't Pritchard's vehicle—would be in the living accommodation in the back. Not lurking in the cab. Roberta crept ahead. Veronica followed. They closed in, staying low, placing each foot carefully, steering clear of dead branches and dried-up twigs. When they were ten yards out they split up, with Roberta on the left, Veronica on the right. They covered another five yards. Then Roberta stood up and ran straight forward.

"No, no, no," she yelled. "Don't you dare."

She had spotted a hosepipe like the one they'd found in the garage Pritchard had been using in his neighbor's yard. Only this one wasn't attached to a water inlet. It was connected to the RV's tailpipe. It hung down from there, ran along the ground, then went up and in through a neat hole in the bottom corner of the main door.

Veronica caught up with her sister. The vehicle's engine wasn't running. Roberta laid her hand on the hood. She shook her head and said, "Stone cold." Then she took off her sweater and wrapped it around her head. She took hold of the door handle and pulled. The door swung open. A faint gray-blue mist drifted out from the interior. Roberta hesitated for a moment then climbed inside. She found a kitchen area with a tiny sink, a single burner cooktop, and a mini-fridge. A flimsy table with a bench seat on either side. A narrow door that opened into a basic bathroom. And a couch at the very back of the space. It took up the RV's whole width. Neville Pritchard was sprawled out on it. His eyes were open, unfocused, completely still. Everything in the place was coated with a thin, oily film. Including Pritchard's skin, which made him look more like a ghost than a man.

Roberta jumped down onto the ground outside and broke the news to Veronica.

Veronica screamed and stamped her foot. She said, "This can't be happening! It ruins everything." She was quiet for a moment, then said, "Do you think he did it to himself?"

Roberta said, "No way. No one escapes and then kills themselves. People kill themselves because they *can't* escape. No. The eighth man did it. To keep his ID secret. There's no other explanation."

Veronica slumped against the side of the RV then slid down until she was sitting on the ground. "It was all for nothing. Pritchard's dead and our only chance of learning the eighth name died with him. Shoot me now."

Roberta gave Veronica's leg a gentle kick. "It's not for nothing. Not even close. Seven of the assholes are dead. That's all but one of them. We swore we'd make them pay for keeping quiet and letting Dad take the blame. We've done that. In style. And aside from Buck with his cancer, their deaths stink of suicide. Reek of it. So it's their families' turn to live with that, now. How different would our lives have been if we hadn't had to? If Mom hadn't felt like she had to flee the country? Richard would be alive. Ryan wouldn't be in jail. We wouldn't have had to join the army to escape the madness. We could have done anything we wanted. Plus, I'm not giving up on getting the eighth name. Or the money the asshole made out of Dad's misfortune. I have an idea. Maybe there is another person who can help us figure it out."

"Who?"

"We'll talk about it when we're back on the road. We need to find a phone. Call 911. There's no point Pritchard being dead if no one knows about it."

Chapter 18

It took two hours and cost a dozen favors but Neilsen came through with the satellite photo. Or a faxed copy, at least. Which was the best anyone could hope for under the circumstances. He collected Smith, who had already fetched her map from her car, and together they went back to Reacher's room.

Neilsen placed the picture on Reacher's desk and said, "I have to duck out for a while. I heard from a buddy. He has information about 192. Something important going back to the sixties. He wouldn't discuss it on the phone. If I'm not back before you wrap up here, I'll see you in the bar."

Smith stood by Reacher's shoulder and tapped the center of the photograph with her finger. She said, "That's Pritchard's house. Does it tell you anything?"

Reacher studied the image for a minute, then said, "If you want to find someone, you have to think like they do. So imagine you live here. You're a little paranoid. Worried that hostile agents could come for you in the night. What would you do? You know the house is vulnerable from two directions. The front and the back. There's nothing you can do about that. Attackers could hit the front and watch the back. Or they could hit the back and watch the front. Or they could hit both simultaneously. So you would create an escape route out of one of the sides. Not the east. It's too exposed, and you'd have nowhere to go from there. So you'd use the west. Construct some kind of concealed exit leading out of the garage."

"How?"

"Doesn't matter. Lots of ways you could do it. The important point is that it would bring you out, here." Reacher's fingers were too thick so he pointed at the picture with the tip of his pen. "You'd be invisible. You'd be screened by the vegetation, here and here. And from there you'd have clear access to the fence. It would be easy to rig an unobtrusive way through. Then you'd be in the neighbor's yard. The hard part would be done. And then, what's this?" He pointed to a small rectangular structure.

"Looks like a shed? No. It has a driveway. It's a garage."

"All the houses in the subdivision have attached garages. What's an extra one doing there? It's nowhere near the house. Not very convenient. If the neighbors needed more space, why didn't they build an addition? My bet is that Pritchard leased the space and had the garage built. No. I bet he bought the whole property and rented the rest back to the occupants. And uses the extra garage to store a getaway vehicle. See how the driveway sweeps away from his own house? It's way longer than it needs to be. Why pay for that? So that he could coast down to the road, almost in silence. No wonder those agents missed him."

"The getaway vehicle will be registered in a false name. You can be sure of that. But what kind will it be? How do we find it?"

"Depends on what his goal is. If he was looking to flee the country, it'll be a car. Something comfortable. Nondescript. Dependable.

With a gas tank big enough to get to an airport, or a seaport, or even over the border. If that was his plan, he's long gone. We'll never find him. He'll be holed up on a beach someplace in a country with no extradition treaty."

"That doesn't sound promising."

"On the other hand, fleeing the jurisdiction is a young man's game. It's stressful. Physically demanding. You have to move fast, and carry lots of stuff, and airports are natural pinch points. They have security. Cops. A limited number of exits. And Pritchard's old. He's retired. The kind of guy who's more likely to use his experience than his muscles. Let his brain do the heavy lifting. I can see him tucked away by a quiet lake somewhere pleasant, fishing, waiting for the fuss to blow over. Or for his buddies to pull enough strings to nix whatever caused the danger. In which case he'd pick an RV. The garage looks big enough for one."

"The RV gets my vote. So where would he go in it? Could be anywhere in the country. Canada, even. Or Mexico. RVs are mobile. That's the whole point of them."

Reacher thought for a moment. He had no experience with RVs but he figured they would be similar in principle to army infantry fighting vehicles. Designed to provide shelter and mobility. So maybe like a Bradley but with more home comforts and fewer guns. Able to carry a certain quantity of supplies. Water. Fuel. And food, in a civilian context. But there would be a limit. Pritchard would need the ability to resupply. Reacher assumed specialist facilities existed to meet that kind of need. He took the map from Smith and spread it out next to the photograph.

He said, "How fast can an RV go?"

Smith shrugged. "I don't know. Sixty?"

"I figure Pritchard would want to be on the road for less than an hour. So here's what we need to do. Find every place that could sup-

LEE CHILD and ANDREW CHILD

ply a vehicle with fresh water within a forty-mile radius of his house. Contact the local cops. Fax them the most up-to-date picture of Pritchard you can get your hands on. Have them send an officer to each potential location and find out if anyone there has seen him. Tell them to be discreet. If they get a confirmed sighting, to report it. Not to make an approach. Pritchard's paranoid. He's in flight mode right now. But that could easily change."

"The businesswoman, scientist person? Why her?" Veronica Sanson settled back in her seat.

"Because she was there." Roberta shifted into Drive and lifted her foot off the brake.

"In India? How do you know?"

Roberta eased out into a gap in the traffic. "I guess you're too young to remember the press conferences on TV. Her picture was all over the newspapers at the time, too. She was the spokesperson for the chemical company."

"That was her? I didn't realize. Didn't make the connection. But she was a civilian. Not CIA. Not army. How can she help?"

Roberta leaned on the gas. "When I was in Pritchard's house I let the fourth agent cuff me. I put myself at a total disadvantage. So how was I able to send the watchers away? How come he was on the floor, unconscious, when you arrived? Because he underestimated me. A woman. Men are always underestimating women. And now what are you doing? Susan Kasluga is smart. Capable. Resourceful. Probably curious and inquisitive, too. She must be, to have achieved everything she has. Who knows what she saw over there? What she heard? What dots she was able to privately join? I bet no one bothered to ask, because she's a woman. She was young. And even if she doesn't realize the significance of it, she could have the secret locked away in her brain. We can't call this thing quits until we at least find out."

"OK. I see the logic. But how do we get close enough to ask? She's the CEO of a gazillion-dollar corporation. Her husband is the Secretary of Defense. We can't just stroll into her office. We can't just knock on her front door."

"We'll do what we always do. Watch. Wait. And when we see an opportunity, we'll take it."

The phone in the Pentagon rang at 2:27 P.M. Eastern. Not a scheduled time for a call.

The guy who answered it listened, hung up, then dialed the number for the study at the rear of Charles Stamoran's home.

Stamoran was sitting in his armchair, lost in thought, when the jangling sound disturbed him, so it took him several rings to move across the room and pick up. He cleared his throat and said, "What now?"

The guy recited the message he had memorized a minute before. "Neville Pritchard is dead. The cause was carbon monoxide poisoning. He was in an RV and a hosepipe had been attached to its exhaust, presumably by himself, though no note has been found. His body was recovered following an anonymous call to 911. The ME provisionally estimates that he's been deceased for four days."

Stamoran stood still and held the receiver down by his side for a moment. This wasn't suicide. If Neville Pritchard was going to kill anyone it would have been the agents who broke into his house, or the women who were gunning for him. Not himself. And something was off with the timeline. If he had been dead for four days, he'd have had to be killed the same day as Geoff Brown, down in New Orleans. That had been an intricate affair. All decoy phone calls and

LEE CHILD and ANDREW CHILD

toad venom. It would have taken time to set up. And it was too far away. The logistics wouldn't work. The ME must have been out with his conclusion. Just by a few hours. Pritchard must have been killed the same night he bolted from his house. The women must have followed him. It's hard to outrun someone in an RV, after all. It must have been the women who spooked him. Not the agents he'd sent to bring Pritchard in. But that was a minor wrinkle. The real question was whether Pritchard had talked. Whether he had revealed the secret. Probably not, given that the women went on to kill the other scientists. *Probably* not. Which was very different from *definitely* not. And it would make a kind of sense for them to leave the biggest prize till last.

Stamoran raised the handset. He said, "Three things. Find out if there were any signs of torture or coercion on the body when Pritchard's autopsy is done. Stand down the agents at his house. And leave the task force in place. Tell them to redouble their efforts at identifying these women."

Stamoran didn't like to waste resources. But if there was a chance a pair of killers was coming for him, it wouldn't hurt to know who they were.

Reacher and Smith finished pulling together their list of places where Pritchard could be hiding in his RV. It ran to two sheets of paper. Smith tucked them inside her map and started toward the door, then her pager began to beep. So did Reacher's. His was a semitone lower and it was a fraction out of sync.

Christopher Baglin was standing, looking out of the boardroom window. His back was to the table. Reacher and Smith took their places. Walsh followed them in. Baglin turned and glared at the door. The expression on his face was somewhere between anger and fear.

He said, "Is Neilsen joining us?"

Reacher said, "He's following up on a lead. Could be out for a while."

"Then we'll start without him. I'll keep this brief. Neville Pritchard is dead. He was found in an RV at a campsite thirty-five miles from his house. A hosepipe had been hooked up to the exhaust."

Smith said, "So our killers are six for six and the other team is fresh out of hitters. Do we get to go back to our day jobs now?"

Baglin scowled. "You're lucky to have day jobs. You've all been as effective as toupees in a hurricane. So, no. Not yet. We have a pair of serial killers on the loose. We couldn't stop them, but we can damn well catch them. You know what to do. Go."

Walsh raised his hand. A moment of awkward silence followed, then he said, "I have something."

Baglin was halfway out of his seat. He paused, then lowered himself back down. Reacher and Smith exchanged a glance.

"I know I haven't made much of a contribution when it comes to identifying suspects and I feel bad about that. And I was getting bored of the view out of the window, so I did what I do. I went sniffing for money. I did a deep dive into all the victims' affairs. They were all pretty messed up. Poor balance between income and expenses. Inconsistent approach to assets and debts. Which is to say, normal. Except for Pritchard. To use a technical term, the guy was loaded."

Baglin said, "How loaded?"

"Seriously loaded. I can get you the numbers if you want them."

"Yes. Do that. Where did the money come from?"

"That's the second interesting thing. The superficial answer is interest and dividends from a bunch of fairly conservative invest-ments. But that's chicken feed compared to what the original seed money must have looked like. And where that originated I haven't found out yet."

"OK. Good. Keep working on that. See where it leads. Reacher and Smith—get me an ID on our killers."

Reacher said, "A question first. Pritchard's body. Did it have any physical injuries? Any sign of electrocution? Any drugs in his sys-tem?"

"No. Why do you ask?"

Reacher shrugged. "What can I say? I have a thirst for knowl-edge."

Smith tore up their list of campgrounds the moment she walked into Reacher's room.

"That'll save the police a heap of trouble," she said. "And Pritchard's dead, too. What do you make of that?"

"Reminds me of a time when I was a kid and my dad got posted to the Philippines. Our quarters were a bit shabby, I guess, so my mom decided to grow potted plants. Make the place more homey. Except that one kind she liked kept dying. Whatever she tried to keep them alive, it made no difference. Plant after plant wound up shriveled and thrown in the trash. Getting one to survive became an obsession. Eventually she came across a book about horticulture in the base library. She looked in the troubleshooting section. It cov-ered the exact problem she was having. It said the cause was too much water, or too little water."

"So it's impossible to say what his death means."

"Could bring the sky crashing down. Could make no difference at all."

"What about Walsh springing to life? I didn't see that coming."

"I'm glad, actually. I got a call from my brother. He also works at the Treasury Department. Apparently Walsh was just undercover. A long stretch. Another of these counterfeiting cases that keep cropping up. It didn't end well. Seems he's suffering from PTSD as a result."

"I didn't realize. Poor guy. I thought he was just a lazy asshole. Let's hope he's turned a corner. But what about all this money he says Pritchard had? Significant, do you think?"

"Have you ever investigated anyone, found out they had a secret stash of cash, and it turned out not to be significant?"

Reacher and Smith stayed at the office until their regular knocking-off time. Ten after five. Neilsen hadn't come back by then. He wasn't in reception at the hotel when they passed through at six, and he wasn't waiting for them at the bar when they claimed their usual table.

Smith took the seat opposite Reacher at their table, leaned forward with her elbows on its wooden top, and said, "You're not married, are you, Reacher?"

Reacher smiled. "Me? No. You?"

Smith looked away and right then the server appeared at her side. "Just the two of you today?" she said.

Reacher said, "For now." He saw a flutter of disappointment cross her face. Her tip was going to be a lot smaller without Neilsen's bar tab to build on.

"Can I get you started with some drinks?" she said.

They ordered beer, and their food, as they knew the menu down pat by then, and when the server stepped away Smith held up her left hand for Reacher to see.

She said, "No ring."

Her statement was true, but Reacher felt like he could make out a slight depression around her finger, where one recently could have been.

Smith leaned forward again and said, "Any thoughts for tomorrow? I heard back from my guy who's checking into the Sansons. The wife moved the family to Israel after Morgan's suicide. They didn't fare too well, it seems. One of the boys, Richard, died. A drug overdose. Ryan's in jail. For dealing. And there's no trace of Robert or Ronald yet. I told my guy to keep digging."

Their food arrived and when they were done eating, Reacher said, "What do you make of Susan Kasluga?"

Smith shrugged. "I don't know much about her. Just a few things I've read in the papers."

The server came by to collect their empty plates, and when she was out of earshot Reacher said, "I keep thinking, Kasluga was in India. She might have known Sanson. She might have information that could help us. Then I remember she's married to the Secretary of Defense."

A scowl spread across Smith's face. "I don't see how her husband's job is relevant."

"He ordered up the task force that ties back to some kind of wrongdoing at a chemical plant. And she worked at the plant. I don't like coincidences."

"Sometimes a coincidence is just a coincidence. And anyway, she didn't work at the secret part of the plant. She was with the civilian company. Mason Chemical. And I read a profile on her once. She didn't meet Charles Stamoran until '72. They didn't get married until '75. He was a big noise in the CIA back then. Imagine the security clearance she must have gone through. She's probably the most honest person you could ever meet."

"Then why did she lie?"

"When did she lie?"

"In '69. She said seven people died in that accident. She left out the other thousand."

Smith was quiet for a moment. "It's only a lie if you know what you're saying isn't true. How would she have known about the real death toll? I doubt the CIA and the army gave guided tours of the scene. They probably just stuck her in front of the cameras because she was young and pretty, and trusted she was naïve enough to read out what they told her to read."

"Maybe."

"I think it's a good idea to ask her about Sanson. I think we should do it."

"Let's take—"

There was a loud ripping sound from the doorway, then a crash. Neilsen had arrived. He'd gotten tangled up in the plastic sheet that hung from the frame and overbalanced in the course of freeing himself. He stood up, brushed off his crumpled suit, strolled across, and took the seat next to Reacher.

He said, "Where's the server. I need whiskey. Immediately."

Smith said, "Looks like you've already had plenty of whiskey."

Neilsen tipped his head to the side. "Correct. *Had*. Past tense. Which is why, now, I need more."

"Your informant had a thirst on, I guess."

"Not an informant. And no. Frank doesn't drink. This," Neilsen gestured to his loosened tie and a stain on his shirt, "all happened after he left."

"You've been drinking all afternoon?"

"If I'd met him for breakfast I'd have been drinking all day. So lighten up."

Reacher said, "He had bad news?"

LEE CHILD and ANDREW CHILD

Neilsen said, "Bad? Such an inadequate little word. Here's what he told me. He said the Agency has no record of Project Typhon. Nothing to say it ever existed. It's been buried. That's what they do with time bombs. But he's a thorough guy, Frank. See, I'd asked him who was in charge of it. And when he couldn't answer that, he moved on to what he figured was the next best thing. Who was in charge of the 19x projects. All of them. And all their spin-offs. So including 192 and Typhon. Care to guess?"

Smith shook her head.

Reacher said nothing.

"Charles Stamoran."

Chapter 19

Neilsen got his whiskey. A double. Smith had a glass, too. A single, with water. Reacher switched to coffee. Black, with a sidecar of espresso.

"There's one tiny silver patch in this cloud," Neilsen said. "The question about whether we dig into Typhon? That's answered. It was the Secretary of Defense's baby. We don't touch it with a ten-million-foot pole." He drained his glass. "Here's another thing that sucks. Our fate is out of our hands. It's down to those killer women now. And Neville Pritchard. If he can disappear, we'll be OK. If they catch him and only want to kill him, we'll be OK. But if they catch him and he blabs, we're screwed. No way is Stamoran going to stand still and take the blame for all those dead bodies. He'll be deflecting, left and right. Onto us, or some poor schmuck from the sixties. Wait. That's a good point. We need to give him a schmuck from the sixties. First thing tomorrow, we find one. Or another KGB guy. Smith, got any up your sleeve? Not that you're wearing sleeves, but you know what I mean."

Reacher said, "You might want to order another whiskey."

"Of course I do. Wait. Why?"

"Pritchard's dead."

"He is? When?"

"We found out this afternoon."

"Did he blab?"

"That remains to be seen."

Neilsen signaled for the server to come over.

Smith took a sip of her drink, then said, "There's one other thing to take away from this. We can forget about talking to Susan Kasluga. She either knows about this, or she doesn't. And if she knows, she's not going to say a word. Not with her husband's neck on the block."

Neilsen took exaggerated care navigating the exit from the bar and then stayed a few yards ahead of the others. He was swaying slightly as he walked but he made it back to the hotel without injuring himself. They all rode up to the second floor together in the elevator. Then they made their way along the corridor, Neilsen in front again, and when they got close to his door he pulled out his keys. And dropped them. Reacher started to lean down to retrieve them but Neilsen waved him off.

"Go," he said. "It's only a door. I've got this."

Smith let herself into her room and Reacher continued to his. He shrugged off his jacket and put it on a hanger. Then he heard a tap on the door. Light, but insistent. He turned, checked the peephole, and opened it. Smith was standing in the corridor. She was barefoot. She'd shed her purse. Her key was in one hand. Her gun was in the other.

She said, "My room's been searched. Has yours?"

Reacher gestured for her to come in. He took a look around. His duffel was on the floor beneath the hangers. Maybe an inch closer to the door than where he'd left it. His spare clothes were laid out on the second queen bed. Maybe not quite as straight. In the bathroom, his toothbrush was standing in the glass by the sink. It was leaning a little. Not quite as vertical as it had been.

He said, "A couple of things have moved, I guess. But searched? I don't know. Housekeeping could have done it."

Smith shook her head. "Not with me. Things have been disturbed inside my suitcase. That's deliberate."

"You haven't unpacked?"

"I repack every morning. It's SOP for me. I need to leave in a hurry, I grab my bag and go. No time wasted."

Reacher shrugged. He figured there was nothing in his room valuable enough to come back for in a pinch. He said, "You check with Neilsen?"

Smith shook her head. "I came to you first."

They hurried back out into the corridor and Reacher tapped on Neilsen's door. There was no answer. He knocked again, a little louder. There was no response. He banged, loud enough that he half expected other guests to come out and yell at him, but still Neilsen did not make a sound.

"What do you think?" Smith said. "Passed out?"

Reacher said, "Probably. But we should make sure. I'll get a passkey."

Reacher used the stairs both ways and was back outside Neilsen's room a couple of minutes later. He had a key on an extra-large brass fob in his hand. He worked the lock. Pushed the door. And saw Neilsen's feet. Still in his shoes. Sticking out through the bathroom doorway. Reacher moved in closer. Smith followed. Neilsen was facedown on the floor. He wasn't moving. His head was by the shower tray. There was a smear of blood on the white porcelain and a neat round puddle on the tiles. It was like Neilsen had rested his cheek on a scarlet dinner plate. Reacher leaned down and pressed two fingers against his carotid. He held them there for a full minute. Then he turned to Smith and shook his head.

"Seriously?" There was fury on Smith's face. "The same day he finds out who was running a top secret government program he falls and winds up dead? How stupid do they think we are?" She crouched down and brushed a strand of hair away from Neilsen's open, unseeing eyes. Her voice was suddenly soft, almost on the edge of breaking. "You know, this is worse. Stalin was right. The thousand deaths in India is just a number next to the body of one person you knew."

Reacher was thinking about something else. About how the killer must have been waiting in the room when they said good night to Neilsen. *Goodbye*, as it turned out. About how he was going to find whoever sent that person. And when he did, how they were going to get more than a tap on the head.

Reacher and Smith moved out of the bathroom and closed the door to the corridor. They didn't want any onlookers gathering around.

Reacher said, "How are your acting skills?"

Smith said, "Not great. Why?"

"It's time to sharpen them up. We need to play dumb. Do everything by the book. Make sure whoever had Neilsen killed thinks his knowledge died with him."

"You mean Stamoran."

"Looks that way. So here's the story. We didn't see Neilsen tonight. He didn't come to the bar. We had dinner, came back, found our rooms had been turned over, knocked on his door, and when he didn't answer we got worried. Because of his drinking. We borrowed the passkey, checked, and found him dead. That's all. Agreed?"

"I guess. But what about the bar? The server saw us together."

"I'll talk to her. Remind her about the story of the golden goose. Make sure she gets the reference."

"So we should call the police?"

"No. Baglin. He can deal with the police. The CIA. Stamoran. Whoever. But first we need to get Neilsen's phone records."

"How?"

"The front desk will have them, so they know how much to bill to his room."

"Why does that matter?"

"It doesn't. But we need to find his contact, Frank, and warn him. And see who else he was in touch with. He said he'd been shaking the trees. He might have said the wrong word in the wrong ear. The alarm could have gotten raised that way. You don't get to the top by being overly trusting. Stamoran will have tripwires out there. All kinds of defense mechanisms. We just don't know how many. Or where they are."

Christopher Baglin was on the scene half an hour after Reacher spoke to him on the phone. He assessed the situation then called the chief of the D.C. police. Two detectives arrived within another twenty minutes. A crime scene truck was hard on their heels. Yellow and black tape sprouted all over the place, running between doorframes and across corridors. A fresh-faced uniformed officer was set up with a clipboard to record everyone who came and went. Designated paths were marked for entering and leaving. Photographs were taken. Guys in paper suits and elasticated booties got busy with all kinds of powders and sprays. At some point two guys in dark suits showed up. They poked around everywhere but didn't introduce themselves to anyone. They didn't need to. Everyone there recognized CIA agents when they saw them. Finally, a pair of paramedics wheeled Neilsen's body away on a gurney and the detectives set to work taking statements from Reacher and Smith.

They were moved into separate, makeshift interview rooms. There were no panic strips or one-way mirrors, but the rest of the detectives' repertoire was in play. They tried every trick. Saying the other one had flipped and it was time to get out ahead of the inevitable charges. That there were witnesses. That there was only one deal to be done and the other one was wavering. Nothing worked. And the whole time a CIA guy was lurking in the corner, leaning against the wall, saying nothing.

When the dust had settled and the majority of the emergency personnel had dispersed, Baglin pulled Reacher and Smith aside. He said, "Are you folks OK? It can't have been pleasant, what you've been through."

Smith said, "I can think of better ways to spend an evening."

Baglin said, "Your rooms were searched by the same guy?"

Reacher said, "Our rooms were searched. We assume it was by the same guy. There's no proof, but it would be a hell of a coincidence otherwise."

"I'm sure the detectives asked you this, but can you think of any reason why someone would come after Neilsen? Maybe after all of you?"

Reacher shook his head. "None. It's hard to see how the attack connects with the task force in any way. We know that two women have committed a string of murders, and we have a good idea why, but that's all. We have no IDs. No descriptions. No physical evidence. They're clearly well trained and proficient, so if they believed the net was closing in, the smart play would be to go back to their regular lives. They could serve us coffee every morning at the café on the corner and we'd be none the wiser. They had no need to kill any of us. It would be a tactically retrograde move to try. Very out of character for them."

"So what happened tonight?"

"My guess? A burglary gone wrong. Hotels get robbed all the time. And look at the sequence of our rooms. The guy started with mine. Found nothing worth taking. Moved on to Agent Smith's."

Smith said, "Nothing valuable in mine."

"So the perp moved on to Neilsen's. He was in the process of rummaging around, looking for goodies, when Neilsen stumbled in. It's safe to say from the smell that he'd been drinking tonight. The intruder might not even have been trying to kill him. Maybe he just pushed him, trying to make a run for it."

Baglin crossed his arms and Reacher got the feeling he wasn't buying the story at all. No one spoke for a moment, then Baglin said, "I should apologize. Placing you all in the same hotel, let alone in adjacent rooms, was a tactical error. It exposed you to unnecessary risk. That has been remedied. You're being moved to new hotels. Separate ones, in different parts of town. Effective immediately."

Reacher said, "I don't have a vehicle."

"One has been arranged. It may have been delivered already. Check with reception on your way out."

Smith said, "Thank you. And what about tomorrow morning?" She checked her watch. "This morning, I guess."

Baglin said, "What about it? Be at the office, usual time. We now have three killers to catch."

*   *   *

A car was waiting in the lot for Reacher. It was a rental. A Ford sedan. A tinny thing with thin seats and too many buttons on the dash and not enough room behind the steering wheel. Reacher wasn't worried about its design flaws, though. He wasn't planning on spending much time using it.

The hotel Reacher had been allocated to was pretty much at the opposite end of the scale from the original. If the first had been designed with hordes of raucous Midwest schoolkids in mind, the second was aimed squarely at the political and diplomatic end of the market. His room was enormous. It was two rooms, really. One with a bed and a bathroom and a walk-in closet. And the other with separate sitting and dining areas. There were full-sized bottles of various washing products he didn't recognize set around the sink and basin. The kind of things he would never dream of using. There were giant towels. Fluffy robes. Enough scatter cushions that if you had to escape the building in a fire you could throw them out of the window and they'd break your fall from ten floors up. Reacher wasn't interested in any of those things, though. He just wanted to put the day behind him and start fresh in the morning. He made his way around, switching off lights and closing drapes, and he noticed the door to a little cabinet wasn't closed all the way. It was a minibar. Neilsen would have liked that, he thought. He looked inside. Took out a miniature of Maker's Mark, popped the cap, and drank a silent toast to absent friends.

Chapter 20

Reacher and Smith pulled into the parking lot outside the task force's office within a minute of each other the following morning. Reacher came from the south. Smith from the north. They walked into reception together and saw that two extra security guards were on duty. The stable door's been locked, Reacher thought, and showed his ID. He followed Smith down the corridor and into the boardroom. She sat and he poured himself a mug of coffee.

She said, "Do you think they'll send a replacement for Neilsen?"

Reacher said, "I doubt it. Sending someone from the Agency was a gamble for Stamoran. A misstep, with hindsight. Neilsen was only able to get to the truth because he could tap up his buddy. The guy would never have spoken to us. Or Walsh, now that he's woken up. Stamoran probably figured it would look more suspicious if the Agency wasn't represented. Eyebrows would have been raised then, for sure. He probably hoped a drunk like Neilsen wouldn't be able to do him any harm."

"You know, that makes me sad. We never got the chance to find out what Neilsen's story was. He was a good agent. That was obvious. Even when he was four sheets to the wind. He couldn't have been drinking like that from the start of his career. His liver wouldn't have survived. And if he didn't get killed he would have been kicked out. Something must have happened to him. Something traumatic. I wish I'd known him well enough for him to share what that was."

Reacher said nothing.

Smith stifled a yawn and said, "Did you sleep?"

Reacher said, "I could have gotten more." The truth was that his eyes had closed a minute after his head hit the pillow and he hadn't stirred until a minute before it was time to get up, but he'd learned over the years that people aren't generally looking for a positive answer to that kind of question.

Smith said, "I hardly got a wink. I'm wiped. This is really bad, Reacher. Neilsen's death, Charles Stamoran, Typhon, a thousand corpses—I just kept thinking, what are we going to do with it all?"

"We'll do what we would do if we were investigating any other person for any other crime. Follow the evidence. If it confirms that Stamoran's guilty, then we take him down."

"But he's the Secretary of Defense."

"Like I told Sarbotskiy, this is America. The law applies to him the same as everyone else."

"Makes going after him harder, though."

"So we work smarter."

"Any thoughts?"

"My gut tells me Neilsen's death starts with someone he spoke to at the CIA. He likely mentioned Typhon. Asked if it existed. If there was any proof. Who had run the program. Something that touched a raw nerve. From there I see three possible paths. One, Neilsen's contact came and did the deed himself. Two, he sent someone else to do it. Three, he reported Neilsen's questions to another person and they arranged the murder."

"Stamoran would fit scenario three?"

"Right."

"How do we prove it?"

"We find out who Neilsen spoke to. I'll contact them. I'll let them know I worked with Neilsen and that I know what he knew. Then I'll wait for someone to come snooping around my hotel room. And instead of me winding up on the bathroom floor, whoever shows up will give us a name. Then we'll rinse and repeat as necessary until we get to the top of the food chain. We already know who Neilsen called from the hotel. Now we need a list of his calls from here. Do you think the Bureau could get that for us?"

Smith stretched out and grabbed the phone from the center of the table. She dialed a number, gave a couple of quick instructions that were mostly in jargon and acronyms that Reacher didn't understand, then hung up. She pushed the phone back and just then the door opened. Gary Walsh hurried in. His face was flushed. He started toward his regular seat near the window then turned back and shuffled awkwardly on the spot for a moment. Then he said, "I heard about what happened. I'm really sorry. I guess you were getting close. If there's anything I can do . . ."

The door opened again and the original security guard appeared. He said, "Message from Mr. Baglin. He can't be present at the meeting this morning. He says you all know what you need to do."

Walsh waited for the door to close then sat in Baglin's place. He said, "What happened to Neilsen—was it to do with why he missed the meeting yesterday?"

Reacher and Smith exchanged a glance.

Walsh said, "I know I haven't given you any reason to believe this, but you can trust me. I haven't really been present because I've been processing some stuff but I want to put that right. Please, let me in. I can help."

Reacher said nothing. Smith looked down at the table.

Walsh said, "Reacher? I know your brother. In passing, at least. Call him. He'll vouch for me. And Amber? Two years ago my team did some number crunching for Phil on a sting he was running. He told me—"

Smith said, "Neilsen went to meet a contact. He wasn't back before we left and when we got to the hotel after dinner we found our rooms had been searched. We tried to check in with Neilsen but he was dead. It was staged to look like he'd fallen, but we're not buying that."

"The meeting with his contact. Was it about the Project?"

Smith didn't pick up on the question. She was staring at the side wall.

Reacher said, "It seems that way."

"Then the cops will do some window dressing but they'll be kept well away from the business end. You're trying to find Neilsen's killer yourselves?"

Reacher nodded.

"Made any progress?"

"We have a list of numbers he called from the hotel." Reacher explained his theory about Neilsen causing panic at Langley and the need to figure out who he'd spoken to.

Walsh said, "Can I see the list? Numbers are kind of my thing. Even without dollar signs in front of them."

Smith didn't respond. Reacher nudged her arm. She said, "Sorry. What?"

Reacher said, "Show Walsh the numbers from the hotel."

Smith passed him the page the receptionist had printed for her the night before when she flashed her badge.

Walsh studied the paper for a minute then said, "OK. One number crops up over and over. The one with four zeros at the end. That'll be a switchboard number. Langley? And all these numbers where only the final four digits are different? Direct dial extensions. They'll be Langley, too. Then there are a few with the same area code. Langley people's home numbers, I would guess. And a few outliers. I don't know about those. Friends, maybe? Except for this one. 1-800-266-9328. He called that a couple of times." Walsh grinned and shook his head. "He was out of control."

Smith said, "I don't get it. What's the significance?"

Walsh said, "I guess it will be advertised alphanumerically . . ."

Reacher did the transposition in his head. "1-800-BOOZE 2 U. A delivery service, presumably. Liquor stores across the Eastern Seaboard are going to mourn Neilsen's passing. That's for sure."

Smith said, "What a world we live in. OK. We should focus on the Langley numbers. How do we prioritize? The switchboard number's no good without knowing who he asked for."

Walsh said, "Maybe if we knew if he also received calls from any of the numbers. That would suggest a back and forth interaction. Not just a brush-off or a message left on a machine. It won't be possible for the hotel—calls to the room phones go through the switchboard—but here it should be."

Smith picked the phone up again and made another call. She hung up and said, "They're on it. It'll take a while, though. Anything we can do in the meantime? We should build on the panic. Try and get them to send another hitman tonight. If you're cool with that, Reacher."

Reacher said, "The sooner, the better. Send him now."

"There's maybe something we can do." Walsh sounded hesitant. "It's a long shot, but it wouldn't hurt to try. Anyone know if Neilsen was the kind of guy who was uptight about deleting his messages?"

*   *   *

Roberta and Veronica Sanson decided not to steal a car this time. They knew they were going to be up to their armpits in law enforcement of all different flavors so they figured renting a vehicle would be a sound investment. They thought a Suburban would look the part. It would blend into the kind of environments they were anticipating operating in, but it took them a while to find a place that didn't quibble when it came to doing the deal in cash.

Their outlay proved worthwhile inside ten minutes. That's as long as it took to observe Susan Kasluga leaving the house she shared with her husband. She was sitting in the back of a black Town Car. It nosed out of their fortified gate and merged into the slow morning traffic. Kasluga was reading that morning's *Wall Street Journal*. A chauffeur was driving and there were two other people on board. Men in cheap suits with earpieces and curly wires disappearing beneath their collars. Bodyguards. From a private agency, by the look of them. Perfect, from the sisters' point of view.

Roberta eased away from the curb. She was four cars behind Kasluga. She varied the interval as the traffic sped up and slowed down. Sometimes she was three cars behind. Sometimes five. A couple of times when they were on longer sections with no turnoffs she briefly pulled ahead then let the Town Car retake the lead before it reached a point where it had a choice of directions. She kept up the same rhythm for twenty minutes, then the Town Car pulled off to the right onto the top of a ramp that led down to a garage beneath an office building. It was twenty stories high, mirrored blue glass over a steel frame, rectangular sections, relentlessly symmetrical. The headquarters of AmeriChem Incorporated. The company Kasluga founded when she returned from India.

Roberta continued straight, then took two lefts in quick succession. No one was following them. She didn't expect there to have been, but it pays to take precautions. The street they were on was quiet so she pulled over and turned to Veronica. She said, "What do you think?"

Veronica said, "In an ideal world we would watch her for a week, minimum. But they know there are two of us now. And there are no scientists left. They could start piecing things together. So good now is better than perfect later. Let's check her schedule. If she's in the office tomorrow, and we can pick up what we need this afternoon, I say we do it in the morning."

Roberta shifted back into Drive. She said, "Agreed."

Neilsen's office was locked. Smith took a slim leather wallet from her purse and selected two slender, metal picks. She inserted the flatter one into the keyhole and held it down low. She slid the pointier one in above it, raked it back and forth, and thirty seconds later the door swung open. Walsh went in first. Reacher followed and the feeling of trespass he always experienced when he entered a dead person's room soon descended on him. Smith closed the door behind them. Walsh crossed to Neilsen's desk and hit a button on his answering machine. A smoked plastic lid popped open. There was nothing under it. He turned to the fax machine. Its output tray was empty.

Walsh said, "Well, looks like the Agency cleaned house already. Damn. Although there's one other thing . . ."

Walsh tapped a few digits on the fax machine's keypad. The mechanism began to whirr and a few seconds later a sheet of paper cranked out. Walsh held it out for the others to see. There were columns with dates and numbers and times and durations. He said, "It's the transmission log. Shows us all the faxes Neilsen sent and received." Then he turned to Smith. "Can I grab that call list again for a second?" He checked a detail and nodded his head. "Yes. Look. The same number shows up on both."

"Does that help us?" Reacher said. "Murderers don't generally fax their plans ahead of time."

Walsh said, "I don't think he sent a fax. Look. Duration: one second. Pages received: zero."

"So what did he do?"

"In the office they gave me the phone and the fax numbers are one digit apart. Yours?"

Smith said, "Same."

Reacher nodded.

Walsh said, "Safe to assume it's the same for Neilsen, then. So I think someone called his fax machine by mistake. Then hung up right away."

Reacher said, "Why would they do that?"

"If Neilsen left a message, he could have given the wrong number. Or the caller could have misdialed."

Smith picked up the phone list and the fax log. "The timing works. Neilsen called the number from the hotel right after we'd been to see Sarbotskiy. He'd sucked down all that vodka, remember? Easy to get one digit wrong when you leave a message and you can hardly stand up straight. And the call back came that evening, when we were at the bar."

"So Neilsen leaves a provocative message. The recipient tries to reach him, but can't. And does what? Escalates? And whoever's above him sends someone to take care of the problem?"

Whoever being Stamoran, Smith thought, but she didn't say it out loud.

"It's plausible," Reacher said. "Worth following up. But why did you say the guy would hang up right away?"

Walsh said, "You've never called a fax machine by mistake?"

"How would I know?"

Walsh pointed to Neilsen's phone. "Try it. Call yours, now."

Reacher punched in the number. The call connected. And his ear was instantly assaulted by a howling, screeching electronic cacophony. He slammed the handset down. "The hell was that?"

Walsh smirked. "Sorry, Reacher. That's how fax machines talk to each other. You can see why the guy wouldn't stay on the line."

Smith leaned over and picked the handset back up. She dialed and when she was answered she reeled off the same succession of acronyms she'd used earlier and requested a list of any other calls the number that had tried to reach Neilsen had made. Then she asked to be transferred and gave instructions for the number to be run through a reverse directory. She was silent for a few seconds, then shook her head and hung up. She said, "The list of calls will be faxed to me later. The number's registered to a John Smith. No relation."

Chapter 21

The reception area at AmeriChem's headquarters was an opulent space full of high-end materials and museum quality art, but boil it down to its bones and it was there to do one thing: Keep people out. Unless they had a pass to operate one of the turnstiles. Staff members had them. Legitimate visitors could get them. Veronica Sanson was neither. So her first step toward gaining access to the building started next door, in a Starbucks. She got in line and while she waited she took a lanyard out of her pocket. She'd bought it years ago in a tourist store in Tel Aviv. It was yellow with cartoon monkeys printed all over it. She slung it around her neck and tucked its clip inside her jacket as if she had a pass card but didn't want to display it to the world on her commute to work. She reached the counter and ordered four venti lattes. That was the largest size of drink available. She asked for a cardboard carrier, wedged the giant cups into the cutouts in each corner, and loaded a bunch of sugar packets and stirring sticks into the space in the center.

Veronica made her way out of the coffee shop and through one of AmeriChem's revolving doors. She was holding the drink tray out in front and moving cautiously, as if the whole thing was about to collapse and scald her. She crept all the way to the nearest turnstile. And then she was stuck. She couldn't hold the drinks with one hand. She couldn't free her lanyard with no hands. People were coming up behind her, pinning her in. She was getting flustered. She tried to rebalance her load and almost dropped it. She tried to hold it level and lean down close enough to the sensor to activate the machine without undoing her jacket. Three packets of sugar slid off and hit the floor. She tried to wriggle one forearm under the tray and one of the cups almost fell. Her face turned scarlet. She looked like she was close to tears. Then a guy in a suit with silver hair and a mustache stepped up alongside her. He leaned down and used his own pass to release the turnstile. She tiptoed through and made for the elevators.

"Thank you so much," she said when the guy caught up to her. "I thought I was going to die of embarrassment back there. It's only my second day. I won't forget to have my card ready ever again." She lowered her voice. "You couldn't hit the button for me when we get in, could you? I don't want a repeat of that debacle. I need Ms. Kasluga's floor."

Susan Kasluga had the largest corner office on the twentieth floor. A perk of being the big boss, Veronica figured. She figured another perk would be having the most qualified assistant so she ditched the milky coffees in the women's bathroom near the elevator lobby, rushed down the corridor, and burst into Kasluga's outer office. A woman in a sleek black pantsuit looked up from behind a wide antique desk, alarmed. She had gray hair pulled back from her face, fine bones, and stern blue eyes.

Veronica said, "You're the one they meant, right? You know CPR?"

The gray-haired woman was on her feet immediately. "Someone's having an arrest?"

"Downstairs. One floor. By the elevators. Someone called 911, but you know how long those guys can take to come."

Veronica made as if to follow, but as soon as the older woman was through the door she turned back. She looped around the desk. A computer monitor took up almost half the real estate. It was beige, hulking, bowed at the front, with a thick tangle of wires hanging down at the back. There was a telephone. A big, complicated thing with all kinds of lights and buttons. A leather desk pad. A pair of trolls, three inches high, with wild fluorescent hair. A gift from a grandchild, Veronica thought. There was a pad of paper and a pen. A Rolodex. Veronica wondered how much she could get for some of the names and numbers it must contain. And at the side, on its own, a leather-bound executive diary. Veronica opened it. Flicked through to the current week. Looked at the following day's entries. Saw they started at 6:00 A.M. with *Serge, Press Conference Prep, Boardroom,* and ran through to 6:00 P.M. without a break.

Sorry, Serge, Veronica thought. *You're going to be getting up early for nothing.*

Reacher and Walsh followed Smith out of Neilsen's office. Smith used her picks to relock his door then led the way to her own office. That felt less ghoulish than hanging out in a dead person's space, and it meant they were near Smith's fax machine. The one the information about the phone calls she'd requested would be sent to.

Reacher and Walsh ducked out briefly to fetch the chairs from their offices, then the three of them sat in a loose triangle and waited. The fax machine became the center of attention, despite being completely inert. Smith made a couple of attempts to kick-start a conversation. Walsh offered a few snippets about his take on the country's financial prospects. Reacher said nothing.

After forty minutes the display on the fax machine began to flash and a few moments later a single piece of paper slid into its output tray. Smith grabbed it, took a look, then held it up for the others to see.

"Calls made by the number Neilsen was in touch with," she said. "Only one was made after he dialed Neilsen's fax. A minute after he hung up. Let's see who it was."

Smith picked up the phone and spoke to the reverse directory guy again. She listened. Asked him to repeat what he'd told her. Then she thanked him and hung up. It was a long moment before she turned and looked at Reacher and Walsh.

"The person Neilsen's contact called?" she said. "Charles Stamoran. A private line at his house. His name's on the bill."

Roberta pulled the Suburban over to the side of the road and Veronica jumped down. She ducked into a phone booth and used directory assistance to get the number for the fire department's central office. When she was answered there she introduced herself as a journalism major from Johns Hopkins. She said she was writing a piece on public infrastructure in contrasting urban environments and so she needed to know which firehouses covered certain buildings in the city. She reeled off her list. The National Cathedral. The Dumbarton Oaks Museum. The Library of Congress. The Kennedy Center. And the headquarters of AmeriChem Incorporated.

The firehouse they were interested in was set on a triangular lot where two streets met in a V shape. That made for an efficient configuration. It meant the fire trucks and ambulances could drive in one side and out the other without ever having to turn around or back up. The tall, wide exit doors were standing open when Roberta and Veronica arrived. They had been told that such buildings are considered *public* in the United States and are mainly open, allowing people to walk right in, but it still seemed strange to them.

Roberta parked on the street out of the way of the firehouse's broad apron and led the way inside. There were four vehicles on the equipment floor. Three fire trucks and an ambulance. The trucks were different sizes. One had a giant ladder that ran its whole length. One had a water cannon mounted on its roof. The other looked more like a regular delivery truck, painted red. They were all parked neatly between lines painted on the floor. Boots and helmets and other pieces of personal equipment were set out in parallel groups. Three sets of double doors in the wall to the left led to an inner area. Roberta and Veronica figured that's where the offices and the kitchen and sleeping quarters would be. And the waiting area. The sisters could hear the rumble of voices and the frenzied commentary that accompanied some kind of televised sporting event.

Veronica took up a position where she'd be seen immediately if anyone came through the doors. Roberta hurried around the front of the ladder truck. She stretched up, opened its passenger door, and hauled herself into the cab. She ran her fingers along under the dashboard, below the banks of switches and dials. And found the edge of a stiff, waterproof pouch. It was held in place with Velcro. She pulled it free. Took a knife from her pocket and cut through the cable tie that held it closed. Shuffled through the papers inside, checking each in turn until she found the one she needed. She took a breath. Focused on the information that was printed there. Committed it to memory. Then replaced the papers and fixed the pouch back in its place.

Roberta took the spot near the doors and Veronica crossed to the other side of the space. To where the ambulance was parked. She made her way between it and the wall and suddenly the sound of cheering and yelling became much louder. Just for a second. Two people had come out of the waiting area. A man and a woman. They were both wearing black and green uniforms. They spotted Roberta and changed direction.

"Help you?" the woman said. Her expression was hovering halfway between friendly and suspicious.

Veronica checked over her shoulder. Whoever had come out couldn't see her so she continued until she was standing in front of a large notice board.

"Are you two paramedics?" Roberta said.

The man and the woman both nodded.

"Fantastic. That's why I'm here. I want to sign up. Start my training. So I came to find out what the score is. There'll be forms to fill in, I'm sure. What about minimum educational requirements? How high is the bar?"

"Wait here," the man said. "There's a pack. It lays everything out. You can take it home. Study it. And if you're really up for it, you can get the ball rolling."

* * *

Veronica scanned the pages that had been tacked up on the board. Most were trivial or officious. Some were out of date. But the one she wanted was right in the center. A list of addresses with a history of callouts related to gun violence. There were fourteen, each with a set of checkmarks next to it. The idea was to warn the crews to take extra care if they were dispatched to one of those places. To call for police backup at the first sign of trouble. Veronica compared them for a moment, then memorized the three with the most marks.

The man returned and held out a sheaf of photocopied pages for Roberta. He said, "Good luck," but he didn't stay to talk any more. Neither did the woman. They moved toward the far side of the ambulance. The same way Veronica had gone. And she was still there.

"Hold up!" Roberta took a big step forward. "This is amazing. Thank you. Let me just ask you one more thing. Are there any physical requirements? Do you have to run a mile in a certain time, or carrying some specific weight?"

Veronica dropped to the ground and rolled under the ambulance.

"It's all in the book," the man said. He kept going. The woman had barely slowed down.

Veronica rolled out on the near side of the ambulance. She got to her feet. Checked that no one had seen her. Then collected Roberta and strolled back to their SUV.

* * *

"It's a mistake," Walsh said. "It has to be. Charles Stamoran?"

Smith shook her head. "It's no mistake. My guy triple-checked. It's Stamoran's number. There's no doubt. He even made sure it's not a different Charles Stamoran."

"It's unbelievable."

"You don't want to believe it," Reacher said. "There's a difference."

"The Secretary of Defense set up a murder? That's ridiculous."

"Is it? Why? Only people with certain job titles can be killers? I catch murderers for a living. Believe me, they come in all different shapes and sizes."

"You really believe it's true?"

"I believe it's plausible. There's a clear sequence of events. Neilsen called this *John Smith* guy to *shake the tree*, as he put it. John Smith tried to call Neilsen back but got his fax by mistake. John Smith next called Stamoran. And Neilsen wound up dead. John Smith passed it up the tree when he hit a dead end and Stamoran took no chances. It actually makes sense for the Secretary of Defense to do that. You don't get the top job if you can't make ruthless decisions."

"You're—"

Smith's phone rang. She answered it, listened for a moment, and said, "Why?" Then, "Bullshit. Someone must be able to." And finally, "OK, then. Thanks for trying."

Walsh said, "That didn't sound encouraging."

"That was my phone records guy," Smith said. "We can't get any details about calls to or from the office lines. They're some kind of special Department of Defense spec. There's no data, incoming or outgoing."

"So we only have one lead to go on?"

"We only need one," Reacher said. "If it's the right one."

"The timing works for it," Smith said. "Neilsen's movements—and his drunkenness—tie together, no mistake."

"There's only one way to find out." Reacher stretched out, took the phone, and began to dial. "Now it's my turn to shake the tree."

Roberta Sanson found the way to the first address that Veronica had taken from the ambulance notice board at the firehouse. She pulled over to the curb and kept the engine running. The street number corresponded to a single green door in the long blank side of a single-story brick building. There was no sign of any activity. Not at that time of day.

"Gambling den?" Roberta said.

Veronica said, "Most likely. I don't like it. One entrance. No way to see what's inside. I vote, *pass.*"

"Agreed." Roberta pulled smoothly away and drove to the second address on the list. Right away she could see why gunshot wounds were so frequent in that neighborhood. The windows of the house in question were painted black on the insides. There was a heap of plastic bottles by the front door. Empty cat litter sacks. A stack of buckets, all warped and twisted. And even from inside the vehicle they could smell ammonia. The place was a meth lab. That was clear. And the houses on either side must have been, as well, before they burned down.

The Suburban had been sitting for less than a minute when a man appeared from one of the neighboring houses. He approached slowly from the opposite side of the street. He was tall. Gaunt. He was wearing a Mets cap. A generic baseball jacket. Ripped jeans. And sneakers that might once have been white. Veronica opened her door a crack and slipped out. The guy didn't notice. He only had eyes for Roberta. He kept coming, all the way up to her window. She wound it down, just a couple of inches.

The guy sneered. "You lost, little girl?"

"Spiritually?" Roberta said. "Geographically?"

"What?"

"I'm not lost. I'm here to do business."

"What kind of business you think we do around here?"

Roberta nodded toward the house. "I'm thinking, a little cooking?"

"You a cop?"

"I'm the opposite of a cop."

"Whatever you are, I don't like you. Time for you to leave."

"But I only just got here. And the neighborhood is so charming."

"You're leaving."

"What if I don't want to?"

The guy straightened up and opened his jacket. He had a pistol tucked into both sides of his jeans, butts facing forward so he'd have to cross his arms over his body to draw them.

Roberta raised her voice a little and said, "Two guns, huh? Guess the area's not so great, after all."

The guy said, "Are you on—"

Veronica stepped out from behind the Suburban. She moved toward the guy. Her left arm was out wide. It was swinging around. She was holding a tire iron. She closed in and planted her feet and twisted from the waist for extra power. The flared end of the tool caught the guy in the temple. His head wobbled to the side. His eyes rolled back. His knees turned to pulp. And he flopped down onto the pavement right at Veronica's feet. She leaned in and took the guns. Checked his pockets for additional ammunition. Found two spare magazines. Took those, too, then looped around and climbed back into her seat.

Roberta said, "That's our community service done for the day. Now it's time for some shopping. We need clothes and radios. And some props, just in case she won't play ball. Which do you want to get first?"

Reacher and Walsh were still in Smith's assigned office when all three pagers went off. They made their way down the corridor together and filed into the boardroom. Christopher Baglin was already at the head of the table. Reacher and Smith took their places. Walsh made for the window. They all did their best to avoid looking at Neilsen's empty seat.

Baglin said, "I'm sorry to have abandoned you this morning, but I'm sure you appreciate there were certain arrangements to be made. I trust you've had a productive day, regardless. What do you have to report?"

Reacher had nothing. Smith shook her head. Then Walsh raised his hand. He said, "I have more on Neville Pritchard. How he amassed his capital. I had to dig back a long way but I got there in the end. I found multiple records of him selling, then buying, large quantities of obscure foreign currencies."

Baglin said, "Explain, please? How is that significant? Keep it at a level for the non–financially literate."

"It's called the foreign currency loan scheme. Not a snappy name, but highly efficient. It has the effect of covertly transferring funds and simultaneously establishing provenance."

"So, smuggling money and laundering it at the same time?" Reacher said.

"Kind of. Only it's legal. And there is some skill to it. You have to accurately predict which currency is about to lose a lot of its value. Here's how it works. Imagine I bought a million dollars' worth of Venezuelan bolivars and lent them to Reacher. He could immediately sell them, and he'd have a million dollars. Right?"

No one objected.

"Now imagine the value of the bolivar falls by twenty percent. Reacher could buy back the same quantity he just sold, but it would only cost him $800,000. He could return the bolivars to me, discharging the loan in full. And he'd be $200,000 better off. Yes?"

Smith said, "I guess."

Baglin said, "Ingenious."

Reacher said nothing.

Walsh said, "Not only would Reacher have the two hundred grand, it would be clean. He *earned* it through currency speculation, which is legal. He'd have a legitimate paper trail for all the trades he made. Much better than trying to account for money made by selling drugs or guns."

Baglin said, "Pritchard was doing this? You're sure?"

"Pritchard did it. Back in the early seventies. And yes, I'm sure."

"Any of the other scientists?"

"I've found no evidence."

"Keep looking. Good work. And Reacher? Smith? I can appreciate you having a slack day today. But tomorrow? No. Be back here in the morning with your heads on straight. Understood?"

Walsh waited for Baglin to leave then he moved closer to Reacher and Smith. He hesitated for a moment, then said, "Guys, there's something I didn't mention just now. I didn't know if it was safe, or sensible, with Baglin in the room."

Reacher said, "What is it?"

"The loans that Pritchard benefited from? They were all made by the same company. AmeriChem. So I also looked into it. Before Susan

Kasluga established it, she set up another corporation in Grand Cayman, with a partner out of the Virgin Islands. Its stated purpose was to compete for a contract to build a chemical plant in Pakistan. That was unsuccessful so the company was dissolved. Kasluga got her money out, and she also sued her partner. She came out of it with a huge settlement."

"So was that good luck? Or bad luck?"

"It was another way to bring money into the country and also legitimize it. It happened right before the business with Pritchard and the foreign loans. And guess who one of the directors was? Charles Stamoran. Which isn't illegal. He stepped down in '79 when his political aspirations started to bear fruit. And AmeriChem has never had any iffy government contracts. But still. Given our suspicions . . ."

"You were right to be discreet. That was smart. And there's that name again. Kasluga."

"What do you mean?"

"Her name's cropped up a couple of times recently. Maybe I'm just more tuned in to it, with everything that's going on with Stamoran. Do you know anything about her? I bet there's a file over at Treasury."

"I don't know about a file. I've read a few interviews with her, though. A few articles and profiles. She's a major figure in the industrial world. A trailblazer. Her career path's been almost flawless."

"Almost?"

"She started small, grew enormous, and pretty much everything she touched along the way turned to gold. The only blip was when her company was still quite new. It got sued. Some issue with a product it was developing. Not unusual, really. I can't remember the details. I could find more out though, if you'd like?"

"Definitely. Please do."

"Give me twenty-four hours."

"Perfect. Now, anyone hungry?"

Smith said, "Sure. But let's find somewhere else to eat, OK? I don't ever want to set foot in that wacky half-built bar again."

Chapter 22

Reacher was a fan of symmetry. Someone had left Neilsen's body on a bathroom floor, so Reacher naturally wanted to leave that person's body on the same bathroom floor. The problem was, that floor was in a hotel. And not only had Reacher moved hotels, breaking the potential pattern, but hotels have people in them. People hear things. They report things to the police. Like sounds. The kind that might get made if the guy who had killed Neilsen proved uncooperative. So when Reacher spoke to *John Smith* on the phone and told him he knew everything that Neilsen had known, he said he'd be waiting in an abandoned church, two miles outside the city, at 10:00 P.M. that night.

Reacher got to the church at 8:00 P.M. His golden rule of ambushes is to always get there first. That gave him the chance to learn the lie of the land. The old building was in a sorry state. Its roof was entirely missing. Some of its walls were crumbling. It had one stained-glass window left above what would have been the altar.

Two parallel rows of columns ran alongside the overgrown nave. And there were a few disconnected stubs left where the buttresses used to prop the structure up from the outside. Reacher found a place where a heap of fallen masonry cast a good, deep shadow and settled in to wait.

Neilsen's killer arrived at 9:00 P.M. He was also early. Just not early enough.

Reacher considered himself a fair man. He made an effort to avoid jumping to conclusions. And he always gave his opponents the opportunity to surrender. Almost always. That night turned out to be one of the times he didn't. Because from minute one the other guy made his intentions known. They were crystal clear. He had come prepared. He had a flashlight strapped to his head, like the kind miners wear on their helmets. He had brought a stepladder. And a rope. He fashioned the rope into a noose then took a moment to survey the ruin. He selected a surviving arch between a pair of columns. It was right where a pair of headlights would pick it out if someone arrived by car. A striking image, no doubt. Which was no doubt his intention. The guy was hoping to win the battle before the fighting even began.

The guy draped the rope around his shoulder and wrangled his ladder into place. He climbed three-quarters of the way up and started to swing the rope back and forth, preparing to toss the noose over the arch. He was looking up. Reacher emerged from the shadow. He inched forward, careful to avoid the debris and any loose stone slabs. He closed to within a couple of feet. Then leaned down, grabbed the base of the ladder, and jerked it into the air. The guy flew forward like a bike rider crashing over his handlebars. He hit the ground. His flashlight fell and landed pointing upright, casting weird shadows. He rolled, struggling for air. Reacher stepped forward and placed his foot on the guy's neck.

Reacher said, "There's one reason I haven't crushed your larynx. Yet. You know what that is?"

The guy tried to squirm away. Reacher increased the pressure with his foot and said, "Because you need to be able to talk. So you can answer my questions. Ready? Here's the first one. Did you kill Kent Neilsen last night?"

The guy stopped moving but he didn't reply.

Reacher said, "I might not crush your larynx for a while, but you have plenty of other body parts." He lifted his foot then stamped on the guy's left hand.

The guy howled.

Reacher moved his foot back to the guy's neck. "Tell me about Neilsen."

"I was sent to kill him. I did. What's to talk about?"

"Who sent you?"

"Same guy who sent me to kill the science freak. Don't know his name. Haven't worked for him very long."

"How do you get your instructions?"

"Phone."

"How do you get paid?"

"Dead drop. Cash."

"How did you meet?"

"We've never met. Friend of mine said he knew someone who was looking for help. I was looking for work. It's all done at arm's length."

"You said you killed a science freak. Neville Pritchard?"

"Yeah. Sounds right. I don't really care about names."

"Two in one day?"

"No. Pritchard was five days ago."

"You sure?"

"Dates are the kind of thing I remember."

"How did you find him?"

"I was told where he'd be."

"At his house?"

"At an RV camp. In his RV. That's how I knew to take a hose."

The shapes and patterns in Reacher's head were shifting and re-arranging themselves like the shards in a kaleidoscope. Charles Stamoran was already in the frame for Neilsen's death but they'd chalked Neville Pritchard's up to the two women. Now this guy was admitting he'd killed them both. On the same person's orders. So that put two murders at Stamoran's door. Not one. And Pritchard had been dispatched days earlier than they'd realized. Stamoran hadn't just used the other scientists as bait. He'd used them as cover. He was even colder than Reacher had thought.

Reacher said, "I'm going to give you a choice. You can repeat what you told me to a detective. Or you can die right here, right now."

The guy was looking at his crushed left hand, and he was waving it around as if he was trying to cast out the pain. But his right hand was also moving. It was creeping toward his waist. To his pocket. Through the shadow cast by his fallen flashlight. That made Reacher late seeing it. He was slow to lift his foot. The guy's hand had reap-peared. He was holding something. A piece of metal, round, with vicious spikes sticking out in all directions. He bent his wrist. He was shaping to flick his hand up and launch the thing. He had plenty to aim at. Reacher's thigh. His groin. His stomach. Even his face or his neck. Plenty of major arteries in those places. Lots of critical organs. A wound from that kind of weapon could be seri-ous. Maybe fatal. So Reacher stamped down. Harder than he'd in-tended. He caught the guy's hand square on. Drove it back down.

Straight into his abdomen, along with the razor-sharp disc. Reacher couldn't see the resulting damage. The shadow was too deep. But right away he could taste a telltale bitter, metallic tang at the back of his throat.

The guy looked up and grunted in pain. He whispered, "Guess you know what you can do with your detective now."

It was almost midnight when Reacher got back to his new hotel. Smith and Walsh were waiting for him in the bar. Reacher didn't feel like being around strangers so he suggested they reconvene in his room. He took a cup of coffee with him. Smith brought a whiskey. Reacher got the impression it wasn't her first. Walsh was sticking with water.

When they were all settled in the living room side of Reacher's suite he told them what had happened at the ruined church. He couldn't hide his frustration. He'd been hoping to convert their suspicions into facts but all he'd come away with was more theory. And it was a theory that made Stamoran look worse, not better. Neilsen's killing could still be seen as a panicked reaction to an imminent threat but given the timing, Pritchard's was looking more like a cold, calculated maneuver.

"I'm just glad you're OK," Smith said. She shivered. "A noose? He was going to hang you? My God."

Reacher said, "That was never going to happen."

Walsh said, "He gassed Pritchard."

"I'm not Pritchard," Reacher said.

Smith said, "At least the guy from tonight can't kill anyone else."

"He's just a foot soldier. It's the general I want. And I'm running out of patience. It's time to shake things up."

"What have you got in mind?"

"I'm going to talk to Stamoran. Show him the phone records. Look him in the eye and see how he reacts."

"You can't be serious." Smith stared at Reacher. "Oh shit. You are serious."

"You can't do it," Walsh said. "He's the Secretary of Defense."

"And that puts him above the law?"

"No. That puts him behind a bunch of bodyguards. You can't just walk up to him and start making accusations. And how would you find him? They don't print his schedule in the *Post.*"

"I'll wait outside his house. Then it doesn't matter where he's heading. And I've got an idea that will take care of his security detail."

"You can't—"

"In a non-harmful way. And don't worry. I'll be acting alone. If there's any blowback, it won't touch either of you."

The conversation rambled on for another ten minutes then Walsh finished his water and stood up to go. He paused on the way to the door and pulled an envelope out of his satchel. He set it down on the counter near the minibar and said, "Here's that information you asked for. About Susan Kasluga. Let me know if you need anything else."

Smith got up and went to use the bathroom. She was gone long enough for Reacher to start worrying that she'd had too much to drink. When she finally did come out she went back to the couch but she wouldn't meet Reacher's eye. She rocked back and forth for a moment then curled forward until her face was almost pressed against her knees. She wrapped her arms around her head and Reacher saw her whole torso begin to heave. He heard her sob, deep and hard and raw.

Reacher didn't know what to say. The best he could come up with was, "Amber? Are you OK?"

Smith didn't respond for a minute then she straightened up and wiped her cheeks and said, "The other night at the bar, you asked if I was married. I said no. Which is true. If you go with the whole till-death-do-you-part thing."

"Your husband died?"

"His name was Philip. He was killed. By a KGB agent. Danil Litvinov. Who's now back in Moscow. Where I can't get to him."

"That's why you fed all those agents' names to Baglin?"

She nodded, which set another plump tear careening down her cheek. "It happened a year ago. Everyone says that's long enough. That I should move on. My mom. My sister. My friends. I figured they might be right. Told myself the next guy I meet who I like . . . But the only one I can think about is Philip. I'm stuck. I don't know what to do. My personal life's turned to stone. My professional life's turned into a disaster. I . . . I'm sorry. I don't know why I'm telling you this."

Reacher sat on the couch next to her and put his arm around her. "You have nothing to be sorry for. You can't put a clock on these things. They take as long as they take. And they're no one else's business. Maybe one day you'll feel ready to move on. Maybe you won't. Either way, you're not doing anything wrong. The asshole who killed your husband was the one who did wrong."

Smith leaned against Reacher's chest. He felt her start to sob again, silently this time, then after ten minutes her body went slack. Reacher picked her up and carried her to the bed. He laid her down and folded the comforter over so that she was covered up. Then he went to the other half of the suite and picked up the phone. He called the duty sergeant at his base and gave an order for his Class A uniform to be delivered to his hotel before 6:00 A.M. that morning.

Then he lay down on the couch and closed his eyes. He wondered what kind of machine down in the bowels of the building would have made a record of his call. And he wondered if that sort of record would ever be used as a clue if he was found bled out on a bathroom floor.

Chapter 23

Four hours later, at 5:00 A.M., Roberta and Veronica Sanson coasted down the ramp that led to AmeriChem's parking garage. Roberta stopped at the barrier and entered the override code she'd found in the pouch in the fire truck the day before. Nothing happened for a long moment. Her pulse spiked. There was no guarantee that the fire department kept its emergency access information up to date. If they couldn't get the vehicle into the garage their whole plan would be left in tatters. But she needn't have worried. The barrier rose and she drove through. She parked the Suburban as far away from the elevators as possible. Then they settled down to wait.

Susan Kasluga didn't read in the car on the way to the office that morning. It was unlike her to waste twenty minutes when she could be doing something productive—ten minutes, at that hour—but she was exhausted. She was stressed. She hadn't slept because she'd been waiting for a phone call that never came, and she had a grueling session ahead of her with Serge, the media coach. She was going to announce her new, groundbreaking merger deal in the next few days, with her in the starring role, and she needed to be at the top of her game to prepare. Needed to be. But knew she wasn't. And now that she had lost the chance to sleep, the only thing she wanted to do was shut her eyes.

Roberta and Veronica watched the Town Car enter the garage. It stopped at the bottom of the ramp and the two bodyguards got out. They made a show of scanning the area, then Susan Kasluga joined them and they headed to the elevator. Roberta and Veronica waited ten minutes after the shiny door closed, just in case, then Veronica dribbled some chloroform onto a rag. Roberta fired up the engine, drove toward the ramp, and stopped next to the Town Car. Veronica climbed out. She gestured for the chauffeur to lower his window. He did, and she leaned in and clamped the rag over his mouth and nose. When he stopped struggling Roberta helped her wrestle his body around the side of the car and into the trunk. They gagged him, tied his wrists and ankles, and Veronica took his place behind the wheel. She drove up the ramp. Roberta followed in the Suburban. Ten minutes later they drove back down, together. The Town Car was now on the top deck of a public garage three blocks away.

Veronica used the chauffeur's security pass to activate the elevator then hit the button for the twentieth floor. They rode up, stepped out into an empty corridor, and Veronica led the way to Susan Kasluga's corner suite. Roberta opened the door to the outer office. Veronica moved aside in case the assistant worked the same hours as her boss. She didn't. The only people there were the two guards. One was sitting behind the desk, playing with the trolls. The other was sprawling on a two-person couch.

Roberta stepped through the doorway and said, "Fellas, thank goodness we've found you. We've got a problem. Two guys, Middle Eastern–looking, clean shaven, carrying backpacks. They just went in the men's room by the elevators. Come on."

Roberta darted back into the corridor. The guards followed. She led the way to the bathrooms then stood aside. The guard who'd been sprawling said, "Thanks, ladies. We can take it from here."

The guards pushed the door to the men's room and rushed inside. Roberta and Veronica went in after them. The first guy spun around. He said, "I told you. We can handle this."

Roberta said, "Can you? Can you handle him?" She nodded toward the far corner of the room.

The guy turned to look and Roberta punched him in the side of the head. One hit was all it took. He went down like a switch had been thrown. Veronica took a two-step approach with the other guard. First she kicked him in the balls. Then when he doubled over she drove her elbow down into the base of his neck. Twice the number of blows, but the same end result.

Roberta stood outside the inner door in Susan Kasluga's office suite and held up three fingers. Then two. Then one. Then she pushed down the handle and burst through. Kasluga was sitting behind her desk. It was a cantilevered glass-and-chrome affair with nothing on it except for two stacks of index cards. Her chair was chrome and green leather and it looked like it had sprouted an exoskeleton.

Roberta said, "Ms. Kasluga, we need to get you out of here, ma'am. Right now. This is a tactical evacuation."

Kasluga dropped the card she was holding onto the left-hand pile and said, "The hell it is. I have work to do. And who exactly are you?"

Roberta said, "Ma'am, please. This isn't a subject for debate. You need to come with us, now. We're going to take you home. Mr. Stamoran has been briefed and he's waiting for you there."

"I said, who are you? And where are my regular guards?"

"My name is Erica Halliday. My colleague is Caroline Burton. We've rotated in for the duration of the emergency. It's standard operating procedure. Rules out the possibility of collusion with hostile parties."

"What kind of emergency?"

"There was an incident in the area in the early hours of the morning. A man was killed. Your name was mentioned by an individual who was taken into custody. Further details are still emerging, but we feel it's wise to take every precaution. So, ma'am." Roberta gestured toward the door. "Please."

Susan Kasluga took a long look at Roberta, and then Veronica. They were wearing gray pantsuits. Unflattering, medium quality, but appropriate. They were armed. They had earpieces with curly wires like the ones her regular guys had. And they had ID cards clipped to their jackets, even if the photographs were too small to make out properly. Also just like her regular guys. A voice at the back of her head started to speculate about how she could play this to her advantage. *Industry titan survives assassination attempt. Foreign rivals running scared of new powerhouse forged by audacious takeover.* She hesitated for another moment then scooped up her index cards and dropped them into her purse. She said, "All

right. Let's go. But you bring me back the moment the panic's over,
OK?"

Smith left Reacher's room at a little after 5:30 A.M. He was already awake. He heard her leave then got up and took a shower. He
shaved and did what he could to tame his hair. He dressed and went
downstairs and checked with reception. There were no deliveries
for him. He ate breakfast—bacon and a full stack plus two mugs of
coffee—then went back and inquired again. A canvas suit-carrier
had just been dropped off. He signed for it and returned to his room
to change.

Traffic was light that morning so Reacher got to his destination
ahead of schedule. Charles Stamoran's residence. A gate covered a
driveway to the right of the house. It was armor-plated and eight
feet tall. Reacher circled around the block to make sure there were
no other ways for vehicles to leave, and when he was satisfied he
returned to the main street and pulled up near to the curb. The river
was to his left. He rolled down his window, did his best to get comfortable in the cramped space, and settled down to wait.

Susan Kasluga didn't balk when Roberta and Veronica Sanson
ushered her into the backseat of their Suburban. She'd ridden in
vehicles just like it more times than she could count. Roberta drove
smoothly and cautiously. The seats were soft and supportive. The
heat was cranked high and Kasluga found herself fighting the urge
to close her eyes. She rested her head and let the familiar landmarks
drift by as they closed in on her home. The trees were welcoming
and Kasluga knew the river was close. She could feel it. She found
it reassuring. Then Roberta took a sudden right onto a short, steep

hill. Kasluga had never driven that way before. There were brick buildings on both sides with a special sloping design to accommodate the gradient. Roberta turned right again onto a service road. There was a dead end ahead and blank, featureless walls on both sides. She leaned on the brake, shifted into Park, killed the engine, and swiveled around in her seat. Veronica jumped out and scrambled straight into the back. Kasluga reached for her own door handle but Roberta was too quick for her. She hit the button on the center console that locked it out.

Kasluga blinked. She said, "The hell's going on? Are you kidnapping me? It had to happen eventually, I guess. But let me tell you, you're making a big mistake. You'll get your money. For sure. But you won't live to enjoy it."

Roberta said, "This is not a kidnapping. We just need to talk to you."

"You ever heard of making an appointment?"

"Would you have agreed to see us? I doubt it. Especially when we told you what we need to talk about."

"Which is?"

"India. In 1969."

Kasluga was silent for a moment. Then she swallowed and said, "India. I was there, of course. In a very minor capacity. There's not much I can tell you."

"There might be more than you realize. We need you to write down the name of everyone you can remember from that time. Everyone. No matter what job they did. No matter where they were based. Please. It's important."

"Why is it?"

"Because one of those people murdered our father."

Kasluga was silent for a moment. Then she said, "I'm sorry. I don't know how to react to that."

"By grabbing some paper and starting to write."

"OK. Sure. Of course I'll try to help. But I have to ask. I haven't been in India for more than twenty years. If your father was murdered that long ago, why are you looking for names now?"

"His murder is new information."

"You think the murderer worked at the Mason Chemical plant?"

"Worked at, or was connected with it in some way."

"A lot of people worked at that plant. And staff turnover was sky high. They'll be all over the world now. Some will be sick. Some will be in seniors' homes. Is there any way to narrow the field? Give yourselves a better shot?"

"Actually, yes. Because there was this one particular research team. I'm sure you saw them around the plant. They mingled with everyone else in the normal way. But the work they did was secret. The regular team members all knew one another, but there was one extra person associated with them in some kind of a detached role. A supervisor, maybe, or a support person, or a technical specialist. And due to all that paranoid Cold War obsession with secrecy, only one team member knew who this associate was."

"You don't know which team member it was who had the contact?"

"We have an idea."

"Could you ask him?"

"Tricky. He's dead."

"Could you try the other team members? Just in case?"

"They're all dead, too."

"Then how did you find out about this whole thing?"

"One of the team members told us before he died. Owen Buck. Did you know him?"

"Never heard of the guy."

"He knew at the time that this extra associate killed our father but he did nothing. Then he found out he had cancer and he had a sudden attack of conscience."

"That sucks. It's a shame he didn't act earlier. Like, right away. So listen, I'll write my list. And I'm still in touch with a few others. I could ask around, if you like? Discreetly? I wouldn't have to fake any office emergencies or impersonate any security personnel."

Roberta shook her head. "Thank you. But I think we'll start with what you know. Then go from there."

"Sounds like a plan. I do have to ask one other thing, though. Sorry if it's insensitive. Am I right to assume your father worked at the plant?"

Roberta nodded.

"Mind if I ask his name? Maybe I knew him."

"I'm sure you knew of him, at least. His name was Morgan Sanson."

Kasluga didn't say anything. She just stared.

"I'm Roberta. This is Veronica."

Kasluga felt like she couldn't breathe. Her chest was tight. She told herself it was just the stress. The lack of sleep. She said, "Robbie and Ronnie? I heard your names. I always assumed you were boys."

"Most people did."

"I remember all the things they said about your dad." Kasluga was feeling light-headed. Maybe if that phone call had come when it was supposed to, she would be more in control. "I can see why it's important to set the record straight."

"The record is straight," Veronica said. She opened her satchel and took out a dog-eared manila folder. "This is his personnel file. It confirms everything about his character. Our father's only concern was safety. He found out that someone was stealing money. Maintenance standards were slipping as a result. That's what caused the leak that killed those people. Not sabotage. Dad was going to blow the whistle so someone had to shut him up."

Kasluga took the folder and pressed it against her lap. "How the hell did you get this?"

"Owen Buck gave it to us. He took it when he left the plant. Said it was proof he always meant to help."

"I'll help. And I don't *mean to* do things. I do them." Kasluga's heart was beating so hard it felt like it might break a rib. She was feeling hot. She was worried she was going to faint. "But listen. All the same, don't get your hopes up. There's a lot of time gone by. A lot of water under the bridge. Finding this eighth guy will be no kind of cakewalk. It might not even be possible. You should prepare yourselves for that. Now, could we get going? I really need to be back at the office."

Chapter 24

After more than an hour Reacher saw the big heavy gates twitch then slowly begin to pull apart. He fired up his engine, pulled forward, stopped, and jumped out. Then he stood in the mouth of Stamoran's driveway with his car parked directly behind him.

By any reasonable measure it was a reckless thing to do. Reckless, and stupid. The Secretary of Defense is one of the best protected people in the world. Anyone executing a hostile maneuver directed at him is likely to get shot. Or tackled to the ground at the very least. And the secretary's official limousine could brush a lightweight rental car aside like a bug. But that morning none of those things happened. The Class A uniform did its job, just as Reacher had gambled it would.

Stamoran's car slammed to a halt and rocked on its springs. Reacher stepped forward and approached its left-hand rear door. For a moment he could see nothing because of the heavy tint on the glass, then the window purred down about four inches. Stamoran glared through the gap and said, "This had better be a dire national emergency, Captain."

Reacher said, "I believe it is, sir. On the grounds that it pertains to the task force that you yourself established. I have a document that calls for your urgent review."

Stamoran wasn't expecting that. He didn't like surprises. He was inclined to send the MP away with a note of reprimand to pass on to his CO. But if he was there on task force business, that could mean the killers had been identified. Or that some indication had been found that Pritchard had given up what he knew. Either way, it was ridiculously overzealous for the captain to show up in person. And either way, it wouldn't hurt to see what he had brought.

Stamoran opened his door. He said, "Whatever you've got, pass it here."

Reacher took a sheet of paper from his jacket pocket, unfolded it, and handed it over. It bore a single line of text. One call record. The one from *John Smith* to Stamoran's private line. The one that preceded Neilsen's murder. Reacher kept his face completely dispassionate. Stamoran didn't betray even a flicker of recognition.

Roberta shifted into reverse and began to back out from between the blank brick buildings. She made it halfway then put her foot on the brake. She turned to look at Veronica. She could see that the penny had dropped for her, too. Veronica pulled her gun. Roberta shifted into Drive and nosed forward again, off the street.

Roberta swiveled around and said, *"This eighth guy?"*

Kasluga said, "What? Don't shoot the messenger. I was just being realistic. I don't want you to be disappointed after everything you've been through. Twenty-three years is a long time. It might not be possible to find the guy you're looking for by now."

"Why did you say *eighth,* specifically?"

"Because I can count?"

"For the extra guy to be the eighth, there would have to be seven on the regular team."

"Obviously."

"There were seven. Only we didn't tell you that."

"Yes you did."

"We didn't."

"I thought you did. But anyway, you didn't need to. I remember the team you're talking about. I knew there were seven people on it."

"Bullshit. You said you didn't know who Owen Buck was. He was on that team."

"I don't remember all the names. Sure. But I know there were seven guys."

"You knew there were eight guys. You know who the eighth guy is. You better tell us."

"I do not know. How could I? You're defying your own logic. You said only one person on the team knew who the eighth guy was. I wasn't on the team. Ergo I don't know."

"Veronica?"

Veronica shook her head. "All these frantic denials don't pass the smell test. You hit the nail on the head. She knew there were eight. She knows who the eighth is."

Kasluga said, "How many times do I have to say it? I do not."

Veronica said, "There's another way of looking at this. If she really doesn't know who the eighth guy is, then she's no use to us. No one knows she's with us. No one saw us leave together. She's trash. We should throw her in the ocean."

"You can't make knowledge magically appear by threatening me, you know."

"Or here's another idea. She's a big-shot scientist, right? Scientists like experiments. So we could do some experiments on her. See what impact that has on her knowledge."

"Bluster all you want but I'm not going to bite. Look, I get that you're hurting. Losing your father and thinking he'd killed himself and hearing all the smack the knuckleheads were talking about him—that must have taken a toll. Pushed you to do crazy things. But you haven't crossed a line yet. So let's say no more about this eighth guy nonsense, and my promise to help you find the name you need still stands. What do you say? Deal?"

Charles Stamoran handed the piece of paper back to Reacher. He said, "When I hear about a document to review, I'm expecting a hundred pages, minimum. Often two hundred. Always a bunch of jargon and buzzwords and empty verbiage that sets my teeth on edge. So in a way I applaud your brevity. But here's some free advice. Next time you write a report, you're going to need to use some words. Include an argument of some kind. A conclusion. A call to action. This—what is it? A prank? A joke? A little act of rebellion against your recent demotion?" Stamoran gestured toward Reacher's car. "Now get that piece of junk out of my way before I have my driver crush it. Then return to your unit. You're off the task force. You may well be saying goodbye to your silver bars as well as your oak leaves. I'll be having a full and frank discussion with your CO in the very near future."

*   *   *

Susan Kasluga was hanging upside down.

Veronica Sanson had made her sit on her hands and she kept her covered with her gun while Roberta drove. She backed out from between the sloping brick buildings and navigated to a water pumping station on the east bank of the Potomac. It was a twenty-foot-tall rectangular structure that dated back to the 1930s. An era when public buildings were made to last. Pipes were strong. Walls were thick. Sound waves produced by all the engines and machines and other pieces of equipment had a tough time getting through them. So did the sound of people screaming.

Roberta got out of the Suburban first. She took a pair of bolt cutters and a rope from the trunk and crossed to the building's double doors. She cut the hasp of the lock and went inside. Veronica led Kasluga to a spot almost in the center of the main space. They were beneath a six-inch water pipe that was suspended from the ceiling on stout metal brackets. Roberta tied a loop in the rope and laid it on the floor. Veronica maneuvered Kasluga back a couple of steps so that she was standing in the middle of the loop. Roberta yanked the rope, hard, jamming Kasluga's ankles together. Veronica shoved Kasluga in the chest and she pitched back onto the floor. She screamed. Part pain. Part surprise. Part indignation. Cement dust puffed up all around her. She tried to roll onto her stomach and lever herself upright but there wasn't time. Roberta tossed the rope up and over the thick water pipe. Veronica helped her to pull and together they hauled it up until Kasluga's fingertips could no longer touch the ground.

Roberta pushed Kasluga and set her swinging slowly like a pendulum in a giant clock. She said, "One name, Susan. That's all we need. Give it to us and you'll never see us again."

"I don't know the name."

Roberta took a piece of paper out of her pocket. "See this? It's our list. Seven names. You can write the eighth one down if you like. Then you can always say you didn't *tell* us."

"I don't know the name. Please. You have to believe me."

"Why do we have to? Because you're rich?" Roberta put the list back in her pocket. "Because you're used to getting anything you want? To buying your way out of trouble? OK. Here's an idea. Imagine that eighth name is money. It's the last currency that exists in the world. It's the only thing you can use to pay for your freedom."

"OK. Fine. I'll tell you. It's Ernst. Richard Ernst. Now let me down."

Roberta shook her head. "Really, Susan, I thought a businesswoman would be a better liar. Do you think we don't read the papers? Richard Ernst won last year's Nobel Prize in Chemistry. So here's what we're going to do. We're going to leave you to think for a little while. To get your priorities sorted out. And while you're doing that, we're going to get a little device ready. See, we thought we might be in a position where we're dealing with someone who needs a little persuasion. We just didn't bank on it being so soon."

Roberta and Veronica returned a quarter of an hour later. Kasluga was still swinging. Faster than before as a result of trying to break free. Her face was red. She was struggling for breath. Veronica was carrying a large goldfish bowl. It was full of clear liquid and an olive green spherical object was rolling around on the bottom. She placed the thing on the floor near Kasluga's head and stepped well back.

Roberta said, "Have you heard of the Sword of Damocles, Susan?"

Kasluga said, "Long time ago."

"Good. Then you'll get the principle. We call this the Grenade of Damocles. It should maybe get a nod to Molotov as well. The branding needs work, I guess, but as a scientist I think you might like it. See the liquid? That's ordinary gasoline. And the green globe? A standard M67 grenade. Only we've removed the spoon and stretched an elastic band around it to hold the striker in place. Now, what happens to rubber when it's bathed in gasoline?"

"It dissolves."

"Correct. And when there's nothing to stop the striker from activating the fuse?"

"It explodes."

"Correct. The only thing we're not a hundred percent clear on is how long the elastic band will hold out. It's not a very thick one, to be honest. Not very good quality. We're thinking twenty minutes? Half an hour, tops? But we may be wrong so we're going to the other room now. It's very unpleasant having to wash body parts out of your hair. Believe me. We've done it. Oh, one other thing. The kill radius of the M67 is sixteen feet, so if you do decide to take the name with you to the grave, at least you won't suffer. No matter how high you swing."

Kasluga tried to bend at the waist and pull herself up, but her stomach muscles just weren't strong enough. She tried to squeeze her ankles tighter together and slip one free, but the rope was too tight. All she did was increase the agony. She started to swing again. Tried to grab a cluster of vertical pipes. They were too far away. She craned her head, searching for something she could use as a weapon. There was nothing in sight. She looked for her purse, then remembered it was in the Suburban. It was no good to her there. She could feel the despair building throughout her body. Overwhelming her. The pressure behind her eyes was building. Becoming unbearable. Her ankles felt like they were on fire. She held out for another seven minutes then gave up the fight. She called for Roberta and Veronica. She said, "You win. I'll tell you. I'll give you the name. The eighth man? It was Charles Stamoran. My husband."

Chapter 25

Reacher didn't move. He stayed standing next to Charles Stamoran's car and said, "Understood, sir. But let me clarify one thing before I leave. These phone numbers. You're saying you don't recognize them?"

"Correct. I do not recognize them. Why should I? Do I look like a walking telephone directory?"

"One belongs to a suspect in a murder case. The other terminates in your house. As you can see, a call was made from one to the other."

Stamoran snatched the page back and scanned it again. He said, "I've never seen either of these numbers before. Let alone owned one or taken a call from one. You don't know what you're talking about. You've been given bad information. Now, conversation over. I've wasted enough time on you."

* * *

Roberta and Veronica Sanson lowered Kasluga to the ground, loosened the rope, and gave her a minute to catch her breath and regain her balance. Then they took hold of an elbow each and led her to a room at the side of the building. It was small and square. One wall was covered with all kinds of gauges and valves and levers and indicators. And on another there was a small red cabinet. *Emergency Use Only* was stenciled on the side in bold white letters. Roberta opened it. A telephone was inside.

Roberta said, "Call your husband. Tell him you're a hostage. Tell him we'll kill you if he's not here, alone, inside thirty minutes."

Kasluga folded her arms.

"Or I could shoot you in the head and call him myself."

Kasluga said, "You could. But I wouldn't recommend it. He'd send every SWAT team on the Eastern Seaboard to storm this place. The only way he'll come is if I call. We talked about situations like this. Made a plan. We have a code."

"So go ahead."

"I will. On three conditions."

"You're in no position to negotiate."

"I'm in the best position. Strength. I have something you need. Something you can't achieve your goal without."

The sisters looked at one another, then Roberta said, "Conditions?"

"First, you can't hurt Charles. He's a good man. He didn't kill your father intentionally, I'm sure. It must have been part of something bigger. Part of his job. Defending the United States. You've got to find some way for him to make amends that doesn't involve violence."

"OK."

"Second, I don't want to be hung upside down again. I don't

want my hands tied, or my feet. If I'm going to be a Judas goat I'm at least going to do it with a little dignity."

"Done."

"Third, I need the bathroom. Which means I need to get my purse from your car."

Stamoran slammed his car door in Reacher's face but before the window had wound all the way up his car phone began to ring. He picked it up and Reacher heard the first couple of snippets of his conversation. He said, "Susie? My God. Have they hurt you? Where . . . ?"

Reacher ran to his car. He jumped in, fired it up, and reversed rapidly out of the way. Stamoran's car lurched forward then took a right, as tight as the great heavy barge could manage. Reacher jammed his into Drive and chased after it. Return to unit be damned. He could worry about explanations later.

When Reacher saw Stamoran's car arrive at what he assumed was their objective his heart sank. It was some kind of old industrial building on the bank of the river, to the east of the city. It was a generous single story high, like it had been designed for machines, not people. The walls looked solid. They were well maintained. There were no windows. No skylights in the roof. And worse still, there was only one way in. A double door. It was made of solid-looking wood. And it was closed. There was no view inside.

Outside, there were no surveillance teams. No support vehicles with additional troops or armor or weapons or ventilators. And there were no helicopters in the air. It was your basic nightmare scenario. Disaster was written all over it. No competent commander would let his troops within a hundred miles of the place. There was no way an entry should be attempted without knowing the occupants' numbers and weapons and disposition and morale. Even then any assault would need to be carefully planned and launched at an optimum time with suitable decoys and diversions.

The only saving grace was that Stamoran was still in his car. It looked like he was arguing with his bodyguards. Then Reacher's heart sank further. Stamoran got out. Alone. He started walking toward the door. He was reckless as well as ruthless, Reacher thought. And then he was inside.

The bodyguards jumped out the moment Stamoran disappeared. They ran to the entrance. One opened the door. The other covered him. The first guy went inside. The second followed. The door swung shut.

Reacher heard a gunshot. A second. Then silence.

Reacher leaned on the gas and his car lurched forward. He steered past Stamoran's and swerved around the Sansons' Suburban. He kept going until he was as close to the entrance as he could get. Then he slid out. Drew his gun. Ducked low and weaved across the last of the open ground until he got to the door. He slipped inside and right away he saw the bodyguards. They were sprawled on the ground in the entranceway. There was no need for him to check their vitals. Neither of them had enough of their heads left. Big chunks of their skulls had been blasted away and blood and bone and shiny gray slime lay glistening on the wall and floor. Someone inside the building liked to do their wet work up close and personal. That was clear.

Reacher took cover behind four blue water tanks that were fixed to the floor. The space was surprisingly bright given the absence of windows. There were lines of giant lights running along the ceiling. They threw weird shadows through the forest of blue and red pipes that sprouted up and branched out at all different heights and angles. There was a constant, low throbbing sound from some kind of nearby equipment. The air was heavy and stale and had a slight odor of oil and chlorine.

Reacher listened. He heard nothing so he left his cover, darted forward, and took up a more advanced position behind a long gray equipment cabinet. Then he heard more shots. There were three this time. They were loud and echoey in the enclosed space and it sounded like they'd been fired close together. There was the rattle of metal against concrete. A gun had fallen. Then a solid, heavy thump. A body had hit the ground. Then two more thumps, similar but lighter. A second body. And a third.

A woman's voice shrieked, "Charles!"

The echo died and silence returned. Reacher risked peering around the cabinet. At twelve o'clock he saw Susan Kasluga. She was standing with a rope around her waist, secured to a pillar. Her purse was at her feet. Her hands were empty. Her eyes were wide and desperate.

Charles Stamoran was at two o'clock. He was lying on the ground, on his back, his right leg folded under his body. His shirt was soaked with blood. His hands were empty, but a Ruger pistol was lying on the ground in front of him.

A woman was on the ground at four o'clock. She would be in her late twenties. She was slim and her dark hair was pulled back tight. She had a Sig Sauer pistol in her hand, but she wasn't moving. A bullet had hit her in the forehead. It had left a gaping hole there like a third, sightless eye.

Another woman, almost identical, was at five o'clock. She was on her back, immobile, eyes blank, with a diagonal swathe of blood cutting across her white blouse from her neck to her hip. A bullet had torn a jagged hole at the tip of the stain, dead in the center of her chest. She also had a pistol in her hand. An identical Sig Sauer.

Reacher straightened up and came out from behind the cabinet. He kept his gun angled down, covering the bodies, just in case. He stepped forward and kicked away their weapons. Then he crouched to check Stamoran's carotid. There was no pulse. He waited until he was certain then he got back to his feet.

"Stop!" Kasluga yelled out. "Where are you going? Leave those others. Help Charles. You've got to save him."

Reacher said nothing. He moved across to the first of the women and leaned down to press his fingers against her neck. He couldn't feel even the faintest flutter of blood flowing in her artery. She was dead, too. That was no great surprise. He straightened, ready to pivot around and examine the second woman. Then he heard a hard metallic click, close behind him.

Kasluga yelled, "Watch—"

White-hot pain exploded in the back of both Reacher's legs. It felt like a thousand volts had been blasted into his joints and ligaments. His legs buckled and he dropped forward. One knee crashed into the hard concrete floor. The other slammed into the dead woman's sternum. A part-formed thought flashed through his mind—*Odd, that doesn't feel like bone*—then he twisted around sharply from the waist so he could look back. He was suddenly angry. Someone had landed a blow from behind. He should not have allowed that to happen. He couldn't remember the last time he had. And he wasn't going to let it happen again. That was for damn sure.

He raised his gun as he spun around, searching for a target to fire at, and at the same time he pushed up from the ground with his left hand. He got halfway onto his feet and caught sight of someone. The second woman. She was alive. She was standing up. He saw a glint of metal against a rough black background peeping through the tear in her shirt. It was the remains of a bullet, mushroomed against Kevlar. The blood on her clothes must have come from someone else. One of the dead agents, probably. She must have been hit after she killed them, but only wounded. Because she was wearing a vest. So was her lookalike. That's what he'd felt under his knee. Good against a shot to the chest. No help at all against a hit to the head.

The woman was holding something in her right hand. It was slender. Made of metal with a ridged grip and a matte black coating. It was two feet long with joints every six inches, and its diameter stepped down slightly at each one. So it was telescopic. Easy to carry and conceal. Easy to extend. All it would take was the flick of the wrist. And it had a rounded tip, half an inch in diameter, which would concentrate the force of impact. Destructive against glass or wood or metal. Devastating against flesh and bone. A hit on the chest would fracture some ribs. A blow to the neck could be fatal. Or to the side of the head.

The woman brought the baton slashing down. She was aiming for Reacher's right wrist. Looking to shatter the joint. Trying to make him drop his gun. Reacher twisted faster. He hauled his arm out of the woman's range. Just. The round metal tip cut through the air. It was close enough for Reacher to feel its draft on his skin. It scythed all the way down to the ground, kicking up a faint blue spark. Reacher grabbed the woman's wrist with his left hand. He squeezed. His fingers dug into her skin, mashing the tendons and ligaments until she screamed. Her grip slackened and the baton clattered to the concrete. Reacher kicked it away. The woman jabbed at his face with her free hand. Her first two fingers were spread wide. She was trying to gouge his eyes. At the same time her right knee was jerking up, aiming for his groin.

Reacher lowered his shoulder twelve inches and launched himself forward. He slammed into the woman's chest. It was a heavy contact. The woman was thrown back like she'd been hit by a dump truck. She landed on the ground and slid away in a thin cloud of dust.

Reacher said, "Roll over. Face down. Hands behind your head."

The woman coughed but she didn't move.

Reacher raised his gun. "I'm trying to think of a reason not to shoot you but I've got to admit, I'm coming up empty."

The woman rolled over.

Reacher said, "Who are you?"

"My name is Veronica Sanson." She jerked her head toward the other woman's body. "That's—" She brought her right arm up and clamped it over her face so that her eyes were buried in the crook of her elbow. She didn't move for a moment. Didn't breathe. Didn't make any kind of sound. Then she raised her arm and dropped it back down at her side. Her eyes were red. She blinked away a tear and said, "That's my sister, Roberta. Our father was Morgan Sanson."

Roberta and Veronica, Reacher thought. Robbie and Ronnie. Two of the four kids taken to Israel by Mrs. Sanson after her husband's death. He said, "You were in the Israel Defense Forces?"

Veronica nodded. "Combat Intelligence Collection Corps."

"Your sister, as well?"

Veronica nodded again. "We came to avenge our father. But listen, please. I was a captain. Same rank as you. So I'm asking as a courtesy from a fellow officer, let me stand up. Explain our circumstances. Maybe we can—"

"Oh my God!" Susan Kasluga's eyes were wide and her face was suddenly deathly pale. "Where is it? What did you do with it? How long till it goes off? You—army person—you've got to do something."

Reacher said, "What are you talking about?"

"The crazy sisters. They made a bomb. An improvised thing. A grenade, a bowl, gasoline, an elastic band. They used it to force me to give up Charles's name. It could blow up any second. It'll kill us all."

Reacher did not like what he was hearing. He had seen photographs from Vietnam. Guerrillas would sneak up to parked US Army jeeps and drop grenades wrapped with elastic bands into their fuel tanks. It turned the vehicles into moving time bombs. The results were not pretty. Even less pretty if anyone was on board or close by when the elastic finally gave way. He looked at Veronica and said, "Is this true?"

Veronica lifted her chin. "Roberta invented it. She called it The Grenade of—"

"Where is it?"

"I'll show you. On one condition."

"There's no time for bargaining. Get it now."

"If it goes off now, you two are dead. There's no escape for you. But down here? I might survive. I'm happy to roll the dice. Are you?"

"And if I shoot you in the head? How do you like those odds?"

"You'd shoot an unarmed prisoner in front of a witness? Hello, court-martial. Plus you'd still have to get out of here. How much time do you have before, boom?"

"What do you want?"

"If I make the device safe, I want you to listen. I want you to know the truth about my father. I want everyone to know. I want you to tell them."

Reacher nodded. "Go."

Veronica stood up. She moved across to a spot where three large pipes rose out of the floor, turned 90 degrees, and were fixed to another set with heavy bolts and flanges. Reacher covered Veronica with his gun. She leaned over, stretched down into an obscured area, and lifted out the goldfish bowl. She tiptoed toward Reacher. She was holding the bowl out in front. The grenade was still inside. The elastic band was intact. She crept closer. Then when she was ten feet away she flung the bowl at Reacher's face. He stepped back. Gasoline sloshed over the front of his tunic. Veronica dived to the side. She hit the ground, rolled, scooped up the Sig that Roberta had been holding, and scrambled onto her feet. Reacher caught the bowl. He trapped it between his chest and right forearm. Thrust his left hand inside, into the dregs of the gasoline. It was a tight fit, like trying to cram a baseball mitt into a cookie jar. He pushed harder. Scrabbled for the grenade. Brushed it with his fingertips. And snapped the elastic band.

Chapter 26

Reacher shook his head and set the bowl down. Veronica Sanson threw herself over another tangle of pipes and disappeared from view. Susan Kasluga started to scream.

"The hell are you doing?" Kasluga yelled. "The kill radius of that thing is only a few feet. Get it out of here. Get it outside. Or throw it as far as you can. Or there's a control room. Over there. You could—"

Reacher stepped across so that he was standing between Kasluga and Veronica's concealed position. "There's no need. The grenade's made of plastic. It's a toy. You were tricked."

"What? No." Kasluga started to cry. "I thought it was real. I believed them. That's the only reason I gave Charles up. They're such liars. They promised not to hurt him. And now . . ."

"Don't beat yourself up over it. Those women were not playing games. They'd have made you talk some other way if you had seen through their bluff."

"Correct," Veronica called from behind her cover. "We're not playing. I'm not. So stand aside, Captain. I have no argument with you."

Reacher figured it made sense for Veronica Sanson to need to kill Kasluga. She'd used her to lure her husband. Kasluga knew what had happened to him. Probably saw it happen. It would be crazy to leave a witness. So by the same token Reacher didn't believe for a second that Veronica planned to let him walk away.

Reacher said, "You want to tell your father's story? I can help you. Make sure people listen. But only if you put your gun down. Surrender now."

"You don't understand. Step aside."

Reacher didn't move.

The Sig's muzzle poked out from between a pair of valves and Veronica fired. Dust kicked up a couple of inches from Reacher's right foot. The bullet whined up and away past Kasluga's head. There was a clank as it slammed into a pipe. Then silence.

The muzzle disappeared. Reacher couldn't see Veronica. He couldn't get a shot. But she could pick him off at will. Then there would be nothing to stop her from getting Kasluga. Reacher knew how many people Veronica and her sister had killed. He knew how ruthless she was. How relentless. Reacher had served temporarily with IDF personnel and had great respect for them. She would have been well trained so would have a degree of patience. But there would be a limit. She had no way of knowing if reinforcements were on their way. Any delay could compromise her chances of success. Which told Reacher he couldn't afford to wait very long.

Reacher heard sounds behind him. A hiss, then a gushing noise. He glanced over his shoulder. The pipe that had been hit by Veronica's ricochet had now burst. It was blue. And it was leaking water. Which gave Reacher an idea.

He turned back. There was still no sign of Veronica. Nothing to aim at. Not even a foot or an elbow or an ear. So he picked a different kind of target. A red pipe. He pulled the trigger. The pipe shattered. And the surrounding space was engulfed in clouds of scalding steam.

Veronica screamed. She dived out into the open, rolled to the side, and came up half sitting, half kneeling. She had the Sig lined up on Kasluga's chest. Reacher could see tension in the ligaments of her wrists.

Reacher stepped closer. He said, "Stop. Don't do it. Shoot her and your father's story will never be told."

He could see in her eyes that Veronica was not going to stop. She raised her Sig a fraction higher. Her ligaments tightened a notch more. Reacher pulled his trigger. He was never going to miss at that range. The bullet hit her in one temple and burst out from the other. All the electrical activity in her brain was shorted out. The signals to her nerves shut down. Her muscles relaxed and her tendons sagged and she tumbled sideways, landing like a mirror image of her sister.

Reacher kicked Veronica's gun away and checked for a pulse, although that was just a formality. She was way beyond saving. He crossed to Kasluga and untied the rope from around her waist. She pushed past him and threw herself toward her husband. She knelt beside him and her tears flooded his chest and mixed with the blood on his shirt.

Reacher heard a sound from behind him. Footsteps. There were two sets. He spun around, gun raised, ready.

"Blue on blue." It was a man's voice. "Federal agents. Reinforcing Secretary Stamoran's protection detail."

"Clear," Reacher called.

The agents stepped into view and stayed still, trying to make sense of the scene. The first one said, "Stamoran?"

Reacher shook his head. "I guess you'll be needing another secretary to protect."

Susan Kasluga stood up. Her tears were still flowing and she was trying to control her voice. She said, "I think the danger's passed, don't you? So I would like a moment alone with my husband now."

Chapter 27

An aged TV on a tall stand had been wheeled into the meeting room at some point during the night. Christopher Baglin used it to get the task force's final meeting under way with a VHS recording of the previous night's press conference from the White House. A suitably somber spokesman announced Stamoran's death. He spent a couple of minutes running through a bunch of weasel-worded platitudes, then signed off with the minimum of details.

Smith said, "They won't get away with that for very long. Questions are going to be asked."

"They'll be hoping things heat up in Serbia soon," Reacher said. "Nothing like bad news to hog the spotlight."

Christopher Baglin switched off the TV. He said, "I spent most of the night ass deep in crime scene photos and the ME's reports and all the physical evidence I could lay my hands on. What a messed-up situation. I guess we could frame it as one story of redemption. One of disgrace. And another of, well, I don't know. Someone else can be the judge of that."

Smith said, "Charles Stamoran *was* a disgrace. The secret program he ran in India, and all those other places. The money he and Pritchard stole. The leak it caused, and the thousand lost souls that resulted. May he rot in hell."

Reacher said, "And what value can we put on Morgan Sanson's redemption?"

Baglin said, "His personnel file showed he was a good person. He was worried about safety, not pay or promotions. He was about to expose the corruption and was killed for it. He wasn't a saboteur. He wasn't a suicide. I for one am glad the world now knows."

"And his daughters?" Reacher said. "What have they got to show for it?"

Smith said, "Some of the blame has to go to the scientists. If Owen Buck, for example, had acted at the time, instead of dithering for decades and then giving Roberta and Veronica partial information and provoking this crazy quest of theirs, how different would things have been?"

"Owen Buck," Baglin said. "He wrote the original list of names, I guess. It was in Roberta's pocket when she died. One strange detail about it. Six names were written in one person's handwriting. And the other two in two different hands. Anyone have ideas why that should be?"

Walsh said, "Sorry."

Smith shook her head.

Reacher said nothing.

"Never mind," Baglin said. "It's probably not important."

Smith suggested a drink when the meeting wrapped up but Reacher didn't see the point. The only unfinished business was Neilsen's wake in a day or two and he wasn't thrilled about attending. He figured how you treat people when they're alive is what matters. No amount of drinking and storytelling is going to make a difference after they're gone. So he went back to his hotel. He figured he would grab his things, drop his car keys at reception, and slip out of town without making a big fuss.

It took twice as long as usual for Reacher to pack because he had his Class A's to square away. The pants were going to need some attention from a tailor after getting worn at the pumping station the day before. And the whole thing would need a thorough clean after getting doused with gasoline. He zipped up its garment bag and dropped it on the counter, ready to sweep his other clothes into his duffel, but he noticed something on the side next to the minibar. An envelope. The report Walsh had brought for him the other night. About Susan Kasluga's career. He hadn't read it. Events had overtaken him. And it would be moot now, anyway. The case was closed. Reacher picked up the envelope and started toward the trash can.

He stopped. He slid the contents out of the envelope and began to flick through them. He had time. He figured it would be good to get a sense of the woman whose life he'd saved. He wound up reading every word, and studying every picture. And when he was done, his travel plans were back on hold.

Reacher stepped into Susan Kasluga's outer office at a minute to nine in the morning, two days later.

Kasluga's gray-haired assistant looked up from behind her giant computer and said, "Captain Reacher?" She gestured toward the door to the inner office. "Go ahead. She's ready for you." Then she lowered her voice. "You know, Ms. Kasluga is the backbone of AmeriChem. She's the life and soul of the company. Everyone here is so grateful for what you did to save her."

LEE CHILD and ANDREW CHILD

Reacher said, "Don't thank me yet." Then he gave the inner door a cursory knock and went through.

Susan Kasluga came out from behind her desk to greet him. She was wearing all black. She looked tired and there were dark circles under her eyes. She gave him a gentle hug and said, "I'm glad you're here. Welcome to my sanctuary."

Most of the furniture in the place was a blend of chrome and leather and pale Scandinavian wood. Exactly the kind of tone Reacher expected to find in a chief executive's office. But along one wall there was a surprisingly personal collection of things. Almost sentimental. There was an old lab bench with a jumble of test tubes in wooden racks spread out all over it. There were tongs and Bunsen burners and round glass flasks in various sizes. And on the wall above it there were clusters of framed pictures of experiments in progress and people wearing white coats and safety goggles. There was also a group of five canvas facsimiles of handwritten chemical formulae, complete with crossings-out and scribbled annotations. Reacher guessed they were copies of Kasluga's own work. Presumably milestones that were significant to her in some way.

Reacher shifted his focus back to Kasluga and said, "I'm sorry for your loss."

Kasluga shrugged. "Thank you. It's a complicated situation. I loved Charles. I still do. I always will, I guess. But I have to face facts. He was a murderer. Have you seen what they're saying in the press? It's like they're trying to take away my right to mourn. To shame me. They don't get that I'm a victim, too. Anyway, enough of them and their vindictiveness. Can I offer you some tea? I have orange hibiscus, peppermint leaf, lemon lavender, or huang ju hua. That's yellow chrysanthemum flower. It's delicious." She moved across to a shelf that held a slim electric kettle, a set of mugs in contrasting pastel colors, and half a dozen cylindrical silver caddies.

Reacher said, "Thanks, but no. This won't take long. I just have a couple of loose ends to tie up. Some of our paperwork got lost, unfortunately. A screwup by the admin guys."

"After what you did for me, nothing is too much trouble," she said. "Tell me what you need."

She moved across and sat in a chair by a low coffee table in the center of the office. Reacher took the one opposite.

Reacher said, "The first thing is new, actually. My CO is a bit of an innovator. He's started a study to see if graphology could be applied to our work in any way. The study of handwriting."

"OK?"

"He's looking for samples for his expert to analyze. It's totally anonymous and unofficial, but if I could take him a real-life example it would earn me a load of kudos."

"You want me to write something down?"

Reacher took a notebook and a pen out of a briefcase he'd borrowed and passed them to her. "If you wouldn't mind. A couple of words. *Clears marathons.* Sounds weird, but apparently it's important for every sample to say the same thing and that's what our guy came up with."

Kasluga scribbled on the first page. "Done."

"Thank you. And while you've got the pen, could you give me your phone number? Not your office. I have that one. A home number. In case I have any follow-up. When I have paperwork backed up I tend to work late."

"No problem." She added a string of digits to the second page and handed back the pad.

Reacher hesitated, then said, "I'm sorry if this is an insensitive time to ask, but how much did your husband tell you about his involvement in Project 192?"

"It's OK." Kasluga took a moment to bring her emotions under

LEE CHILD and ANDREW CHILD

control. "He didn't tell me much. Just that he suspected someone was killing the scientists from the sixties in order to force one of them to give up the identity of the eighth man on their team, and that he was the eighth man. He didn't want to breach state secrets or anything, but he was worried the killers would come after me to get to him. Which is exactly what did happen, of course."

"What did he tell you about Project Typhon?"

"Nothing. I don't know what that is."

"OK, well I think that pretty much wraps everything up." Reacher started to heave himself out of the chair, then sank back down. "Actually, let me ask you one more thing. I'm curious. I came across an early draft of a press article about your role following that accident in '69. Made you sound a lot more heroic than the one that got published. Heroic is closer to the truth, right? From what I've seen I can't picture you as a passive, talking-head type of person."

Kasluga looked down and smiled. She said, "I didn't realize that original version is still making the rounds. But you're right. It was pretty much spot-on. When the gas leaked, and what a nightmare that was, by the way, there were no senior managers to be found. They all buried their heads in the sand. Someone had to take action, so I did. I organized the work to neutralize the gas that had leaked. And to treat people who had been exposed. Then to clean any contaminated water and repair the damage to the soil."

"And when you'd done all the heavy lifting the bosses resurfaced, took the credit for themselves, and downplayed your role."

"I was seriously pissed at the time. I won't lie. It's one of the reasons I quit that job and founded AmeriChem. But you know what they say. The best revenge is massive success. And look at me now."

"They also say that pride goes before a fall."

Kasluga tipped her head to the side. "What do you mean by that?"

"The gas that leaked in '69 was a product of Project Typhon. So you did know about it."

"It wasn't. It was a new kind of disinfectant from the Mason Chemical plant, where I worked. And look, seven people died which makes it—"

"One thousand and seven." Reacher took a photograph out of his briefcase and laid it on the table. Flemming had given it to him the previous afternoon. It was the wide shot of the bodies strewn out across the desolate field. "You knew which chemicals to use to neutralize the gas. So you knew what kind of gas it was. That's the truth."

Kasluga didn't reply.

Reacher said, "In fact, it's only part of the truth. You didn't just know about the Typhon gas. You stole the formula. And when you set up AmeriChem, it became the basis for your first blockbuster product. In a watered-down form. Your big-deal disinfectant. I bet it's one of the ones you have hanging on the wall."

Reacher saw Kasluga glance at the left-hand canvas.

She said, "That's a lie. I devised the formulas for AmeriChem's first five products myself, on my own, and only after I had established the company."

Reacher set a second photograph on the table. Another from the leak in '69. A close-up of a victim's face. He set a third photo next to it. Also a close-up of a face. With skin stained with the exact same kind of weird purple blotches. Walsh had dug it up when he threw a searchlight on Kasluga's professional life. It was in the envelope he had left at Reacher's hotel.

Reacher said, "That picture was evidence when you were sued after AmeriChem had a gas leak."

Kasluga glanced at the canvas again but didn't say a word.

Reacher said, "Same symptoms. Same gas. No question."

Kasluga picked up the first picture from '69. "Where did you get this?"

Reacher shrugged. "I'm an investigator. I find things."

Kasluga turned the photograph over. There was a stamp on the back, in blue ink, pale to begin with and faded by time. Kasluga brought it closer to her face and peered at the letters. "Copyright Spencer Flemming. And a post office box number. Interesting."

"Don't try to find him. You'd be wasting your time. He's somewhere you'd never expect."

Kasluga got up, crossed to one of her bookcases, and opened a cupboard that took the place of the lower three shelves. There was a machine inside. A document shredder. She fed the picture into it then slammed the door. "Oops."

"That won't help you. Flemming has copies."

"So what are you going to do? Arrest me? Drag the grieving widow out in handcuffs? Good luck with the optics on that one."

Reacher stood. "Not me. Not my jurisdiction. If you were in the military you'd already be in a cell. My next meeting's with the FBI. I'm going to give them everything I have. I'm sure you'll be hearing from them soon. I just wanted to see the look on your face, first."

Chapter 28

Spencer Flemming was sitting on the floor, surrounded by his books and papers and files. He had taken a shower so his hair was hanging down even lower on his back than usual. His clothes had been washed so his shirt was brighter and there were fewer stains on his jeans. A plate was on the desk. A sandwich was spilling over the sides, loaded with tomatoes and peppers and red onions and spinach. His favorite combination. Usually. It was out of his reach, but that was OK. He didn't have the stomach for it just then. He was too busy second-guessing himself. Change was coming. Good things were going to happen, he hoped. But before the sunshine, the storm. Reacher hadn't hidden that from him when he'd asked for his help. It was just a lot easier to be brave when he wasn't on his own.

The guy at the postal store was stubborn. He waved off Susan Kasluga's threats against him and his business. He wasn't interested in her bribes. He wouldn't budge an inch until she spotted the photograph he kept in a frame behind the counter. It showed a woman and two little boys, all hugs and smiles and happiness. Kasluga suggested that two of the men who were with her could track the trio down. She suggested a few things they could do when they caught up with them. Then the guy changed his tune. He gave up Spencer Flemming's address in a heartbeat. He even warned Kasluga that the premises it corresponded to were extremely unorthodox. He didn't want her to think he'd tried to stiff her. He didn't want her coming back. He was extremely clear about that.

Kasluga's driver stopped the Town Car at the end of the asylum's driveway, in the same spot Smith had used six days before. He killed the engine and climbed out. He drew his gun. The other three guards followed and reached for their weapons. Kasluga got out last. The four guys formed up around her and they stood for a moment and stared through the fence at the building. A dark cloud hung low in the sky over the whole site. It felt like some kind of warning. The crumbling brickwork and the rusting screens over the windows seemed to scream, *Run*. Kasluga nudged the guard in front of her. She said, "Come on. What are you waiting for?"

The guard made a gap in the fence and led the way toward the portico and the huge wooden door. He was carrying a set of bolt cutters and he used them to slice through the padlock and knock its rusty remains loose. Then it took two of them to heave the doors apart far enough to squeeze through. Daylight filtered in. They could see the filthy space on the other side. Kasluga pointed at the footprints in the dust that covered the black and white floor tiles. She said, "That way. Let's go."

They stayed close and followed the track past the ruined desk and under the crusted chandelier and all the way out to the courtyard. Kasluga pointed to the line of travel trailers on the far side. "He must be in one of them."

The drapes in the left-hand trailer were drawn but its door was latched open. Kasluga nudged the guard and said, "Try that one."

The guard set his foot on the bottom step. He took the next one slowly, and stepped inside. He paused in the doorway, then crept forward. He disappeared from view. He was gone for a minute. Two. Three. There was no sign of him bringing Flemming out. No sign of him returning alone.

Kasluga called out, "Hey. What's going on in there? What's taking so long?"

There was no reply.

She nudged the next guard. "Go see what's happening."

The guy took the steps at a snail's pace then rushed forward, gun raised. He vanished inside. And did not reappear.

A voice called out from behind them. A man's. Firm. Authoritative. It said, "FBI. Drop your weapons. Lie facedown on the ground. Do it now."

The two remaining guards did as they were told. The pair who had gone into the trailer stumbled back out, disarmed, their hands cuffed behind their backs, followed by two agents. Four more agents swarmed around the guys on the floor. They cuffed them. Hauled them onto their feet, and dragged them away.

Susan Kasluga was alone. She remained on her feet. Reacher and Amber Smith approached from the glass doorway. Smith said, "You heard. Get on the ground."

Kasluga folded her arms. She stayed standing.

Reacher stepped in close. He leaned down and loomed over her.

His voice was barely more than a whisper. He said, "I killed a woman because of you. A woman I shouldn't have. So if you think I won't take any chance to rip you to pieces . . ."

Kasluga brushed the ground in front of her with one foot. She lowered herself to her knees. Pushed away a couple of rocks and eased down until she was lying on her front. Smith cuffed her then pulled her back upright and began a search. She was thorough. She checked under Kasluga's arms. Around her chest. Her waist. Her thighs. In the seams of her clothes. Even in her hair.

Kasluga poked at the ground with her toe and sneered. "So what was this about, this wild-goose chase?"

Reacher said, "It's about actions speaking louder than words. Any competent lawyer could have gotten that photo I showed you excluded from a trial. The one with all the bodies from '69. There's no way to prove when it was taken. Where. Whether the people were really dead, or just posing. Whether you even knew about them. But you going to such trouble to find the photographer? That's as good as a guilty plea, all day long."

"Not in a court of law."

"We're not talking about a court. Or the law. Not any longer. I'm not sure society will be best served by you going to jail. Maybe there's another way for you to make amends."

"I'm listening. And I'm betting this has to do with money. How much do you want?"

"AmeriChem made you a very rich woman. You could use that money to provide for the families of the victims you left behind in India. For Morgan Sanson's wife and surviving son. For Kent Neilsen's daughters. A guy from the Treasury Department has drawn up a document. It'll make everything legal. You should sign it."

"Are you insane? I'm not responsible for any of those deaths. I'm not helping those people."

"How much time did you spend in chemistry labs, Susan? Because something's clearly rotted your brain. Start with India. A thousand people died because that gas leaked? Why did it leak?"

"Poor maintenance." She scuffed the dirt with her foot. "Nothing to do with me."

"Everything to do with you. The maintenance was bad because you stole the money that was supposed to pay for it."

"That's a lie."

"You stole the formula to give your new company a head start. You stole the money, too."

"I never—"

"The Cayman Islands, Susan. The property development company. The failed bid. The bogus lawsuit. We know about it all."

Kasluga didn't respond.

Reacher said, "Your stealing caused the leak, and the leak is why you had to silence Morgan Sanson."

"Sanson was a sad loser who messed with the cooling equipment in a fit of temper because he wasn't good enough to get a raise. People died and he couldn't live with it so he killed himself."

"We've read his personnel file, Susan. Safety was his concern. Not pay."

"Speculate all you want. I can listen to this garbage all day long and when you're done I can tell you one thing: I'm not going to jail because some poor people died in a gas leak and I'm not going to jail for killing Morgan Sanson."

"Maybe not," Reacher said. "But you will go to jail for killing your husband. That's for damn sure."

Spencer Flemming struggled to his feet. He was stooped at first, as usual, then he forced himself to stand up straight. He couldn't remember the last time he'd cared about his posture. Or that his skin hadn't been dirty. Or that he'd felt carpet under his toes. He moved until he could catch his reflection in the mirror. He didn't like what he saw. He looked so different, next to the people who had helped him since Reacher and Amber Smith had brought him to the hotel. His hair. His clothes. He was stuck in time, he realized. Not his fault, given that he'd been forced to live in the shadows. And not his choice. But now he could choose to change. He would have to, if he was going to take advantage of this second chance he was being offered. If it actually happened. Reacher had told him the woman most responsible for his plight would be going to jail for the rest of her life. He prayed that was true. But deep down in his gut he didn't believe it. He couldn't. He had a premonition. She was going to skate, and he would wind up back in the asylum.

"You're framing me." Kasluga's voice was practically a shriek. "You're actually trying to frame me. It's unbelievable. You know I didn't kill Charles. You were there. You know Veronica Sanson killed him. She would have killed me, too, if you'd showed up a moment later."

Reacher shrugged and said, "And I used to think punctuality was a virtue."

Kasluga turned to Smith. "Try to arrest me for this and I'll have my lawyer put Reacher on the stand. Make him perjure himself. He'll be the one who winds up in jail. Not me."

Smith said, "Oh, you're getting arrested."

Reacher said, "Try to keep me off the stand."

"This is insane." Kasluga raised her eyes to the sky. "You saw what those women did."

Smith grabbed her by the right arm. "Enough of the histrionics. Come on. Time to go."

Kasluga instantly pulled away. Her right arm appeared from behind her back. Maybe Smith hadn't secured the cuffs properly. Maybe Kasluga's wrists were particularly narrow. But either way, she had somehow wriggled free. Her left arm appeared. She ducked down. Scrabbled in the dirt. Then straightened up with an object in her hand. A four-inch nail, all bent and rusty. Kasluga twisted around behind Smith. She wrapped her right arm around Smith's head, covering her eyes. She used her left to jam the tip of the nail into Smith's neck. She hit a spot right above Smith's carotid. A drop of blood ran down her neck and soaked into her shirt. The nail was still sharp despite the rust. That was clear. A few more ounces of pressure and Smith would be dead.

Kasluga stepped back. She dragged Smith with her and simultaneously pulled her head, stretching her neck and arching her back. She said, "Drop the gun."

Smith did as she was told.

Kasluga shifted her focus to Reacher. "You too."

Reacher raised his hands to shoulder height but he kept hold of his gun. It was side on to Kasluga with its muzzle pointing harmlessly at the sky. He said, "I didn't see those women do anything to your husband. He was already dead when I got there."

"Because they shot him. The younger one did."

"Did she?"

Kasluga pulled back farther. "I said, drop the gun."

Reacher moved the hand holding his gun a little to the side and a little lower, but he didn't let go. "I found the two agents, dead. Then I heard three shots. They were close together. In time, and origin."

LEE CHILD and ANDREW CHILD

Smith started to struggle. She tried to twist her head away from the nail but she couldn't wriggle free. The nail just bit deeper into her skin.

Kasluga said, "Veronica had already shot the agents. Charles fired twice. He hit Roberta and killed her. He hit Veronica and knocked her down but she survived because of her vest. She shot back at the same moment and killed Charles."

Reacher shook his head. "I heard three shots, then a gun hitting the ground. You shot all three of them. Your husband, then the women. Then you tossed your gun at your husband's feet. But you made a mistake. You didn't kill Veronica. And that almost cost you your life."

"Check the police report. See how many shells were missing from each gun."

"I did. Two from your gun. One from Roberta's. Three from Veronica's."

"Two from Charles's gun. Which proves what I said."

"From the gun found by Charles's body. Which proves you're good. For an improvised plan it was adequate in several respects. You asked for time alone with your husband. And you used it to switch one bullet from Veronica's gun into your own. You even noticed it was a different brand. You use Browning. She used Federal. So you unloaded your gun and reloaded it so that her bullet was at the bottom of the magazine."

"I did nothing while I was alone with Charles. With his body. I was too upset."

Smith started to scuffle her feet, trying to pull away. Kasluga elbowed her in the ribs and she stopped moving.

Reacher said, "You switched one bullet. You moved the spent cartridges. The police report noted they were in an odd position. And you wrote your husband's name on Roberta Sanson's list."

"I did not. Now drop the gun. I won't tell you again."

Reacher moved the gun a little lower. A little farther forward. "Remember those words you wrote for me? *Clears marathons?* That's an anagram of *Charles Stamoran*. Same letters, different order. And guess what? The handwriting is a perfect match."

"Drop the damn—"

"The bigger question is why did you write his name at all? Why not leave the list at seven names? Why make him the eighth?"

"He was the eighth. I didn't make him anything."

"Right. He was some kind of a supervisor, 7,500 miles away. He made no difference to the project, day to day. Unlike the ninth person, who was there, on the ground, getting their hands dirty. Cleaning up after the leak. Paying off the relatives and the witnesses."

"There was no ninth person."

"There was. It was you."

Reacher saw Kasluga's knuckles turn white around the nail. He saw her eyes narrow. The tendons in her neck tense up. So he brought his gun the rest of the way around to the front. He was an expert marksman, with a pistol or a rifle. At that moment the range was negligible. There was no wind. No glare. His target wasn't moving. He wasn't out of breath. There were multiple spots he could have picked with minimal risk to Smith. Kasluga's head. Her shoulder. Either knee. Either shin. Either foot. Reacher pulled the trigger. He hit Kasluga dead in the center of her right instep. She screamed, dropped the nail, and fell hard to the side.

Smith stepped back and clamped her hand over her neck.

Kasluga howled and curled up and clenched her teeth. She managed a strangled, "Help me."

Reacher said, "Help you? The way you agreed to help those kids after you killed their parents? To help those bereaved families in India?"

"I was wrong." She was gasping, barely able to breathe through the pain. "Please. I'm begging you."

"I want information. Two questions."

"Anything. Just get me to a damn hospital."

"Who did you call to set up Neilsen's murder?"

"That wasn't—"

"Do you want to lose your whole leg?"

Kasluga shook her head.

"Then stop lying for ten seconds. We know who Neilsen called, asking questions. That person called you. They used the number you wrote in my notebook."

"That's because . . ." Kasluga was panting. ". . . he was calling Charles. We lived together. Same house. Same phone."

"He wasn't. Charles had a whole bunch of Defense Department phone lines in that house. Those lines don't generate records. Why would he take incriminating calls on a line that did?"

Kasluga hissed, "Fine. David Sullivan. Vice president, client satisfaction, Total Security Solutions. They have the AmeriChem account. I have a problem, a lawsuit, someone making trouble, anywhere in the world, he makes it go away."

"Good. I'll give him a call. See if he can make himself go away. Now, Neville Pritchard. What was the deal with him?"

Kasluga let out a long, deep groan. "Hospital. You promised."

"You answer first. Pritchard reported to Stamoran. We pieced that much together. So did he recruit you in-country?"

"Don't make me laugh." Kasluga whimpered for a second from the effort. "Pritchard was an idiot. A pencil pusher. I figured out what he was doing inside a day. Forced him to let me in."

"You stole the money together. Split it later."

"No. I—"

"That's why you gave him the bogus currency loans right after your property development scam. To funnel his share of the laundered cash to him."

Kasluga nodded. Her face was pale and gleaming with sweat.

"When you figured that Buck had spilled his guts to the Sanson sisters you made a call to your buddy Sullivan. Had Pritchard taken out because he was the only one who could identify you."

Kasluga managed a thin smile. "The funny thing? It was Charles who told me about the scientists getting killed. That was why I called Sullivan. Charles thought he was protecting me. He was an idiot, too."

Reacher turned and started toward the glass door. Smith hurried after him and grabbed his sleeve.

She said, "Hold up. You promised we'd get her to the hospital."

"I didn't say how. She can crawl to the car. Or she can bleed out here. Either way is good with me."

"Reacher, that's cold."

He shrugged. "She really should have agreed to help those kids."

Chapter 29

Reacher didn't believe in fate but he had heard it said that the harder a person works, the luckier they become. He thought it would be fair to say he'd worked hard that day. So when he was halfway through putting on his freshly cleaned Class A uniform in preparation for Kent Neilsen's wake and the phone in his hotel room rang, the orders he received seemed fitting. He was being sent back to Illinois with immediate effect. Irregularities had been uncovered with the inventory at the Joliet Army Ammunition Plant. His recent experience at the Rock Island Arsenal was expected to be valuable. And given Joliet's proximity to Chicago, he figured if he worked really hard the case might just expand to include Agent Ottoway . . .

The final flight to Midway airport left in four hours so Reacher decided it would be safe to show his face at the wake. There would be time to pay his last respects to Neilsen and his new posting would be a perfect reason to leave if the whole occasion turned out to be too dire. The venue was easy enough to find. It was an old movie theater, all neon and art deco curves and flourishes, and it had recently been converted into a concert hall. It turned out that Neilsen had been a bit of a musician in his younger days. His thing was the flugelhorn. He was bigger on enthusiasm than technique, according to a woman who'd known him when he played. She was part of a makeshift band that had been rounded up for the evening. It included a couple of his old buddies. They had set an extra place in their semicircle on the stage and propped up a thing that looked to Reacher like a trumpet on the empty chair.

Reacher gravitated to the back of the room and the first person he recognized was Spencer Flemming. Although it took a moment for Reacher to place him. His hair was still gray but it no longer hung down on either side of his face. It was short now. It had been cut into an actual style. And he was wearing jeans and a shirt that didn't look like they were decades out of date. Reacher shook the guy's hand and their conversation quickly turned to the future. Flemming knew Joliet, or had in the sixties. He'd covered a story about a string of accidents at a motor racing track near there. He was hoping to be covering more stories very soon. He just needed to sort out his accommodations. The hotel hadn't worked for him so he was back in his trailer. The FBI had arranged for it to be towed to an RV park. The same one Pritchard had been murdered in, but Flemming didn't know that.

Flemming wandered away after a few minutes, and moments later Reacher bumped into Amber Smith. She had a Band-Aid on her neck as a result of Susan Kasluga's efforts with the rusty nail, and she was wearing a black dress with heels. Reacher had only ever seen her in jeans and boots before. Another person whose appearance had changed. All part of spinning out of one orbit and moving into another, Reacher thought. A natural transition at the end of an intense case.

"Heard anything about Kasluga?" Smith said.

Reacher shook his head. "Done anything about Sullivan? Her wet-work guy?"

"I briefed my supervisor. He said I can run with it. I have a good feeling about it. A chance to do something right again. Get my career back on track."

"And outside of work?"

Smith shrugged. "OK, I think. This is the first funeral I've been to since Philip's. I didn't know how it would be, but I'm handling it. Maybe time really is all I need."

Pretty soon after that Reacher figured he'd had his fill so he started to drift toward the exit. He bumped into Christopher Baglin and Gary Walsh. He heard the band start up for a second session. He saw a man and a woman making for the valet station with an urgent look in their eyes. And when he made it to the foyer he nearly ran into a pair of men in dark suits who were clearly escorting some kind of a bigwig. The guy glanced at Reacher then stopped and backtracked. He said, "Captain Reacher? I thought I might find you here. My name's Jon Essley. Acting Secretary of Defense. I want to thank you for what you did for my predecessor. The fact that we can mourn him as a man who did his duty, albeit in tune with the sensibilities of a bygone time, rather than condemning him as a cold-blooded murderer, is a huge comfort to me personally, and to the nation. If this position becomes mine permanently it's safe to say it won't be long until your silver bars will be gone and your oak leaves will be back."

Reacher said nothing. In his experience, a verbal promise from a politician wasn't worth the paper it was written on.

About the Authors

Lee Child is the author of the #1 *New York Times* bestselling Jack Reacher series and the complete Jack Reacher story collection, *No Middle Name*. Foreign rights in the Reacher series have sold in one hundred territories. A native of England and a former television director, Lee Child lives in New York City and Wyoming.

jackreacher.com
Facebook.com/LeeChildOfficial
Twitter: @LeeChildReacher

To inquire about booking Lee Child for a speaking engagement, please contact the Penguin Random House Speakers Bureau at speakers@penguinrandomhouse.com.

Andrew Child, who also writes as Andrew Grant, is the author of *RUN, False Positive, False Friend, False Witness, Invisible,* and *Too Close to Home.* He is the #1 bestselling co-author of the Jack Reacher novels *The Sentinel, Better Off Dead*, and *No Plan B*. Child and his wife, the novelist Tasha Alexander, live on a wildlife preserve in Wyoming.

andrewgrantbooks.com
Facebook.com/AndrewGrantAuthor
Twitter: @Andrew_Grant